The Pirate Queen's Daughter

The Pirate Queen's Daughter

William Frank

Terra Nova Books
SANTA FE, NEW MEXICO

Also by William Frank
Young Blood and Old Paint, 2022

Library of Congress Control Number 2022945953

Distributed by SCB Distributors, (800) 729-6423

Terra Nova Books

Published by Terra Nova Books, Santa Fe, New Mexico.
www.TerraNovaBooks.com

ISBN 978-1-948749-83-1

Tommy McNaul sat alone in the cramped booth, unfolded his last flour torilla, and examined its burned spots. They didn't form the face of anyone he knew, so he tore off a hunk and sopped up the remnants of Rosie's napalm, the best red chile in Santa Fe. He removed a manila envelope from a wounded leather backpack and laid it on the table like a second entrée. Although there was no return address, the Boston postmark meant Colleen, or maybe her lawyer. He hadn't talked to his wife in three months, but he knew she was preparing divorce papers. He bit the corner off another sopapilla and grabbed the plastic honey bear containing the best-known antidote to Rosie's red. The grinning bear stuck to his hand like it was afraid of the table. As he tried to pry it loose, a shadow darkened his plate.

"Mind if I sit down?"

Tom rolled his head toward the smooth female voice and stared back into a pair of amber eyes set within an oval face as attractive as any woman deserved. Her hair curled a bit near the shoulders and was some sort of light brown that a wise man would avoid labeling. She looked to be a bit shy of thirty. Nice figure. Casual jeans and blouse outfit. Roper boots. The clothes looked new, and there was no mud on the boots. No rings. A thin, unscratched leather briefcase hung from one shoulder.

"Please do." He felt honey oozing down his hand as he set the bear next to the tired menus.

The woman slid down the opposite bench, folded her arms, and leaned forward until her elbows rested on the table. "You're Thomas McNaul, aren't you?"

"Tom, but you've got the right guy. I'm sorry. I don't recognize you." He angled his head a few degrees to the right. "Have we met?"

"No." She glanced at the envelope, then back at Tom. Her smile seemed sincere but forced, and the stress revealed a few more creases than her scant makeup could handle. The silence began to get awkward.

"Well, nice to meet you, but what can I do for you? And by the way, how did you find me?"

"I went to your office. The woman in the front room, Ms. Myrna Malloy, I believe, said you were here. She said she wouldn't normally give up your whereabouts, but today you could use a lift." The smile became more relaxed. "So, do you feel lifted?"

"Depends on why you're here, but yeah, a little. There are lots of loose—sorry, single—women in this town but not many under thirty." He arched his eyebrows into a question, but she didn't take the bait. "I'm older than that myself. But then, if you talked to Myrna, this is probably a business matter."

"That's right." She scanned the cozy confines of Rosie's. "Will you be going back to your office now? This seems a little public."

"We can hoof it to the office, if you like. Are you a local? If not, I could give you the Cook' s Tour on the way back."

"Maybe some other time. I'm a bit rushed right now. I've got a class at four."

"Grad student?"

She shook her head. "Professor. University of New Mexico. I started a month ago."

"Well, at least tell me your name."

"Sorry." She produced a gray business card with red letters: Aoife O'Malley.

Tom squinted at the fine print, then leaned back. "O'Malley I get. I'm part Irish myself. But how do you pronounce your first name?"

"E'fa."

"Unusual. Haven't heard that one."

"It's the Irish form of Eve."

Tom paid near the door and steered Aoife through a horde of September tourists mobbing the plaza—in town for Fiesta, he assumed. After five minutes, they reached Staab Street and the squat, irregular building housing McNaul Brothers Detective Agency. Sometime in the past, an owner had tried to inflict a measure of Santa Fe style on the structure, but it retained a misbegotten look. Red ant colonies thrived between broken pieces of sidewalk and were swarming like the tourists. Tom chose a short detour through the adjoining packed dirt and withered grass. He wanted to escort Aoife past Myrna's desk and into his interior office without a gab session, but his hopes were dashed faster than most battle plans. Willie, his older half-brother, sauntered out of the inner room and parked his hairy bulk in the connecting doorway, eyes agog.

"Little brother. Who's the fine lady?"

Aoife rolled her eyes in obligatory contempt, though Tom caught her failing to bite back a smile. Myrna shifted her ample frame, rousing audible complaints from her chair. She lurched to her feet and cooed a near-perfect Mae West imitation. "Hiya, Aoife. Glad you found your way back."

Aoife adroitly parried a couple of Myrna's probing questions until Tom and Willie managed to escort her into their inner office and close the door. Tom seated Professor O'Malley next to his desk and rolled back his own chair. Willie parked his feet in the lower side drawer of his battered desk, laced his fingers behind his head, and continued his perusal of Aoife from a flanking position. The lady seemed in no hurry to speak, so Tom decided to wait her out.

Aoife's gaze settled on a blue FBI coffee mug next to Tom's computer. "A G-man, eh? I guess you must be the real deal."

"I hope so, Ms. O'Malley, though the mug came from an earlier employer. Would this be a convenient time for you to tell me what you want?" Tom watched as Aoife's eyes resumed their study of the undeniably shabby decor, Willie included. She turned back to Tom. There was something familiar and vaguely unnerving about her eyes, but he couldn't place it. He was sure he had never met her. He shook it off, rolled his chair a few inches closer to the lone window, and waited.

"I understand you are an art detective, Mr. McNaul." She ignored Willie, but his brother didn't seem to mind.

"Yes. I handle stolen property cases, primarily ones involving fine art." He gave a slight nod toward Willie. "My brother handles most everything else."

Aoife glanced toward Willie. "I hope you don't mind, but my business here is somewhat sensitive. I don't want to offend you, but I'd like to speak to Tom alone." Willie returned his boots to the floor with more thud than necessary. "Sure. I'm hungry anyway."

Tom waited until he heard the front door of the outer office rattle shut. From the mix of footsteps, he deduced that Myrna was joining Willie, perhaps for a second lunch. He turned back to Aoife and tried to avoid being distracted by her disconcerting gaze. "You were about to say, Ms. O'Malley?"

She stiffened her back. "I want you to recover a painting. It belonged to my family."

"Uh-huh. What happened to it?"

Aoife altered her posture for no obvious reason and began to show signs of discomfort. "We think it was stolen. I don't know all the details, but it's missing, and we need to get it back."

"We?"

"My mother and I. The painting is quite valuable, and to be honest, we need the money. Or rather, my mother needs it. She's partially disabled from an accident, and her medical bills are mounting up."

"Is the painting by a local artist? Someone from New Mexico or Arizona?"

"No."

"No?" Tom's patience was racing for the exit. He tried to head it off. "Are you going to give me a clue? The artist's name, perhaps? I'd like to know if the work is valuable enough to make this case worth our while." Tom rolled back to his desk and leaned on both elbows. "You see, I don't charge all that much for my time—just fifty an hour, plus expenses. I make most of my living off the finder's fee. That would be 20 percent of the recovered value. It wouldn't be worth it to either of us if we're only talking about a painting worth, oh, say, a thousand bucks."

"It's worth much more than that, Mr. McNaul."

"That's fine. So who painted it?"

"Monet. Claude Monet."

Tom tried not to look as dumbstruck as he felt. He didn't think he succeeded. "Monet?"

Aoife nodded.

"Are we talking about a real painting? Not just a sketch, or maybe a litho?"

"Yes. It's a fairly large piece. Well, framed, or at least it was the last time I saw it. Good condition, I'm told."

"What did it look like?"

"About this big, I'd say." Aoife held her hands somewhere near four feet apart. "Or maybe bigger. I haven't seen it for a long time."

"What was the subject?"

"Water lilies. A pond full of them."

"Naturally." Tom rolled his neck a full circle, which produced a few cracking noises. At age forty-seven, the bearings seemed to be grinding. "Anything else you can tell me about how it looked?"

"Well, it was mostly green."

"Most water lilies are." Tom got up and began to pace laps of the room, his hands in his front pockets. "Do you have more specific identification? Title? Date? That sort of thing?"

"No, I'm sorry. I haven't seen it since I was seven, but my mother says it's a genuine Monet."

"Okay, we'll get back to that. Any Monet painting will be worth a lot, but you must know that some of them are worth a fortune."

She arched an eyebrow his way. "Like millions?"

"For starters. Enough to make me sit up straight, anyway. Did your mother give you photos or copies of sales records?"

Aoife dropped her gaze without moving her chin. After a few seconds, she drew a deep breath and looked up. "You want to know the provenance. I understand that. But the truth is, we have no records at all. My grandfather kept the painting in his private library and rarely showed it to anyone outside the family. He treasured it, but he never told my mother or me where he got it."

"Is your grandfather still living?"

She shook her head. "He died over twenty years ago."

Tom stopped his laps of the office and faced the small, grimy window at parade rest. He kept his back to Aoife. "Well, surely there is at least a record of your mother inheriting the painting."

"No. She never actually received it."

Tom froze for a moment and then tried to turn slowly without seeming melodramatic. He was deflating rapidly and worried she might hear the hiss. "Professor O'Malley . . ."

"Aoife."

"Aoife. Are you telling me you have no proof of ownership?"

"I'm afraid so."

Tom felt emptier than a wallet after Christmas. "Lady, I'd really like to help you, but there doesn't seem to be much hope. If I find your painting, what good will it do? You won't be able to take possession of it, let alone sell it to anyone. Isn't there anyone besides you and your mom who can vouch for your family owning this Monet?"

Aoife shook her head but tightened her jaw and doubled down the intensity of her stare.

Tom bit his upper lip. "I'm sorry, but I can't help you. As I said, I work mostly for the finder's fee. My dreaming lamp was lit when you told me it was a lost Monet, but I don't see a dollar in this for either of us. You'd be wasting your money hiring me just to find out whose wall it's hanging on."

Aoife continued to stare at Tom, but a barely perceptible smile appeared. "You don't seem to understand, Mr. McNaul. I don't just want you to find my mother's painting. I want you to steal it."

When Tom's mind refocused, he wasn't sure how long he'd been sitting on his desk or just how hard he'd landed there. The amber eyes widened a hair as he stood up and stared into them. "Listen, Ms. O'Malley. Aoife. You must have me confused with somebody else. I don't steal fine art. I recover it. I spent twenty-five years in the FBI, the last few on the Art Crimes Team."

"And then they gave you the boot, or so I'm told. What happened? Did you souvenir some little Degas on the side?"

"Word does get around. But no, I didn't swipe anyone's masterpiece. I shot a couple of bad guys just outside of Boston. They deserved it at the time, but the second one must have put me over the limit."

Aoife loosed her broadest smile yet. "Tough guy, eh? Well you sound like you might be up to the job." She flowed to her feet and closed to within arm's reach. "So, can you help us?"

Tom deepened his breathing to enjoy her scent. He loved women's perfume, though he couldn't tell one from the next. "I'll hear some more. Start at the beginning. When did these water lilies disappear?"

"We're pretty sure it was the night of the murders."

Tom collapsed back onto his desk. "Murders? I'm beginning to feel sandbagged, toots. But please, do go on."

"My father and grandmother, Peter and Maureen O'Malley, were shot dead in my grandmother's house." Aoife made a faint choking sound and failed to disguise it as a cough. "The police said they probably surprised a team of burglars. The home had been ransacked and the walls stripped bare. Lots of things were missing. My grandmother rattled around that house alone, and the police couldn't find any kind of inventory. The murders were never solved."

"I'm sorry." Tom extended his right hand toward Aoife's shoulder. She edged out of reach, and he let it drop to the desk top. "Where did this happen?"

"Ireland." Tom could feel his eyebrows converging. Aoife looked like she was enjoying this.

"Could you be just a bit more specific? Ireland isn't very large, but short distances can make big differences there."

"Indeed. My grandmother's home was a few kilometers west of Armagh. It was a manor house, seventeenth century, I believe. She still owned considerable grounds. I remember a stable of horses."

"With hounds?"

"Not that I remember. My father used to take me riding through the fields on a pony, though. I haven't been there since I was seven, and he was killed not long after that last visit."

Tom searched his memory banks. "Armagh. That's up north in the Orange country—Northern Ireland. I was there once. It's near County Tyrone, where we McNauls came from. Was your grandfather a Protestant? Mine was a Presbyterian."

"No, he was a devout Catholic. The O'Malleys somehow managed to hang on to most of their lands despite the frequent English land grabs." She turned her back toward Tom and began to wander around the room. She didn't seem to be put off by the Goodwill decor.

Tom tried to sound sympathetic. "Not many did. Probably an interesting story there." He glanced at the coffee maker atop a battered metal file cabinet, but the oily remains of the morning's brew were far below client quality. "When did the killings take place?"

"I think it was in the fall of 1997. I'd have to look up the date. Is it important?"

"Maybe later. But that was over twenty years ago. Mind telling me why you folks took so long to start looking for this painting?"

Aoife took a deep breath and exhaled loudly as she turned back to Tom. She seemed more resigned than angry. "I don't know why my mother didn't hire an investigator years ago, but last week, she got a call from an FBI agent in Washington. A member of your old art crime group. The agent got a tip from a Sotheby's broker in Boston. A man came to their auction house wanting to sell a Monet water lily painting. He showed some pictures, but he wouldn't bring the piece in for examination. The broker got suspicious and called the FBI to see if it was hot."

"Was it?"

"They weren't sure. Mom had reported her painting as stolen—I'm not sure when. I gather there must be some sort of international stolen art list. Mom's description of the painting jibed with the one given by the Sotheby's man, but the seller didn't leave the pictures, and as I said, we don't have one. Anyway, the FBI agent called Mom to ask some questions, and then suggested she call you."

"Me? Who was this agent?"

Aoife shrugged. "No idea. A woman, though. Mom did say that much."

I'll be damned. Has to be Kate. Katherine J. Bacon. Tom grinned. "Sounds like it was my former partner. Did your mother tell you anything about the painting's history? Where your grand-dad got it, or when?"

She shook her head, a little more than necessary, and her hair whipped around to practiced effect. "I'm sorry, but I have to get back to campus." Tom could hear pens rattling as Aoife's hand thrashed around in her briefcase. It emerged with a business card. "Give me a call this evening if you want to talk more." She turned toward the front room.

Tom guided her out, but Aoife paused inside the front door. "I'll be home after six." She stepped through the doorway and didn't turn around, so he moved back to his desk and peered through the one clean spot in the lower-right corner of the window. Aoife wrenched open the driver's door of a last-resort Ford with mismatched fenders, sun-chalked blue paint on the roof and hood, and one visible hubcap. Must be an assistant professor. She drove off. Tom examined the card. It sported a UNM logo and the address of the Department of Anthropology. He wondered why a babe like her would be home taking his call on a Friday night.

*   *   *

At six-thirty, Tom handed Stella the last third of his green chile cheeseburger, counted his fingers, and killed three seconds while she dined. He wrapped the leash around his wrist and let the young corgi tow him up the hill to his condo. Stella was short but pulled like a tank. Five minutes later, she staked out a claim on his purple armchair while he sprawled on the sofa with a shot of Black Bush in a square-based tumbler. The whiskey was almost gone when the Clancy Brothers erupted into a live recording of "Whiskey, You're the Devil" in his right shirt pocket. The voice on his phone was female and Irish, but it didn't belong to Aoife.

"Mr. McNaul?"

"None other."

"My name is Grace O'Malley. My daughter tells me that you've agreed to help us recover our stolen painting."

"Not exactly—I said I was willing to talk about it. But I'm definitely interested. Did Aoife tell you my terms?"

"Yes, and they sound fine. What do you want to know?"

"For starters, tell me more about the theft and murders. And then, why you didn't go after the painting right away? Aoife seemed a little fuzzy on the details."

"She doesn't know much about it. My husband used to travel to Ireland every summer to visit his mother near Armagh. One night in '97, he and his mother returned home late from a dinner in town. They were found shot to death early the next morning when the cleaning lady arrived at the house. She called the police. Most of the paintings in the house were gone, along with various silver items and some tapestries."

"And the Monet was missing in action?"

"Missing, anyway. It wasn't in the house that morning, but there wasn't any proof it had been taken at the time of the murders. Every time I saw the painting, it was hanging in my father-in-law's private office, and he rarely took friends or outsiders in there. After he died, my husband's mother kept the room locked. The police couldn't find a witness who remembered seeing the painting anytime during the previous five years. And there was no listing of it in the insurance policy."

"Your daughter said the police haven't found the murderers. They find any of the art?"

"Not really. A few pieces of the silver surfaced, eventually. I submitted a list of the paintings I thought were taken, and the police sent it to some international database, but there has been no trace of the Monet or any of the others. Not until two days ago, when an FBI agent called me—Agent Katherine Bacon. She said a Boston art broker with Sotheby's was approached by a man trying to sell a painting that sounded a lot like our missing water lilies. The FBI looked into it, but they couldn't identify the seller. Agent Bacon suggested I call you." Grace paused, but he waited her out. "Was she right?"

"Yes. With so little to go on, and your rather shaky provenance, the FBI can't afford to spend much time looking. It's a job for a private investigator who specializes in stolen art, and that would be me."

"Are you a good one?"

"I don't know of a better one, but that's not a guarantee I can find your lily picture." Tom stood up and began pacing around his tiny living room. "Mrs. O'Malley, in a case like this, I will need to move fast. Kate Bacon is my former partner. I'll find out what she knows, and then I'll need to fly to Boston by tomorrow morning to see if I can run down the shy art peddler. I'd like to stop by your home to have a longer chat. When would be a good time?"

Grace took a couple of loud breaths before she replied. "I'm sorry, Mr. McNaul, but I don't want to meet with you in person. You may think me vain, but I haven't adjusted very well to my new life in a wheelchair. I don't receive anyone but close friends and family at my home. I'll be happy to talk on the phone, and you can contact me by email if you like. I have a helper during the day, and she can fax you copies of any papers you need to see."

"That's rather unusual, Mrs. O'Malley."

"Perhaps, but I value my privacy. Anyway, consider yourself hired." The phone disconnected.

Tom poured himself another drink, dug out Aoife's card, and tried her number. She answered on the third ring. "Hello?"

"Hi. Tom McNaul here. I just got off the phone with your mother."

"Yes, I told her to call. She's the one hiring you, after all. Did you two decide anything?"

"Yeah. I'm heading to Boston. Probably on tonight's redeye. Anything more you can tell me before I go? How about if I stop by your place on the way to the airport?"

"Sorry, I'm going out. I believe I told you most of what I know, but if I think of anything, I'll call you."

*   *   *

A tall blonde woman in jeans, scuffed boots, and a blue REI hiking shirt smiled down from her porch as Tom tried to herd Stella along her sidewalk. Once the pooch spotted Laurie, she bounded up the steps and crooned a low howl. Tom considered doing the same but settled for, "Hiya."

"Hi, Tommy." Laurie took the leash while Tom returned to his pickup for the rest of Stella's sleepover gear. The threesome moved inside to a living room in disarray. It occurred to Tom that Stella was the more housebroken of the two females. Laurie reached for a bottle on the bookshelf. "Time for a drink?"

"Always." Tom removed several sections of the New Mexican, Laurie's employer, from the sofa and claimed the spot. Laurie handed him a jelly jar, poured him a couple of fingers of Jameson, and clicked it with her own. "Tilt your kilt."

"Still drinking the Catholic whiskey, I see."

"When it's on sale."

"It'll do."

Laurie shrugged and settled onto the other end of the sofa without removing the remaining debris. She drained most of a finger. "Is this the big showdown with Colleen?" Her tone feigned cheer, but the question was loaded like a howitzer. Six months ago, Tom had returned to Santa Fe and Laurie, on the run, a refugee exiled from the FBI and banned in Boston. He hadn't seen his former flame for almost twenty years—not since he'd left Albuquerque and her for MIT and, as things turned out, Colleen. A few hours of whiskey and a drive-by shooting reignited old passions, but Laurie called an abrupt ceasefire. She didn't want to be burned twice by the same smoldering female. Time enough for love after the divorce was final. She didn't doubt that Tom would go through with it—Colleen had set Tom up to be shot. But still, "fool me once. . . ." Meanwhile, they shared joint custody of Stella.

"No, I've actually got a hot case. A woman in Boston wants me to track down a Monet that may or may not have been stolen in Ireland twenty years ago over her husband's dead body. Also her mother-in-law's."

"I hope you get your expenses upfront."

"Myrna will take care of that. You working on any hot stories?"

"I wish. We're so understaffed I have to help check out lost dogs."

"Well."

"Yeah. Anyway. You're not really going back to Boston, are you? Last I heard, the mob boys said they'd shoot you on sight."

"Have to. This could be a big one. I'll keep my head down."

"Yeah, right. Just make sure you shoot first." Laurie set down her glass. Tom took the cue, did the same, and stood up. He was reaching for the front door handle when she caught his arm and spun him into a tight embrace. After six months of her smacks on the cheek, he now struggled to coordinate squeezing, kissing, and breathing. It reminded Tom of his failed attempt to learn the bagpipes.

She abruptly pushed Tom away. "Don't read anything into that. I just figured I might never see you again."

* * *

Kate Bacon finally returned Tom's calls ten minutes before boarding time for his Albuquerque-to-New York redeye, with a morning connection to Boston. It was after one in the morning in Washington, but Kate was a hard-ass who lived alone and prowled the night. "Tommy! Where the hell are you?"

"En route to Beantown, toots, on the trail of some lost lilies. I understand that you got me into this, so?"

"Not much to tell. I assume you know the basics. We got some crummy photos of the would-be seller from a Sotheby's surveillance camera. I'll email you a couple of the best. No luck matching them to any of the usual suspects. We couldn't put more time into this one—no firm ID of the painting itself, no provenance, not even firm evidence that this Mrs. O'Malley ever owned a Monet."

"Get a surveillance shot of the painting?"

"Nah. The seller didn't have it with him. He had photos, and he carried them in a small portfolio case. When he gave the Sotheby's man a peek at the photos, he used his body to shield them from the robot paparazzi. We're left to trust the broker's judgment, and, of course, even if the photos are real, it doesn't mean the seller has the painting."

"True enough. Thanks anyway."

"So, Tommy. You got time to stop by here on your way home? I could show you my scars."

Tom bit his upper lip. Times with Kate always went down easy, but Colleen's divorce lawyers were circling like buzzards during a rabbit shortage, and then there was Laurie. Too much just now.

He realized he had paused too long. "Maybe, but chances are I'll have to catch an express to somewhere from Boston. Ireland maybe. Rain check?"

"Uh huh. Just make sure you don't wait too long to cash it. Call me from Boston if you need anything. I could always hop up to give you a hand. The locals there still owe me one for taking those slugs while they loafed around in the woods."

"Will do, thanks." Tom clenched his teeth and stared at his dark phone. He should have been the one with slugs in his chest, but on the night of the sting, he froze. Let her go into the house alone. He always seemed to make that same mistake in the clutch—think too long, then shoot too fast. No wonder the FBI ditched him.

~ 3 ~

Tom clutched the overhead strap and took shallow breaths to minimize ozone damage as the MTA swayed two stops inbound from Logan. He got off at Aquarium and lugged his leather backpack and wheeled metal case up to street level, where the predominant smells shifted to a blend of auto exhaust, full dumpsters, and deceased aquatic life. The midmorning air was already muggy, but he survived the fifty-foot trek to the Harbor View Hotel before his shirt soaked through. It proved to be a quiet boutique oasis situated conveniently close to an Irish pub shamelessly named The Quiet Man. The chances of a big payday at the end of this job were slim. He figured he'd juice the expenses while he could.

The tidy young desk clerk wore a nametag saying "Molly" and a smile wider than Tom's rumpled appearance called for, but she stood firm that he was way too early for check-in. The lobby was empty, so Tom rolled his metal case behind a large stuffed chair and out of sight of the front desk. He knelt, transferred a thirty-eight special from the metal case to a clip holster on his belt and stashed a small leather bag of bullets in his inside jacket pocket. He wasn't licensed to carry concealed in Massachusetts, but he was a marked man in Boston, and he wasn't heading into these mean streets unarmed. He returned to the desk, checked the metal case with smiling Molly, and headed for a small business office off the lobby. The three surveillance photos from Kate's email produced prints as grainy as a '50s TV, but two were profiles and the third almost a head-on shot. Good enough for an ID if he could find the guy. He headed for Sotheby's.

Twenty minutes, four long stares, and a handshake later, Tom was shown to one of two chairs in a cramped office. The floor was cluttered with small paintings leaning against walls and scattered papers, some in folders. A slender young man with a fine suit, Italian shoes, and a sad approximation of a haircut seated himself in the other chair. "Welcome, Mr. McNaul. I'm Joel Lieberman. Agent Bacon told me you would be arriving this morning." Joel emphasized the word "agent" like a man who didn't deal regularly with the FBI.

"Nice of you to see me on short notice." Tom grinned, but Joel just stared at him with as little expression as he could muster. "Kate gave me most of the details, but I'd like to hear some of your thoughts, Mr. Lieberman." Tom took the surveillance photos from his pack and showed them to Joel. "Do you think this man has a genuine Monet?"

Joel seemed momentarily offended by the bluntness of the question, but he rallied and gave an exaggerated shrug. "Could be. The pictures he brought were of good quality, and they certainly looked like a Monet, though not one I'm familiar with. It was not framed. The photos of the back showed details consistent with others I've seen. I think they were of a real Monet, but I have no idea whether the man owned it."

"That's why I'm here instead of the FBI."

"Of course."

"Anything in the photo to give it scale? It would help to know the size."

Joel thought for a moment. "I can't be sure, but the painting was upright on a table and leaning against a white wall. It seemed to be a plain dining table, maybe six feet long or a bit more. So I'd figure the painting to be a little less than four feet wide, and it seemed rectangular—maybe just a few inches wider than tall."

"Anything else?"

"Not of any importance. It was sitting on plain brown wrapping paper, and there were some short pieces of masking tape stuck to the paper. I'm afraid that's all I noticed."

Tom tapped the top surveillance photo. "Tell me how this guy left. Did you follow him to the door?"

Joel nodded. "I didn't want to lose a possible sale of that magnitude, and I don't mind telling you I was nervous. I'm new in this department, and it would have been my first big coup." He uncrossed his legs and began tapping the floor with the toes of his right foot. "After the seller took back his pictures, I told him he'd need to bring in the painting for appraisal. He just stood up and headed for the door. Didn't say a word. I stayed with him, of course. I asked him how I could get in touch with him, but he just laughed. More of a snort, if you know what I mean. He said maybe he'd call me someday."

Tom tilted his head and rubbed his right ear on his shoulder. "That's it?"

"Not quite. I got desperate and told him I'd talk to our manager to see what could be done. The man wrote a phone number on the back of a business card and said not to wait too long."

"Can I see the card?"

Joel dug through his pockets like a prospector chasing a nugget and finally handed Tom a card for Paddy's Oyster House. The card was stained and had wrinkled, bent edges, suggesting the seller used it to pick his teeth. "Agent Bacon said the number is for a disposable cell phone. She had me call it several times, but nobody ever answered."

Tom took out a small spiral notepad with a pen clipped to the cover and wrote down the phone number and the address of the restaurant. "When the man left, did you see where he went? Was anyone waiting for him?"

Joel's shoulders slumped. "Sorry. The guy turned left at the sidewalk, crossed Chestnut Street at the corner, and disappeared down River. Not a word from him since."

*   *   *

The desk clerk managed a softer smile on the second time around. Molly seemed to be fond of tossing her straight, black hair in various directions and looking through it sideways.

"What brings you to Boston, Mr. McNaul? Business, or just visiting?"

"The fine art business. A Monet, to be precise."

Her eye scan switched to a higher frequency, and her brow furrowed. "Is it in the art museum? I've seen quite a few there." She obviously wasn't taking Tom for a buyer.

"No, and seeing this one may prove to be something of a chore. I don't know where it is, but with luck, it may turn up at your local Sotheby's."

"Really! Did you come here to buy it? That's exciting." Tom's stock was rising like a dot-com IPO.

"Not exactly. Somebody stole it, and the owner hired me to get it back." Tom figured he shouldn't say much more, so he dug out a credit card and looked hopeful.

His room was ready, complete with a mint on the pillow. There was a message to call a Mrs. Grace O'Malley. The O'Malley girls could wait. Tom pulled the curtains and crashed until six. He jolted awake with no clue of what he'd been dreaming about. He never remembered dreams. Someday he'd have to find out what that meant. Although his jacket had lost a few wrinkles, Tom still saw forty-seven years' worth in the bathroom mirror. A shave, wash, and assorted ablutions failed to evoke a feeling of freshness. He adjusted the position of the revolver on his belt to make it less visible beneath the jacket and headed out into a still-sweltering Boston night.

Paddy's was on the harbor, close enough for Tom to walk most days but not after a redeye night. The cab wound through the rat's maze of Boston's one-way streets and took twenty minutes to reach a spot less than a mile from the Harbor View, as the seagull soars. The cabbie assaulted Tom with a stream of stories and recommendations for three Indian restaurants before they turned down a pier and rolled to a stop. Signs were clearly not a priority at Paddy's, but the front door was easy to find. The exterior was the type of chic-shabby favored by would-be boat people. The interior was dimly lit and draped with the obligatory nets and starfish. For seven on a Saturday night, the patrons were sparse. Maybe the beer was expensive. The clientele seemed determined to liven the empty spaces with audible cheer.

Tom picked up a fresh version of Paddy's card at the cashier's station. He took an isolated seat along the near side of the race-track-oval bar in the front room. Two men in black suits, white shirts, and ruddy faces argued on the far side of the clubhouse turn. The more portly of the two ripped his tie askew, propelling a shirt button into his double whiskey. Each combatant had two empty glasses behind the fresh ones. Seemed like Tom's kind of place.

The bartender looked like a Southie kid—young, Irish, and bored. He was slender but hard, and his dark buzz cut allowed good viewing of a single hoop earring. He wiped his way down the bar to Tom using a rag grim enough to keep a sober man from leaning on his elbows. The lad slapped down a recycled beer coaster sporting a shamrock.

"Kin I getcha?"

"Pint of Guinness, thanks." Tom didn't trust the water in Boston and usually survived on Bushmills. This was an oyster bar, though, and nothing pairs with oysters like Dublin's smooth, dry stout.

The barkeep didn't seem too friendly, so Tom nursed his pint until the kid was around the other side of the track. He chugged the rest and waved over a blonde waitress in a stressed black top and jeans. She didn't look like a veteran oyster waitress—maybe a student working a weekend shift. She might have looked pretty good in a larger-sized outfit. When she sashayed back with a second pint and a dozen fried oysters, Tom slid the plastic basket to one side and laid his short stack of surveillance photos on the bar. "Don't get excited. I'm not a cop, but I need to find this guy. He come in here often?"

She pulled away and scanned the room. Satisfied, she leaned back in. "I don't know. I'm only part-time here. I'll get Sean." She skipped around the bar and whispered in the young barman's ear, then took off on an imaginary errand. Tom gritted his teeth. Gambit rejected.

Sean sauntered over flashing a tight smile and greasing his hands with the gray rag. He tossed the rag on his shoulder and shoved the mug of Guinness aside, sending a slop down the bar. He picked up the top photo and stared while he rubbed its surface with a wet thumb. Then he spun it into the pool of Guinness and moved on to the other two. When they were all marinating in the pool of beer, he put his hands on his hips and turned to face Tom.

"The fuck are you?"

Tom relaxed his face into a dead stare and removed his business card from an inside breast pocket. He pinched it between the index and middle finger of his left hand and extended it toward Sean, who looked like reading it was a stretch. The kid finally looked up.

"The fuck are the McNaul Brothers? You one?" He grabbed the card and started to flip it into the pool of Guinness, but Tom's right hand struck like a viper and clamped around the kid's wrist.

"That's not polite, sonny." Tom kept the kid's wrist in a vise, plucked the card back with his other hand, and let him go. "Not looking for trouble, and like I told the lady, I'm not a cop. Not looking to shoot the guy either. I just need to talk to him. He was looking to sell something, and I'm interested." Tom tried to force a business grin. It wasn't working, so he went back to earnest. "Maybe I'm in the wrong place, but if you see the guy, ask him to call me."

Sean smirked but said nothing, so Tom held out his card again. Sean took it and paused. He frowned at his right hand as he slid the folded C-note away from the card, but he slipped them both into his pants pocket and locked eyes with Tom. "That doesn't buy much these days."

"I'm not asking for much. Just give him the card if he comes in."

Sean shrugged and went back to wiping the bar. When he reached the far side of the oval, he veered toward a door in the rear wall and disappeared. He returned five minutes later and spent a while pretending to tend the bar top opposite Tom's stool. Tom looked toward the front door as two hard-looking men entered and stopped a couple of steps inside. The rangy one was wearing a tweed Irish cap and clashing vest despite the sweltering weather. His companion was sporting a largely yellow, upscale Hawaiian shirt covered with blue coconut trees and straining buttons. He looked like he spent his days working out time-and-a-half while eating for two. The pair tried to look casual as they scanned the clientele with quick eyes. Fat boy's eyes hesitated for a second as they flitted over Tom. The men became ambulatory and disappeared through the door last used by Sean. Tom wolfed down the oysters and left cash on the bar.

The last gleam of twilight winked goodbye as Tom strode out into the night. Paddy didn't seem to like spending money on lights, but Tom aimed toward a street lamp at the land end of the wharf. He opted to walk back to the Harbor View. Never could think straight sitting down. He was halfway to the lamppost when the shadows started moving. He spun to his left but knew he was too late. A fist like a hand sledge caught him flush on the temple. He staggered one step before the lights went out, and he fell into darkness.

The dark didn't last long. It took Tom a few seconds to realize he was under water, but he stopped thrashing and let himself float to the surface. The water felt like diesel and reeked of ripe fish guts. He treaded water for a minute to keep his head above the surface film while he looked for a route to shore. His breaststroke wouldn't win any prizes, but eventually he hit firmer slime and crawled onto the shore next to the pier. He checked his pockets. Nothing was missing, but his room key had migrated from front left to front right. The thirty-eight special was still snapped in its holster. His phone wouldn't power up—no surprise. He didn't have a submersion app. The Timex on his left wrist kept on ticking.

The streets of Boston were abuzz with scurrying young Saturday night hopefuls. Few heads turned his way. A drenched, middle-aged man in a sport jacket must not be unusual. Tom's shoes were still squeaking as he sloshed through the hotel door. Molly's lips twitched until she finally lost it, whooped a shrill laugh, and nearly choked trying to swallow it. She ducked into a supply closet and returned with a couple of towels.

"Is it raining out there? I didn't hear anything." She stretched across the counter toward him and craned her neck toward the door.

"No, the Boston monsoon isn't active this time of year. I fell in the harbor."

Molly withdrew behind the front desk. "Are you all right? I could get you to an emergency room."

"Thanks, but I won't need serious repairs. Could stand some medication, though. Would you have the bar send me up a bottle of Black Bush?"

"Good choice, but it might not dry you out."

"Mmm. A good whiskey glass too, if you don't mind. I'm partial to the ones with square bases. Might need two if you bring it up yourself."

Molly smiled annoyance with a hint of maybe. Tom squished to the elevator and headed for drier ground. He threw his clothes in the tub to soak, tossed in two tiny bars of hand soap, and wasted fifteen minutes blasting his phone with the hair dryer. The room phone would have to do.

Tom peeled through the soggy pages of his spiral notebook. He could still make out the seller's alleged cell number. An unidentified female voice steered him directly to voicemail, so he left his name, the relevant numbers, and closed with, "I'm fond of Monets." He set the notebook on the dresser top to dry and grabbed his change of clothes. As he buttoned the left cuff of his only dry shirt, a bellboy in a green pillbox hat delivered the bottle on a silver tray. The tray also held two square-bottomed glasses, so Tom tipped him a ten.

*   *   *

The phone went off like a klaxon sounding battle stations. All of Tom's muscles contracted at once, and his eyes shot open to total darkness. What the hell? As he fought for consciousness, it blared again somewhere on the far side of the king-size bed. The previous guest must have taken out his hearing aid and turned up the ringer. Tom launched himself toward the distant nightstand but ran aground on the soft shoals of Ms. Molly. She slipped her arms around his back and held fast. Tom's hand stopped inches short of the phone as he lost any sense of urgency. During the sixth ring he sighed, broke free with a clockwise twist, and stretched for the phone. He lay across her sideways as he fumbled with the handset.

"Yeah?"

"Tom McNaul?" The man was trying hard to convey menace, but his voice lacked punch in the bass range.

"Good guess. And who might you be?"

"A guy with something you want."

Tom bought some time with a couple of slow breaths, but his heart rate failed to slow. Molly was carving something into his back with her nails. Tom managed to focus his eyes on the digital alarm clock. It said 3:15.

"I don't want much. I'm a man of simple tastes." Tom winced as Molly dug a bit deeper.

"Don't get smart, asshole. You're a long way from home, and you didn't fly all the way to Boston to visit the museums."

"Says you." Tom's mind snapped into focus. Where was this guy? He tried to sit up to concentrate, but his head spun from the whiskey. He collapsed on his back. The caller waited. "Look, you seem to know a lot about me, so you might guess I'm hung over. Spare me the games and tell me what I'm supposed to want."

"Water lilies."

Hangover be damned—Tom sat up. "Go on."

"Get your head straight. I'll call back." The caller hung up.

Tom turned his back to Molly as she climbed out of bed to reassemble. He felt woozy again, so he collapsed onto the mattress and stared at the red light on the smoke detector. The bathroom door opened, and he turned in time to watch Molly, now mostly dressed, wobble back to the bed. He took his turn. One glance at the bathroom mirror was too much. As he stumbled back into the room, he saw Molly checking out his debris on the dresser. She set something down, but her body shielded it from his eyes. He didn't figure she'd lift his cash, but one never knows.

As Molly turned toward the door, she angled her neck to one side and stared at him with the eye not hidden by a fall of hair. "You fookin better call me, if ya know what's good for ya. I want to see that Monet."

The accent was new. "You can count on it. Sounds like you've spent some time in Dublin." Molly just smiled, and as the door clicked shut behind her, Tom realized he didn't know her last name. He dressed, drained the oily water from the tub, and stared at his sad heap of wrinkled clothes. There wasn't time enough to start a salvage operation, so he wrung out the worst of the slime, stuffed the lot in a plastic laundry bag, and dropped it outside a door down the hall. There was no escape from the wet shoes, so he set them in the outflow from the air conditioner. All the cash was still in his wallet, and no pages seemed missing from his soaked notebook. Tom turned the phone ringer down to a volume less likely to summon the fire department and passed out on the bed.

~ 4 ~

A few rays of sunshine managed to slip below the base of the morning overcast and stab Tom's eyelids. It was almost seven, and the message light on the phone was still dark. The mysterious caller was taking his time. Tom ordered bacon and eggs with coffee and a side of orange juice. The cart arrived half an hour later pushed by a different bellboy. There was only one glass.

Breakfast was over in four minutes. Tom cleaned and loaded his pistol, shaved, and tried to scare a few wrinkles out of his clothes. The wrinkles stood their ground. He rolled the desk chair near the window and watched Sunday morning drivers crawl toward coffee shops, or maybe churches. He put his feet on the sill and stared at the gray sky until his eyes lost focus. The caller had to be the seller, or at least someone who knew the guy. But who was he? The bartender at Paddy's seemed to recognize the surveillance photos of the seller, and only minutes elapsed between the kid's trip to the back room and the appearance of the fat boy and the man in tweed. Neither of those bums looked or talked like the seller, but they tossed Tom in the drink. What was the connection? It didn't seem like the bums were working with the seller. The man on the phone wanted to talk. If the bums wanted information, they would have taken Tom for a ride, not worked him over.

It was clear Tom didn't know enough to solve this one by staring at clouds. He let his feet crash to the floor and made a quick call to Joel at Sotheby's. Joel confirmed that the seller didn't have a deep voice but not much else. Tom sortied to a convenience store a block from the hotel to buy a prepaid cell phone, but they were sold out. As he passed inbound through the lobby, he was surprised to see a statuesque blonde woman behind the front desk giving him a reasonable facsimile of the evil eye. She appeared to be a few years older, and a good deal less friendly, than Molly. He stopped, sauntered to the desk, and returned her glare. "Hi. Is Molly off duty?"

The blonde snorted. "Yes. Thanks to you, I assume. I'm the assistant manager. Molly called me around midnight and asked if I'd finish her shift for her. When she staggered out of the elevator around three, she was damned lucky there were no guests present."

"You two must be pretty good friends."

"We were." The manager turned away and beckoned to an incoming guest. Tom grabbed an elevator.

* * *

The room phone began ringing at ten. Tom sat down in the desk chair and listened to four more rings before he answered. "Yeah?"

"You sobered up yet?"

"What's it to you?"

The caller laughed and dumped his tough-guy voice. "Okay, McNaul. Here it is. I've got a genuine painting by Monet. It's in nice condition, and it has lots of green water lilies on it. I presume you know what something like that is worth?"

"More or less, and somehow, I have a hunch it's more than you could afford. How did you come by it?"

"Long story. You want to see it or not? I heard you were looking for a painting like that."

"Where'd you hear that?"

"I have my connections."

"Okay, but I'd like to hear the story. I'm working for a buyer who prefers not to pay for hot goods. No offense, but did you happen to come by these lilies honestly?"

"Sure. It was given to a friend of mine to settle a debt. My friend would like to convert the canvas to cash for business purposes."

Tom swiveled toward the window and checked out the pedestrians below. He could see at least two-dozen people walking or loitering, but the only ones using phones were a pair of young women in smart business outfits with short skirts and carrying thin brief cases. "Your provenance seems a bit sketchy. Still, it's worth a look to see if it's the real deal."

"Fair enough. It's good, though. I'm not worried about you being disappointed." The seller's voice edged to a higher pitch. He was either eager or good at faking it.

"I'll give it a shot." Tom tried to sound casual and forced himself to breath softly. "When and where? You want to bring it to my hotel room? You seem to know where that is."

"No, I prefer to meet somewhere more private. I know a small house that will do." He read off a Dorchester address. "Noon, and come alone."

"That'll work, but it sounds like a tough neighborhood. Don't get any big ideas. I'll only be carrying about fifty bucks."

"High roller." The phone went dead.

A cab ride to the Apple store on Boylston required ten minutes and seventy honks. A smiling, youthful android separated itself from the random flow of blue shirts with headsets and floated to Tom's elbow. In forty-five minutes, he was out the door with a new iPhone. He placed another call to the seller and left a message with his cell number.

*   *   *

Tom's aging rental car exuded a cacophony of mechanical noises, and the interior stank like the bilge of a tramp steamer. This wasn't the kind of neighborhood where a fresh, mainstream rental would avoid notice. The woman's voice from his shirt pocket had a British accent and told him to hang a left in two hundred feet and then look for the destination on his right. When she announced his arrival, he had to take her word for it since the small brick house was missing two of the address numbers. The glass in one front window was held together by swaths of duct tape. The yards of the houses on each side were littered with pieces of metal, some recognizable as auto parts or former appliances. The grounds of the target house were oddly devoid of scrap, and there were isolated tufts of grass between the sidewalk and the front stoop. Tom scraped the sidewall of his right front tire against the curb and tried to set the parking brake but couldn't find one. There were no people in his sight lines as he approached the steps. The front door was ajar by about a shoe's width. The invitation struck him as a bit too obvious.

Tom stopped short of the steps and scanned the street and adjoining houses. Still no signs of life. He slipped his right hand under his jacket, eased his revolver from the holster in the small of his back, and held it against his side as he moved to the right. A four-foot chain-link fence surrounded the back and side yards. The gate on the right side was closed but unlocked. The latch and hinges squeaked with different pitches. As he moved through and along the side of the building, a dog with a booming baritone barked into action several houses away, but there were no signs of dog turds in this backyard. He peered through a corner of the window beside the rear door and saw a '60s kitchen with Formica counter tops, an empty sink, and a live spider plant hanging from a macrame strap. The plant looked healthy enough. Someone must be watering it. A small bowl with a smiling cat face on one side sat on the floor next to the refrigerator. It was half full of water. Tom raised his gun and tried the door. It was unlocked. Again, too convenient. He edged farther along the back wall and peered around the far corner.

The side wall sported two small windows. The rear one was covered by black drapes, but Tom could see light through the window closer to the street. He crouched, faced the wall, and oozed sideways until his right eye cleared the frame in the bottom corner of the window. He saw a small dining room with fake wood paneling, a rough-pine hutch on the wall opposite the window, and a simple table and chairs set with seating for six. The table was lying on its long side with the top pressed against the end wall to Tom's left. Five of the chairs were clustered around the protruding table legs. The sixth chair was in the center of the room directly beneath a ceiling fixture containing one incandescent bulb shielded by an inverted, bordello-red glass bowl. The chair faced Tom, as did the man sitting in it. The ceiling light was on, but the man's eyes were clearly not. They bulged slightly and appeared to be fixed on the floor somewhere short of the window. The red hole in his forehead explained his inactivity.

Tom spun away from the window and dropped to one knee. He couldn't see anyone watching him, but there were plenty of potential sniper's nests among the junkyard decor of the surrounding properties. The only sounds came from traffic a block or two away. Tom steadied his breathing, stood up, and holstered the gun. He moved back to the window. The seated man was white, slender, maybe five-nine, and was clearly the man in the Sotheby's surveillance photos. He was dressed in aged green sneakers, shapeless jeans, and a Celtics basketball jersey. His arms hung at his sides and were not tied. No doubt the killer had shot the unfortunate fellow first, then placed his body in the chair. Tom's eyes followed the man's arms downward until they fixed on a black object about the size and shape of a coffee can. A wire, also black, protruded from the top of the cylindrical object and connected to what appeared to be an older-model flip phone. Had to be a bomb.

Tom's first instinct was to freeze, wondering why someone would want to bomb a dead guy? A second later, he dove away from the window and landed face down in the grass and grit. This one's meant for me. There was no explosion, but he lay listening and kissing the dirt for a full minute before he pushed it away and regained his feet. He tried to stroll as he moved to the front yard, but both legs twitched. The neighborhood still seemed as dead as the guy in the dining room. Tom walked briskly toward his car. As he reached the sidewalk, an overweight ginger cat loped up the steps and squeezed through the door. The cat's girth forced the front door to yawn wider. Tom slipped into the driver's seat, over-revved the engine, and drove off in what he hoped was a seemly manner. He slowed to a stop at the first cross street. Still no traffic.

A sharp explosion was followed by sounds of shattering glass. Tom jerked his head around to see debris settling outside the windows of the house with the dead man. He stared through the dust and smoke for a few seconds, then turned forward. The orange cat shot past him—eight lives to go. Tom figured it must have been in the kitchen. He hit the gas and kept his speed in the legal zone as he made four turns and pulled to a stop in the parking lot of a dry cleaning shop. Sirens began to wail in the distance. He tried to ignore them.

What the hell was going on? If the guy in the chair really had the Monet, there would be plenty of improper Bostonians willing to kill him to get it. But why the bomb? It sure as hell wasn't meant for the cat. It hadn't gone off when Tom looked through the window. That meant there wasn't a triggerman watching the house. There were two doors and only one bomb. Both doors were probably wired to transmitters. There was a time delay between the fat cat's entrance and the explosion, so maybe the bomber wanted someone to see the dead seller before the curtain fell. And Tom was the target. No doubt about it. The bomber wouldn't have left a trap ready to blow from a visit by a nosey neighbor or some kid selling Girl Scout cookies. Somebody wanted him dead, but there wasn't any need to off him to get the painting—if the seller had it, the bomber had it now. Killing Tom didn't sound like a good business plan. True, the Irish mob boys had told him to stay the hell out of Boston, but this wasn't their style. They'd want to see him squirm first.

One thing was clear—Tom no longer had a live lead to the Monet. Maybe Boston's finest would identify what was left of the presumed seller, but the bomber and his prize were well away now. Would the cops make a connection between the singed body fragments and a stolen painting? Not likely. The FBI Art

Crime Team wasn't even sure there was a stolen Monet in the city, so it was a good bet the local constabulary was clueless. No way Tom could hang around Boston snooping on his own either. For his next swim in the harbor, he might be chained to a string of cement blocks.

Tom considered the odds. He felt sure the seller's Monet was genuine, real enough to be worth two murders, and the dead guy's behavior meant he probably had stolen it—almost certainly from the bomber. That wasn't much help, though. The painting might, or might not, still be in Boston, but Tom would have to find it the hard way. He would have to trace the water lilies from the original theft and murders in County Armagh, Ireland. He wasn't equipped for foreign travel, so he headed to Logan for his return flight to Albuquerque.

The McNaul Brothers Detective Agency met for a rare Sunday morning penary session. The Staab Street office smelled of burnt coffee, stale donuts, and Myrna's latest perfume experiment. Willie rested a pair of worn Ariat ropers on his desktop and stroked his ragged beard. Tom paced laps around their cramped office as he summarized the case. Myrna listened from her perch on the sprung sofa. The surviving springs complained as she adjusted her angle of repose to highlight her favorite assets. The shift released a cloud of dust and toxic pollen from the cushions, causing her to sneeze. As Tom wound up the Boston saga, he stopped at his own desk, gulped some tepid coffee, and stared out the window. "What now?"

Willie cleared his throat with more gargling than was necessary. "Let me see if I've got this straight. A rich Irish woman in Boston, who refused to meet with you, hired you to find an expensive painting that she may not really own. You tracked down a guy who said he wanted to sell it, but when you went to see him, he was dead. Then the house blew up, and the cat made it out alive. That about cover the essentials?"

"Close enough. The question is . . . what do we do now?" Tom turned to face his comrades. "The evidence is sketchy, but I'm convinced the seller, the dead guy to you bozos, had the Monet. Or a Monet anyway. The trail is too cold to chase it on spec, but I called Grace O'Malley before I left Boston. She's willing to foot the expenses upfront."

Willie nodded approval. "Make sure it includes a big lump sum with no receipts kept. We could use the dough but not a clear trail. We could also use a plan. Any ideas?"

Tom folded his arms and leaned hard against the edge of his desk. Its right-front leg stopped a half-inch short of the floor, and the resulting lurch of the desktop sent his UNM Lobos coffee mug over the edge to its doom. Nobody flinched—Tom broke two or three cups a month and replaced them from a thrift shop. "Someone in Boston has that painting, or knows who does, but nobody there is going to talk to me about it. I might add that some of those nobodies would shoot me on sight if I showed up in Beantown and started asking questions." He paused, took a deep breath, and blew it out slowly for show. "The Monet disappeared in Northern Ireland more than twenty years ago. That's where I'll have to start. Someone there knows how it got to Boston."

"Where 'we'll' start, little brother. Tell the shy O'Malley lady that she'll have to pay for two tickets. I'm not letting you play cowboy by yourself."

Myrna came to life. "Ooh, an adventure. You boys pack your guns. I'm with Willie on this one. I don't think even a Bostonian is mean enough to blow up a house to get rid of a cat. Someone wants you dead, Tommy. You take your big bro along. He's not like you—he doesn't stop to analyze things when the bullets fly."

Tom grunted, but Myrna was right. He was a better shot than his ex-Marine brother, but Willie never flinched when a fight broke out. He was born down and dirty. "Yeah, okay. We'll go."

Willie gave a satisfied nod. "Glad that's settled. Where is Ireland anyway?"

"You don't need to know. Just think green. And pack a raincoat."

A group of Irishmen began singing "Whiskey, You're the Devil" in Tom's left shirt pocket. The Clancy Brothers and Tommy Makem provided his favorite ringtone. "Yeah?"

"Time to talk?"

"Kate." Tom recognized the clipped diction of his former partner. "Got another case for me?"

"Still working that Monet caper for you. I just got off the phone with Boston's finest. Seems a man closely resembling your would-be Monet seller went up in smoke in Dorchester. You know anything about that?"

"A little, but you first, toots. You called me."

"Mmm. Not much to tell about the bomb. I assume you know it was a bomb?"

"Yeah. Look, Kate. I was looking through the window just a couple of minutes before it went off."

Kate snorted. "No wonder they call you guys 'peepers.' Well, anyway, the deceased was some sort of low-level Irish hood. For now, the locals are playing it as a gang hit."

"It probably was, in a manner of speaking."

"Play it straight with me, Tommy. You think the fireworks are connected with the lost Monet?"

"I always do. And yeah, has to be a link. Someone took out the seller less than an hour before I was to meet with him. He was dead before I got there, and the bomb was set for me. Someone knew I was coming, and that someone didn't want me to get any closer to the painting."

"Or maybe he just didn't like you."

"Lots of people don't. Particularly in Boston. Is anyone checking up on Colleen? As you'll recall, my soon-to-be-ex tried to take me out over a Vermeer last winter."

Kate hacked out a rare laugh. "I told you to ditch Colleen a week after I met her. She's too much of an artsy social climber to settle for a G-man husband. You need a hard-ass like yourself."

And like Kate, of course. Colleen's jealousy was overblown, but she had sensed Kate's interest in Tom at first sniff.

"But not this time, Tommy. Solid alibi. She was setting up a show in her New York gallery."

"Swell. Look, Kate, I don't know much. I figure the dead seller really did have a genuine Monet, and he probably stole it from the guy who killed him. Looks like that didn't work out too well. I figure he swiped it from a Boston mob guy, probably Irish, and lads will be lads."

"Maybe. Bulldog that you are, I assume you'll stay on the case?"

"Gotta, Kate."

"I figured. So, Tommy, good luck, but watch your ass better than usual this time."

"Not easy to do. I'm getting older, and my neck won't turn back far enough."

"Wiseass. I'm not kidding. Maybe this was just an in-house mob job, but there's the bomb. It wasn't particularly big, but that kind of setup—transmitter, delayed fuse—doesn't feel right for a simple hit on a simpleton detective. I'll know more when the forensics come in, but we might be dealing with a weirdo, or worse."

"Pursued by a mad bomber, eh? Well, maybe, but whoever it was must have had some connection to the painting. He knew I was coming, and when."

"Forewarned, Tommy."

"Yeah, and I'll carry four arms. Thanks, Kate." Tom clicked off his phone and turned to face the smug grins of Willie and Myrna. "Why the shit-eating grins?"

Myrna rolled her eyes a full revolution. "That little fireball of an FBI agent has the hots for you, honey. Why don't you make up your mind? You've been dragging your feet over ditching your witchy wife, and I want to know who's next? I vote you be smart and stay local. You and Laurie have lots of complimentary faults—been misbehaving since high school."

"Stow it, babe."

Myrna pretended to look hurt as she fought her way out of the sofa and sashayed toward her desk in the front room. She paused in the doorway and looked back over her right shoulder. "I'm local too, big boy." She winked and closed the door with enough force to rattle the brass-eagle knocker.

Willie moved his boots from the desktop to the lower bottom-right drawer. "I think you need to make the next move, Tommy. I don't know a living soul in Ireland. Is it one country or two?"

"Two, I think. We'll count when we get there." Tom stood up and resumed pacing laps. "The painting disappeared in Northern

Ireland. Ask Myrna to book us a flight to Belfast. We'll leave as soon as we can."

"How long we staying?"

"Never can tell. Tell her to book something changeable. Mrs. O'Malley is picking up the tab."

"Tommy, not to show lack of confidence, but do you have any police contacts over there? This case is twenty years cold, and we aren't going to find out much eavesdropping in pubs. Not that we shouldn't try."

Tom tightened his jaw and shook his head. "Sorry, but no. I'll see if Kate can at least get us in a door somewhere. Can't count on it, though. Art theft is common in Ireland, but the FBI Art Crime Team wasn't set up until 2004. This case was dead years before that."

"Open return it is." Willie lurched to his feet and headed toward Myrna's desk in the front room.

* * *

Tom swerved his Tacoma to the curb in front of Laurie's house and braked hard enough to chirp the tires. As he bounded up the last step, the door swung open to a chorus of sharp yaps and a charge of brown fur inches above floor level. Stella snarled and bit at his shoelaces as he fought his way inside.

Laurie was nowhere in sight, but he followed the sounds of clinking glass into her kitchen. The clinks dropped in pitch once the glasses were full, and they settled into crude Mexican chairs with fraying rush seats. Iced tea. Laurie must be working on a story. She showed him a tired smile. "What's the news from Boston?"

Tom ran through a discrete version of his adventures and watched Laurie's smile drain away. She stared at her bare feet, wiggled both big toes, and spoke without looking up. "Does this mean you're hitting the road again? Where to this time?"

"Ireland."

"Green or Orange?"

"Probably both, but we'll probably start up north."

"You always were a Bushmills man."

"Only since high school."

Laurie sighed and leaned back enough to lift the front legs of her chair an inch. Her feet came to rest on Tom's thigh. "Who makes it we?"

"Willie."

"Shoulda guessed." She closed one eye and stared at her feet as she ground her right heel into Tom's thigh. "I can never figure out whether you're safer alone or with your homicidal brother looking out for you." She sighed and let her feet drop to the floor with an intentional thud. "You're here tonight, though?"

"Uh-huh."

"So how are things going with Colleen?"

Tom tried for an innocent grin but felt like he was smiling at a camera. "Didn't see her this trip. She was down in New York."

Laurie turned her head and arched one eyebrow until she looked at him like a rooster contemplating an earthworm. "How do you know?" Laurie was well aware that Colleen still had her loft in New York, though she spent most of her time in Boston bunking with Justin, her northernmost gallery owner.

"Kate told me." He cringed as Laurie's second eyebrow assumed the same arch as the first. Shouldn't have said that.

Laurie didn't say anything, but the spark was gone from her eyes as they returned to her glass. Tom once felt he and Laurie would probably double up someday, but there never seemed to be any rush. Anyway, he was still legally married to Colleen. That excuse didn't cut much mustard, though, when the subject of Kate oozed up. Someday he was going to have to think all this over. Meanwhile, he'd be sleeping alone tonight. He finished his tea and made excuses.

*　　*　　*

Tom knew the fridge was bare, save for a couple of pale ales, so he tried his alleged pantry cabinet. The only resident was an open box of generic raisin bran. A small, white moth fluttered out the top. Tom headed for Rosie's. His condo sat on a low ridge overlooking the city and was only a ten-minute stroll from the Plaza. As he turned right onto San Francisco Street, his phone began singing the virtues of the juice of the barley. Aoife O'Malley. He fumbled the phone trying to answer but caught it at knee level. "Hey!"

"Hey back. I haven't heard about your Boston trip. Do you have time to talk?"

"Sure, but I'm a block short of dinner. Can I call you later?"

"Yes, but where are you? I'm in Santa Fe myself, and I'm hungry. Got room for me, or would I make three?"

Tom tried not to sound too eager. "We'll just be two, but let's try someplace a bit quieter than Rosie's." They settled on a steakhouse on Old Las Vegas Highway—at least two levels upscale from Tom's usual enchilada emporiums. He got there first and found a secluded table in a corner of the walled patio. The sun was setting, and the meager lighting struggled to maintain some degree of visibility. The light reached tryst level—seemed appropriate for detective work. Tom ordered a pint of Guinness and settled into a latticed metal chair with his back to the high stone wall.

Aoife strode in a beer-and-a-half later, spotted Tom's glass, and swept up a house margarita (rocks and salt) on the way to join him. The wind flailed a sheaf of hair across her eyes, but she shook it back to her shoulders as she settled in the lee of the wall and angled her head a few degrees. Her faded jeans and embroidered shirt stuck close to their owner and bore the wrinkles of a workday, but her full lips were freshly painted to a red resembling Navajo sandstone. They curled into a melting smile while the silent, amber eyes opened the inquiries. Tom refused the bait. "How do you happen to be in Santa Fe?"

"I'm writing a review paper with my former PhD adviser—early Chaco trade patterns. My Monday class is first thing in the morning, so I drove up here and spent the afternoon digging in the library at SAR. That's the School for Advanced Research."

Tom nodded. "I'm familiar with it. How's that Friday class going?"

"Not bad. It's an intro course. Two sections. It's early in the term, but the students seem halfway motivated. They're mostly girls, but archeology is like that." Aoife leaned back in her chair and flashed Tom a coy grin. "I didn't want to mention this before, but one of them has a familiar name. What was it now?" She gave her chin an exaggerated rub. "Oh yes, McNaul. Cassidy McNaul. Any relation?"

"Surely, you asked her?"

"Actually, no. I didn't know your name until my mother asked me to contact you on Thursday. Although my class did meet Friday, I left it in the able hands of my teaching assistant." She pursed her lips slightly, as if contemplating whether she owed Tom some sort of apology. None was forthcoming.

"You could have asked me. On Friday."

Aoife fidgeted in her chair. "I suppose I should have, but I was late for a meeting with my department head." Her eyes took the offensive, and Tom instinctively leaned back an inch. "So if you don't mind, I'm asking now?"

"Fair enough. Yes, we're related." Tom regained his inch and more as he leaned both elbows on the table. "Cassidy is my daughter." Aoife's eyes appeared to widen, and for a moment, Tom wondered if she had been hoping to hear "cousin." "She's been living in New York, but she decided to move to New Mexico for college."

"Does she have a mother?" Aoife developed a sudden interest in stirring her margarita. She stared at the ice cubes as they rattled against the glass.

Tom stalled with a long pull on the Guinness. The soft stout slid down his throat like a premium motor oil for humans. Aoife extended her tongue fully and licked salt crystals from her glass as she waited him out. "Yes." Tom moved his beer coaster a quarter of an inch to the right and took care to make sure he centered his pint. "Her mother is Colleen McNaul, or at least she was still McNaul as of last week. She's an artist of some note, a painter." He hoped to end it there, but Aoife rolled her eyes to meet his while still licking salt. "I've been married to her for, uh, twenty-six years now. We met in college, winter of my sophomore year at MIT."

"That's a long time these days. Congratulations." She drained the last of the margarita.

"Yeah. We got married a week after graduation. Ups and downs, but it worked for a long time." He waved to a waiter. "But when I got transferred to D.C. a couple of years ago, to the FBI Art Crime Team, she didn't want to leave New York. Maybe the living apart did us in. Maybe we'd already lost it by then. I don't really know. FBI life can be hard." But usually not so hard that your wife tries to have you shot. Best hold off on that story.

Aoife's face softened, and she dropped her hands to her lap. "I'm sorry." She looked almost sincere. "Are you working on it?"

"No. The divorce papers were on the table at Rosie's Friday." The waiter arrived. Tom started to order another round, but Aoife switched to water. He joined her.

Tom fiddled with his spoon as he watched the disappointed waiter shuffle off. "I'd rather not go on with this. You can do the math—I just turned forty-seven. Cassidy is eighteen, a freshman, though I guess you know that." He set down the spoon and cocked his head to the right. "Your turn."

"I'm twenty-nine."

Tom tried for a Gallic shrug. "They all say that."

Aoife laughed. "No, I really am. You've talked to my mother. I was born in Boston, went to Wellesley, grad work at Michigan in anthropology, stayed for a short post-doc, new assistant prof at UNM. Details to follow, perhaps, but let's get on to our case. What happened in Boston?"

"Let's order first." Tom found an interesting cheeseburger with blue cheese, some sort of chile-infused oil, and an organic bun. It wasn't as healthy as Aoife's salmon salad, but he had his principles. When the waiter was out of earshot, Tom ran through an abridged version of his weekend, leaving out his swim in the harbor, the night with Molly, and Kate's worries about the bomber. He felt like he was reading her a Classics Illustrated edition. Aoife shook her head a lot and tossed in a few raw expletives, but she provided no new insights. She seemed to be playing it straight.

"Willie and I are going to Ireland. We have no leads, but we don't have much choice other than to work this as a type of cold case. It may be a bit awkward, since nobody over there has invited us."

"When are you going?"

"I'm not sure when, or even where, but I'll call you before we leave." Tom figured the less she knew, the better. Aoife shrugged and whipped out her credit card before Tom could make things awkward.

As a busboy cleared the nearest table, Tom sank into his chair and tried to read Aoife's face. A diagonal shadow covered all but her lips and chin, and they weren't giving many clues. He gave up. "How's Cassidy doing in class?"

Aoife leaned forward until her eyes sparkled in the light. "I can't really talk about that. Student privacy has become a big deal in colleges."

"I'm paying half her expenses. Seems like I should get some sort of report."

"I tend to agree with you, but the courts have ruled otherwise. No problems, though."

*   *   *

Their feet crunched gravel in the cramped parking lot. Only five cars remained, and they reached Tom's pickup first. He dug out his keys and hesitated, then extended his left arm toward her side. She caught his wrist with her right hand and gave it a firm squeeze. "I enjoyed the evening." She released his arm and gave him a wink. "It's too early in the term to be bribing the teacher, though. I'm sure Cassidy will do fine."

Tom relaxed and couldn't hold back a smile. "I hope she gets a B on her midterm."

~ 6 ~

"Hey, Kate." Tom slouched in his worn purple chair and rested his mismatched hiking socks on the coffee table. He spotted a small hole in the heel of the right. "Working late?" It was four-thirty on Tuesday afternoon in Santa Fe, two hours later in Washington, but Kate never left her office before seven.

"Tommy, my man!" Kate never sounded sorry to hear from him. "What's up?"

"The Emerald Isle, toots. Got to go there in a couple of days chasing water lilies, and I need some help. Can you give me any?"

"Would if I could, but that case has been dead a long time across the pond. Seems like it's dead on this side now. Not sayin' you killed it."

"More like it tried to kill me, but never mind that." Tom could hear Kate's breathing speed up. No doubt she was doing exercises at her desk. Her body seemed to be fully recovered from the near-fatal lung wound she suffered six months earlier, but her rehab would never end, nor would she ever forgive herself for getting shot in the first place. Tom waited as the rhythmic huffing got louder. Kate seemed slightly misplaced in the FBI. She had grown up dreaming of being a Marine, but her five-foot-four stature left her inches short of the minimum height required by the Corps. The FBI didn't care about height, just fitness.

Kate expelled an epic whoosh worthy of a winded quarter horse. "Still there, Tommy? Score one for persistence. Okay, here's what I know. When that O'Malley woman in Boston reported a missing Monet, twenty years after the theft, I called the cops in Northern Ireland and talked to a detective who remembered the case. He wasn't on the original investigation team, but he went through their files for me. This was high-profile. Their team worked it hard but not for long. They played it all the way as a burglary that went bad when the owners got home early. A couple of silver trinkets eventually surfaced in pawn shops, but they'd passed through too many hands to be traced. The major swag, including the art, never turned up. The case went nowhere, and the law soon moved on to bigger things."

"What's bigger than a Monet? Did somebody steal a Rembrandt?"

Kate's snort sounded a bit louder than necessary. "Bigger than art, Tommy. The Troubles. Bombings and shootings were still all the rage in '97. The peace accord, such as it was, didn't occur until '98. So yes, the Irish cops had bigger problems than stolen art on their plates. People were dying on both sides of the Irish Sea. Lots of them."

Tom deflated and sat wiggling his toes while he waited for more. There wasn't any more. "Well, thanks anyway, toots, but I've got to make a living. You think anyone over there would talk to a lonely P.I. from New Mexico if he showed up at their door?"

"You're kidding, right? They've probably never heard of New Mexico. You'd have to show them a map and a passport before they'd believe you weren't from Guadalajara." Kate's voice lowered half an octave. "Kidding aside, Tommy, they won't help you. Security is tighter than a Scot's wallet over there. Everyone in Ireland, north and south, is scared shitless that the peace won't last. If there's even a chance those murders in '97 had anything to do with the Troubles, there's no chance of the police cooperating with you. They'll sit on it. Let the sleeping dogs lie, and all that."

"These particular dogs are dead and buried, toots. I just want to recover a painting and pay some bills. Come on, Kate. Do you really think the O'Malley murders had anything to do with Irish politics?

Kate sniffed. "I wouldn't know. But look at it from the cops' point of view. A couple of rich Catholics are murdered in Northern Ireland. A bunch of expensive stuff, possibly including a Monet, disappears. Were the murders an unfortunate twist of a simple burglary, or were the thefts just the cover for a hit? The Royal Ulster Constabulary had a look and said they couldn't find the killers, or any of the important loot. Case filed, nobody objects. Twenty-some years later, a man in a $50 suit shows up at their door wanting to stir the bones. Best of luck."

"Resent the crack about the suit. Got it at a Brooks Brothers sale."

"Noted."

"Otherwise, yeah, and thanks, I think. Can you at least give me the contact info for the guy you talked to? I don't want to knock on the door of the Royal Ulster what-the-hell and get the bum's rush."

"Constabulary, but you won't find them under that name anymore. They reorganized into the Police Service of Northern Ireland in 2001. No point in going there, though. The guy I talked to was barely willing to talk to the FBI. Alone, you've got no chance." Kate was silent for at least thirty seconds, but Tom could hear no exercise noises. When she resumed speaking, her voice was pure professional monotone. "When are you going?"

"I'm shooting for Friday, but Myrna is still working on the tickets."

"Tell you what, Tommy. I'll go with you."

"Uh. Why? I appreciate the offer, but wouldn't it be more efficient for you to stay home and work the lines from Washington?"

"Maybe, but miracles can happen, and on the off chance that you actually get somewhere, I think I should be there to represent the bureau's interests."

Tom was puzzled. "Enlighten me. What interests?"

"Tommy, your client says she doesn't have any proof of ownership of this allegedly stolen Monet. If the painting is real, and if it ends up in your hotel room, do you really think we're going to let you hand it off to this O'Malley woman before we investigate the provenance? We're talking about an international treasure."

"I suppose not, but this is our case, and we need to make a living. You guys had your shot and gave up."

"Don't panic, McNaul. I'll just be there for the weekend to see if there's any trail warm enough to follow. If there is, you keep us in the loop, and I'll make sure you don't end up stowing away on a tramp steamer to get home. If we smack a stone wall, at least we'll have a weekend in Ireland."

Tom couldn't quite hear Kate chuckle, but he could picture her grin. "A nice idea, but is it really worth your time?"

"It's about time we find out."

Tom was cornered and knew it. Kate was no bullshitter, and if she said he'd never get close enough to an Irish cop to see the whites of his eyes, that doorway was bricked up. He'd need her help. Her ulterior motives were clear enough. Three years ago, when Tom transferred to the Art Crime Team, sparks swirled like July fireflies. He and Kate managed to stamp out the brushfires, but Tom must have smelled of smoke. Kate and Colleen started snarling at each other five seconds after they met. Tom had no idea how women sensed such things. Didn't figure he ever would. For two years, Kate had maintained a pseudo-professional distance from Tom out of a grudging respect for his wedding ring. Then, last winter, someone had set up Tom and Kate to die by tipping their sting operation to the Boston mob. Kate stopped a bullet with her chest, while Tom escaped with a flesh wound and a blown career. Both were sure Colleen had made the phone call, but they lacked evidence. Colleen walked. The marriage died. The stolen Vermeer was still in the wind.

Tom took his time for appearances but surrendered without pretense of resistance. "You win. Better call Myrna to coordinate flights. I was planning on Belfast. What do you think?"

"I don't think so. We'll just get the runaround there, but I have an idea. Get back to you."

Kate called back in less than an hour. "We're cooking, Tommy. I woke up my cop contact in Belfast. He kept barking that he'd said all he would, but I made him give me something to get me off his ass." She paused, and Tom took a few seconds before nibbling the bait.

"So what did he give you, toots?"

"The name of a detective who actually worked on the murders. Paddy McGrath. He's retired now, but here's the deal—he was the lone Catholic cop working the case. In '97, those were pretty rare in Northern Ireland. Still aren't that many of them."

"And we care about his religion because. . . ?"

"Sergeant McGrath was the token Papist on the investigation team—placed there because the two victims were prominent Catholics. There were a couple of leads, but they fizzled. The chief inspector played politics and cut off the investigation. Pissed off McGrath no end, and the sarge mouthed off to the press. The Constabulary buried him in a filing job, so he took early retirement. My contact doesn't have the guy's number, but he figures Paddy'd mouth off some more if we showed up at his neighborhood pub and acted sympathetic."

Tom slid his feet to the floor. "You always were a bulldog, Agent Kate. Nice work. Just where might Paddy's preferred pub be located?"

"Down south, in the Republic. He lives in or near the town of Carrick-on-Suir, in County Tipperary."

"As in it's a long way to. . . ?"

"Can it, Tommy. Just get Myrna to book you a ticket to Shannon, and have her tell me what flight you'll be on. For a genuine Monet, I think I can get the bureau to send me to Ireland for a long weekend. If they balk, I've maxed out my accrued leave anyway—need to use it or lose it."

"Will do." Tom clicked off, livened his glass with another finger of Bushmills, and savored a long pull. It had been ten years since he'd been to Ireland. He closed his eyes and began to reload the memory banks. He tried to remember the name of a hotel in Shannon, but his mind ran off to a weekend in Dublin with a young lecturer at Trinity. Bridget McCory, that was her name. Perhaps he should try to call her. He forced his eyes open. No, best leave that behind.

Tom prowled through his meager book supply but couldn't find any guides to Ireland. He slid a paperback copy of *Ulysses* with a torn dust jacket from his bookshelf. The first three pages had fingerprints, a coffee stain, and two dog-eared pages, but the rest were in mint condition. No matter—there were two days left before Friday. He would walk down to the Travel Bug in the morning and pick up some maps and a travel guide. Maybe he could find an Irish mystery to read on the plane.

*   *   *

"There's not a goddamned green-chile cheeseburger in this dingy excuse for an airport!" Willie was scowling at the menu of an Irish pub at Newark Liberty International. His shaggy mane was unusually clean, and he was sporting the same suede sports jacket he'd worn at their father's funeral. "Pick me somethin' that packs some heat."

Tom flagged a waiter and ordered two shepherd's pies plus a round of Guinness pints. His phone began to buzz like a dentist's drill. Incoming text from Kate—she was only four gates away. Tom captured a third stool for their table as she marched into the pub trailing a trim, black carry-on that looked bulletproof. She smiled at Tom but switched to her FBI stare as she scanned Willie. "Who the fuck are you?"

Tom realized he hadn't told Kate about Willie coming along. He grasped for an out, but Willie beat him to it. "Name's Willie. Willie McNaul. We're half-brothers." He extended a paw. "You Tommy's G-girl?"

"G-woman, bub."

"Beg your pardon." Willie shook her hand without standing up. They fixed eyes for a moment while testing grips. Each seemed satisfied as they let go.

Kate climbed aboard the empty stool, feet dangling six inches above the floor. She arched an eyebrow at Willie. "Heard you used to be a Marine. Any truth in it?"

He nodded slowly. "A gunny. Long time ago, though." He eyed the visible sections of Kate's muscular limbs. "Tom said you had thoughts of being in the Corps."

"Fuckin' A, Bubba. Came up a bit short, though. Four inches."

Willie laughed and headed over to the bar to get her a beer. Tom offered Kate a sip of his own to tide her over. She wiped the trademark creamy foam from her upper lip and cocked her head. "Interesting brother. Glad I finally met him. You bring him along for protection?"

"In a way, but not from you." Tom showed a renewed interest in swilling Guinness. Kate knew plenty of Willie stories, and it would be best if she didn't hear the rest. Willie owned a fierce sense of justice but never showed a shred of concern for the law. There were unmarked graves. Tom grew up feeling he was the anti-Willie, a believer in rules. But the FBI had cast him out, and without his badge and blue suit, he found himself slipping toward Willie's side of town. He shivered, set the empty glass down with a thud, and looked into Kate's bemused eyes. Glad she's coming along.

* * *

Tom jolted awake as the lights came on and the crew announced breakfast. The aisle seat was empty. He craned his neck backward and spotted Willie chatting up a redheaded attendant. Kate's nose was already stuck to the window. He stared past her at islets of black rock, each making its stand against the raging surf. Soon, the United jet descended toward Shannon, and the islands got bigger and grew dense rugs of green vegetation. Tom nodded to no one in particular and recalled his two previous visits. No matter how green you thought Ireland might be, when you got there, it was greener. Greener than the Technicolor palette of *The Quiet Man*.

As they pulled into the gate, Tom saw a ground-crew man standing spread-eagled on the ramp as a security guard ran a metal detector wand over his body. There weren't many legal handguns in Ireland, though everyone figured there were plenty of illegal ones cached throughout the island. Willie was still howling about having to travel naked, but there was no way a couple of private eyes licensed in New Mexico were going to get carry permits here. Kate wasn't armed either, and she was FBI.

Kate renegotiated the Hertz car rental contract down to a subcompact to save gas. She claimed to have the most experience driving on the left side of the road, so she jumped behind the wheel. Nobody argued. Tom rode shotgun while Willie contorted his frame, legs splayed to the pain point, until he was able to close the right rear door.

Kate took off like a stuntwoman in a *Mad Max* film, causing Tom to keep an eye on the side mirror for signs of hot pursuit. He spotted neither villains nor cops and eventually relaxed. The main roads to Carrick were fast and largely straight in the brief intervals between traffic circles. The scenery remained green. Kate brought them to Main Street, Carrick-on-Suir, in an hour and thirty-five minutes, a quarter of an hour ahead of the Google Maps estimate. She swerved to the curb in front of the Carraig Hotel—the city's lone inn. Although the bar beckoned, they were still an hour short of the 10:30 opening, so they opted for naps. The three rooms were tidy, the beds splendid enough for people straight off an overnight flight.

*   *   *

Tom's hunger surpassed his fatigue just after noon. When he reached the hotel bar, Kate and Willie were freshening pints of red ale. The pair returned to a table for three wedged into a dark corner. Their new pints were close to half-mast by the time Tom waited through the traditional pouring period for a Guinness. As he reached the table, Kate terminated a call and jammed her phone into a side coat pocket. She flashed Tom a peevish expression. "No luck, Tommy. McGraths abound in these parts, and the five listed as Patricks or Paddys aren't answering. Of course, we don't know for sure whether our guy lives in the town."

Tom shrugged. "So we start with the pubs. Ask around. You said the guy took early retirement, and that was at least twenty years ago. This Paddy McGrath must be in his 70s. Gotta be well known in a town this small."

Willie stood up, stretched, and sidled toward the young, sturdy barmaid. "I'll get us a list."

Tom clinked his mug against Kate's and did his best to equalize the fluid levels. Willie returned with a battered, and fortunately thin, phone book. He spun it onto the table next to Tom's right elbow. "Barkeep says there are seventeen of them, depending on what you count. She's new here—recent immigrant from the Ukraine. Says she doesn't know any Paddy McGrath, but my guess is she wouldn't tell us if she did."

The page listing local pubs was stained, missing its lower-right corner, and split by a major rip extending to within an inch of the bottom edge, but Tom was able to make out all of the names and most of the phone digits. Carrick was a small city, and he figured there couldn't be more than three or four genuine hangouts. He preferred to visit them alone. Kate's demeanor screamed law-woman, while an imbibing Willie exuded pure menace. The locals would likely take him for a Yankee hit man. The three of them together would clear out any pub in town within seconds. Tom lifted the open phone book with two hands and carried it back to the bar. He eased it down onto a dry spot near the barmaid. She blinked pale-blue eyes surrounded by long, black lashes spiked like a wolfhound's collar. Her frame was more muscular than fat, and she leaned a pair of Popeye forearms on the bar while presenting the usual view intended to increase liquor sales.

"What can I get you?"

Her accent was subtle, and Tom wondered how Willie placed her as Ukrainian? It didn't seem to matter. "A Jameson on the rocks, thanks." He smiled as he placed his own arms on the table close enough to hers for the hairs to tickle. He spoke in a prison-yard whisper. "Listen, I just want to ditch these two for the evening." He made a subtle nod toward Kate and Willie while keeping his eyes locked to the barmaid's. "Which of these are the real town pubs? I'll send that pair off to one of the pretenders."

The barmaid stared back at him for several seconds. Tom couldn't tell whether she was sizing him up or waiting for an invitation. Either he passed, or she gave up. She stabbed the tattered page with a callused finger, muttered three names, and turned to pour his whiskey. Tom paid her but left it untouched on the bar.

Kate and Willie were obviously skeptical of his plan to split up, but they relented after a few grunts and copied down the names and addresses of the less-favored establishments. Tom followed them as far as the front door.

~ 7 ~

Although Tom had never considered the Irish reticent, the name of each pub on his list consisted of a single word—presumably the name of an owner, past or present. This was a welcome difference from English pubs, which typically had whimsical names longer than limericks. He started with Riley's, a well-lit establishment about a block uphill from the River Suir. The half-dozen patrons pretended to ignore his conversation with the large lad behind the bar, who polished a pint glass, extended his square jaw, and slowly shook his head. Nobody looked Tom's way as he left. Murphy's produced an identical result, though this time with only four patrons.

Tommy's was two blocks farther down the narrow street, but as Tom pushed through the black, wooden door, it was clear his reputation had preceded him. He counted eight customers, each ignoring all others present and staring into a pint mug with the intensity of an extra in a B Western. The bartender's mustache resembled a blond Wyatt Earp model with squared tips, and Tom noticed the man's hands dropping out of sight below the bar. Nobody seemed to be holding a phone, but news travels fast in a troubled land, and maybe the pubs had runners. There wasn't much point in trying an indirect approach, so Tom strode to the bar, ordered a Guinness, and aimed his back toward the one empty corner of the room. Several minutes later, when the milky head of the stout was proper for consumption, he drained an inch and lowered the mug onto a coaster stained with more overlapping rings than the Olympic flag. He stood tall, slipped a McNaul Brothers Detective Agency card from his inside jacket pocket, and offered it to the bartender. After a brief hesitation, the man's hands climbed back into view. One of them took the card. He squinted at it for a few seconds and then handed it back to Tom. "What's this supposed to mean? You some kind of traveling entertainer looking for a gig?"

Tom forced a laugh. "Sorry, no. My comedy license is only good in Massachusetts." He leaned across the bar until his nose was six inches from the bartender's, but he spoke in a voice loud enough to be heard in the kitchen. "My name is Tom McNaul. As you surely can tell, I'm an American—from the high plains of New Mexico. I'm a private investigator, not the law, and I'm surely not looking for trouble. I just want to talk to a man named Paddy Mc-Grath to see if he can help me find a valuable item for my client. I was told Mr. McGrath frequents this place from time to time. If he comes in, would you ask him to call me? I'm staying at the Carraig."

The bartender's eyes never strayed from Tom's, and the patrons continued to count bubbles in their beers. Tom noticed a slight movement in the corner to his left. He didn't turn his head, but after a few seconds, he glanced at a mirror behind the bar to check out the only occupied table in that corner. A thin man with a highly irregular gray beard sat watching him. Tom made a quarter turn to his left to get a better view. The fellow looked to be in his 60s, and he was dressed in worn woolen pants, muddy boots, and a green sweatshirt. A blue tweed cap rested on the table next to his pint. The chair opposite the man was pulled back and faced a half-filled glass of ale and a soup bowl containing brown gravy with worrisome lumps. The man with the ragged beard noticed Tom's eyes and dropped his stare into his glass.

There didn't seem to be any point in ruining Tommy's business, so Tom took to the streets. Kate and Willie had more pubs to cover, and he had a bit of time to explore. He pulled out his pocket guidebook and strolled to the center of the fifteenth-century "Old Bridge" across the River Suir. It looked sound, and the scars of its partial demolition by the IRA in 1922 were not prominent. He returned to the north bank and continued eastward. Ormonde Castle, which may or may not have been the birthplace of Anne Boleyn, loomed with quiet dignity, but there wasn't enough time for a formal tour. He returned to the Carriag and gave his liver a break by ordering a steaming mug of coffee with fresh cream. As he settled into a leather wingback with a view of the street, Tom and the desk clerk had the lobby to themselves. The clerk was a slender young man with a narrow blue tie of the sort favored in the '60s.

Tom was still sniffing steam and waiting for the coffee to drop below scalding when the clerk disappeared through a narrow door behind the desk. Seconds later, two men emerged from the same door. The bearded man with blue cap from Tommy's moved to the inside of the front door of the hotel and leaned his back against it with enough leverage to prevent casual entry. He crossed his arms and began scanning the other entrances to the lobby, avoiding Tom's eyes. The second man was heavyset, clean-shaven, and almost bald, showing only a monk's fringe of cropped white hair. He wore a Gaelic football jersey with more rips than patches on the sleeves. Tom didn't know enough about the Irish leagues to place the team from the colors. The second man approached with wary confidence, checked the location of his colleague, and sat in the chair across from Tom without speaking. Tom shrugged and began sipping his coffee.

"Do I take it, then, that you might be a Mr. Thomas McNaul, from America?" He spoke with the even confidence of a man accustomed to controlling the conversation.

Tom set down his coffee and leaned back slightly to lessen the toxicity of the man's beer breath. "I am. And might I be so bold as to assume you are Mr. Paddy McGrath, honorably retired from the Royal Ulster Constabulary?"

"You might." Paddy leaned forward, shed his tight smile, and lowered his voice half an octave. "Now suppose you tell me why the fuck you're asking around about me. Sure, that's not a smart thing to be doing in these times. If you're lookin' for trouble, you've just made a very serious mistake. Best you check out of here and get your arse back to Mexico."

"That would be New Mexico, Paddy, but I take no offense since you're not a Texan. And never fear, I'm not here to ruin your good times. I'd just like to ask you some questions about a cold case you once worked on. If you don't want to answer them, I'm fine with that. I'll just go home, collect my expense money, and find a new client. But my guess is that you'll want to talk about it."

"You're pretty fucking sure of yourself, aren't ya?"

"Actually, I'm not, but you're the only lead I've got. Look Paddy, hear me out. You remember the O'Malley murders? County Armagh, back in '97?"

"Jaysus." Paddy took a deep breath and exhaled with lips blubbering at the approximate frequency of a whoopee cushion. "The fuck you have to do with that?"

"Not a lot so far, but the wife of the late Mr. O'Malley hired me to find a painting stolen by the murderers. A source told me you were upset with the case being terminated too early. If you're willing, I'd like you to tell me why? I'm not a lawman—not looking to track down the killers. I just want to find out what happened to the painting. It's valuable, and my client needs the money."

"You say the widow hired you?"

"Yes, Mrs. Grace O'Malley of Boston."

Paddy's expression changed to quizzical, then stretched into a grin with teeth suggesting a lifelong aversion to dentistry. "Come on, McNaul. Who put you up to this?"

It was Tom's turn to be confused. "What do you mean? I just told you. . . ."

"The name Grace O'Malley doesn't mean anything to you?"

"Nothing special, beyond the fact that she's paying my bill."

Paddy looked dubious. "Grace O'Malley was a famous pirate queen back in the days. Also known as Granualle. Had a taste for plundering English ships until she negotiated a deal with Queen Elizabeth the First. You sure someone isn't having you on? Not many people in Ireland would hang a name like that on their daughter."

Tom was getting annoyed. "Then I presume she was named Grace O'Hara or something, and had the bad fortune to marry a man named O'Malley. Who the hell cares? Look, I heard that you quit the Constabulary because you thought they gave up on the O'Malley murders too soon. Didn't want to stir up the Troubles any more over a couple of dead Catholics. You happy with that outcome?"

"Easy, cowboy. No, I sure as shite don't like how that ended, but you said you're just after one of the fucking paintings. I don't much care about some damned piece of art, so what's in it for me?"

"You've got a point, Paddy, but the only way I'm going to find the painting is to follow its trail from the crime scene. I've got no authority to chase the murderers, but if I find the painting, chances are that'll tell you who snatched it. Best I can offer. What do you say?"

Paddy glanced around the lobby to ensure it was still empty, save for the blue-cap man leaning on the front door. "Like it or not, you're probably going to have to trace the killers. I can't get you files or anything, but here it is. We had two suspects. Couple of known burglars, and both had violent records. A witness said she saw them get in a car and leave the scene, but later on she got scared and changed her story—said she wasn't sure. The RUC kept the names of the alleged witnesses out of the papers, but someone got to her. No end of leaks at the RUC."

Paddy wiped his mouth on his jersey sleeve. "There was no physical evidence to speak of, but it was still early days." He leaned in closer and dropped his voice to a hoarse whisper. "Ten days after the murders, a kid on a bike found the two suspects shot dead and lying in a ditch next to their car. It was parked on a grassy farm track a bit east of Armagh. Clean twenty-two holes in the backs of their heads—an obvious hit, pro all the way, not a shred of evidence, and no sign of the paintings or other swag. Bunch of closed-door meetings, and two days later, the O'Malley murders were dropped. The chiefs made a brief show, wailing about the Troubles, when will it end? You should have seen them—made me puke. As I see it, they were getting nowhere on the murders and conveniently figured they'd cut their losses. They never admitted to any connection between the O'Malley murders and the two dead guys by the car. But I think there was a link. And I don't think the fucking chiefs would have dropped the case if the O'Malleys had been Protestants."

Tom tried to hide his disappointment. "What you figure? Someone found out about the heist, offed the burglars, and ran away with the painting? Seems a bit lame. In my experience, there aren't that many burglars with a taste for fine art."

Paddy shrugged and waited. Tom stared at the floor to his left while he thought. Paddy was right—whoever killed the burglars, in or near their car, was in on it from the beginning. The murders were only ten days apart, and the loot was still missing after twenty years.

Tom looked up. "Occam's razor—the simplest explanation is usually best. It was a double-cross—a gang pulled the heist and then had a falling-out. Like coyotes fighting over a dead rabbit but less noisy."

Paddy gave a slow nod.

"So yeah, they're connected. Too much of a coincidence otherwise. Any evidence that more than two guys pulled the original job?"

Paddy shook his head. "Such forensics as we had, and the one shaky witness, placed only two men at the scene. But like you said, it could have been a gang, and the two stiffs in the car were the unlucky dupes." Paddy's eyes wandered the room like he was looking for a safe place to spit. "Things were tough over here, you know. Shootings and bombs going off, here and Britain. Good people were dying, north and south, Catholic and Protestant alike." He looked back at Tom with pained eyes. "I couldn't prove anything, but I couldn't shake the feeling that the O'Malley murders were the handiwork of one of the fucking Orange paramilitary groups."

"How so?"

"I don't like coincidences either." Paddy hunched his shoulders and leaned forward on his elbows. "Everyone knew the O'Malleys had money, though lord knows how a Catholic family held on to so much land up in County Armagh. Old Mrs. O'Malley lived there alone, but she traveled a lot. Easy enough for anyone to burgle the place while she was gone. Doesn't it seem odd to you that they chose to break in when her son was making his annual visit?"

Tom paused a few seconds before replying. "You think someone wanted to take out the O'Malleys?"

"Not saying I know that, but we should have at least looked into it. Kind of late now."

Tom developed a sudden urge to scratch his right ear. "Doesn't sound like there's much hope going after the second set of murderers, but what about the guys they shot in the car?"

"You want to track a couple of dead guys? There I can help you. They're both about six feet down in a churchyard. Bit north of Armagh."

"Thanks a lot, but I was thinking of survivors. Family maybe. Were there any?"

"Timmy O'Neal was pretty much a loner, as I recall, but the other guy, Michael Fitzpatrick was married. Had a wife and baby daughter in Armagh, but I think they moved somewhere after Michael was shot. No idea where. I think the wife's name was Peggy."

"Know whether the wife was Orange or Green?"

"Not for sure, but I'd say Michael was most likely a Protestant. Not that I ever heard of him going in for church, mind you. I'm just guessing that because the deceased were Catholics."

Paddy unfolded from his chair and extended his hand. "Best of luck, Tommy McNaul. You will let me know if you find anything?"

"I'll do that, Paddy McGrath." Tom's hand disappeared into a paw that would be the envy of any blacksmith.

*   *   *

Tom knew he should have phoned his partners, but he preferred to think alone. Peggy Fitzpatrick, if that was still her name, had a twenty-year lead on him, but Kate had enough pull to stir up a fast search of public and police records. Tom figured Peggy might not have stayed in the part of Ireland where her husband was shot, but Ireland wasn't all that big. Of course, there was no guarantee she was still on the island. The barkeep was delivering Tom's third coffee when Kate and Willie strode through the door. Willie spotted him first.

"Will you look at that? A McNaul brother drinking coffee in an Irish pub. And after noon too." Willie grabbed Tom's coffee and poured it in a planter. Five minutes later, they settled into three leather chairs facing a front window and clutched three pints of Guinness.

Kate took over. "Okay, Tommy. We understand you ditched us, not that some of the dives on the north end aren't charming. Skip the fairy tales and spill it."

Tom rattled off the facts of his encounter with Paddy McGrath and leaned back in his chair. He rechecked the room to make sure there weren't extra ears, but the only other patrons were an elderly couple inspecting menus at the bar. He turned to Kate. "So . . ."

"Ditch the damned 'so,' will you? It doesn't mean shit, and it wastes time."

"Whoa, big girl." Tom regretted his words before he finished them, as his diminutive ex-partner seethed. "Look, Kate . . ." Tom couldn't figure out why "look" was preferable to "so." "We aren't close to anything, but if you can get the locals to clue us in to the whereabouts of this Peggy Fitzpatrick, we might at least have something to do next."

"Fair enough. And, sorry I barked. I just don't like being sent on a tour of the town for nothing. You could have said you wanted to go alone."

"Would you have let me go alone?"

"Hell, no." Kate sucked in her cheeks. "Point taken. I'll go upstairs and get busy. Call you when I find out something." She popped out of her chair and jogged up the stairs. Tom knew she hated waiting for elevators. Willie slid her half-empty pint next to his own.

*   *   *

Tom staggered into his room just after eleven, turned on the dimmest lamp he could find, and collapsed, fully dressed, on the bed. He'd lost count of Willie's calls for another round, but he'd managed to skip enough of them to stay sober. He stared at a plaster rose on the ceiling for a while, then closed his eyes and began to review the case. The room phone jarred him awake. Seven or eight rings later, he managed to locate the cursed device on the bedside table. "Yeah?"

It was Kate. "Wake up, Tommy. Got something on Peggy Fitzpatrick."

Tom stole enough time to take several deep breaths and beat the back of his head on the pillow. "Tell me she's here in the hotel."

"You wish. She's buried in the same churchyard as her late husband. Up in Armagh."

"Oh shit. What happened?"

"Overdose. About three years ago. She'd been working in a Michelin tire plant in Ballymena. That's northwest of Belfast. Lost her job and ended up working the streets."

"Don't suppose she left a draft of her memoirs?"

"Hardly."

"Well, thanks, toots. Looks like we're finished."

"Maybe not. You might be able to find the daughter."

"Oh?" Tom tried to stand up, but the phone cord was too short. He collapsed back onto the bed.

"A young woman named Branna Fitzpatrick graduated from Trinity College in Dublin last year."

"What was her major?"

"Who gives a damn? But if you must know, it was English Studies. The point is, her registration info shows her mother to be a Mrs. Peggy Fitzpatrick of Ballymena. No father listed."

"Ya done good, Kate. You should work for the FBI." Tom scratched his forehead with the receiver. "Does anyone at Trinity know where she is now?"

"Not yet. She got her diploma and handshake and disappeared to parts unknown. Shouldn't take too long to find her, though."

"Unless she's trekking in Nepal."

"Not likely. She was a scholarship student, and her mother couldn't have helped much. She'll have a job somewhere, and I've got some ideas. Come on down the hall, and let's work on it."

Tom's curiosity was rising, but he was still groggy. "Any chance it could wait till morning?"

"Damn it, Tommy. I've been working my ass off all evening while you and Willie sat on yours boozing. The least you can do is help me finish the bloody job. I'm heading home Monday morning."

"Yeah, you're right. Be there in a minute." Tom took the time to splash cold water on his face and tuck in his shirt. He took a look in the mirror and wasn't impressed.

Kate's room was just four doors down. Tom knocked softly, and in a few seconds the door clicked and creaked inward an inch. He pushed it open and stared into darkness. A small, muscular hand clasped his and pulled him into the room. He sniffed a trace of what might have been perfume as the door clicked shut. Tom followed the steady pressure as she led him forward, and he offered no resistance as she spun him around and pushed him backward onto her bed. As she eased herself on top of him, his hands felt her warmth through sheer fabric. There didn't seem to be much of it.

The sound of a passing truck missing most of its muffler caused Tom to lift his left eyelid. The only light in the room emitted from the red digits of a small clock radio on the far bed table. The clock was alone atop the table, the lamp having hit the floor within moments of his arrival. The intrepid clock insisted that it was almost five—technically morning, but the dawn was at least an hour hence. As the sound of the truck faded, Tom could hear Kate's soft breathing. Her outline was barely visible in the faint crimson glow. He noticed that the interval of Kate's exhales matched his own—she was awake. Tom crawled out of bed and pushed the bathroom door open far enough for the nightlight to create an artificial twilight in the room. He heard fabric rustle, and when he found his way back to the bed, the top sheet was missing. They lay facing each other, eyes straining to find details in the shadows. Tom noticed he was smiling. He hoped Kate was. Traces of their scents lingered on the lower sheet.

Neither of them spoke for at least five minutes. The growl of a lone car grew louder, and tiny beams from its headlights swept through small openings around the curtains as it passed. Kate was smiling, though Tom read her expression as more bemused than triumphant. As the light became bright enough to reveal colors, his eyes broke from hers and dropped to her chest. He stared at the ragged scar below her left breast. The entry wound had been small enough, but the emergency surgery left its tracks, and they were still a bright pink. He felt embarrassed and raised his eyes to meet Kate's, but she reached across the bed, took his right hand, and placed it on the scar.

"Let it go, Tommy."

"Easier said, toots."

"Oh, shut up!" Kate threw his hand back with enough violence to bounce it off his chest. She rolled away from him and drew up her legs. "Give me some credit, Tommy. I was in charge of the Lexington sting, and it was my decision to go into the house without you. Mine alone." Her breathing became more rapid, and Tom wondered if she might actually be fighting tears. After several seconds, she rolled back to face him, stretched out her legs, and propped her head on her right fist. There was no sign of a tear—he should have known better. Kate's eyes bored into his. "And it was me who screwed up and let that asshole draw his gun while I stood there like the village idiot."

Tom stared back at her and tried to keep his face as still as a death mask. "I."

Kate blinked. "What?"

"You should have said, 'It was I.'"

Kate's eyes widened in a rare loss of control, and she slugged him in the stomach with her left fist. It hurt like hell, but Tom forced a tight laugh. After a few seconds of pointed glare, Kate unfolded her fist, allowed herself a smile, and began rubbing soft circles on his chest with her index finger. "This has nothing to do with Lexington, Tommy, and everything to do with us. It's been a long time coming."

"Yeah." Tom stretched his neck up to look over Kate at the clock. "And time's somewhat short." He rested his right hand on Kate's waist, slid toward her, and they fought another round.

*   *   *

The sun was just making its appearance on the streets of Carrick when Tom walked into the breakfast room. Only seven patrons were present that early on a Sunday. The traditional Irish breakfast seemed to agree with Willie, who was refilling his plate with sausages, rashers of bacon, eggs, beans, grilled tomatoes, and cheese. He wavered over a piece of bread but left it behind. Tom just grabbed a mug of coffee and stood sipping it until Willie pointed at his table in a rear corner. When they were both settled, Willie paused, his knife and fork six inches above his plate, and pointed his nose toward a couple two tables away. "Do they all keep their knives in their right hands while they eat? Makes 'em look like they're in a considerable hurry to get the food in their mouths."

Tom gave a single nod. "Yep. Europe was a dangerous place in olden times. Nobody dared to let go of his knife at the dinner table."

Willie frowned, pondered this tidbit of cultural evolution for a moment, and then attacked a greasy rasher. Tom cooled off his coffee with fresh cream and drained the mug. He got up for a refill while Willie gorged on. As Tom collapsed back onto his chair, Kate appeared at the door in her usual jeans and a hiking shirt. She waved and moved straight for the coffee urn, bypassing the savory food line. She joined Tom and Willie, and the three sat in silence, sipping and munching. After a few minutes, Willie paused and rested his harried utensils on the plate. He glanced at Tom but settled his eyes on Kate. "You know, you really didn't need to come down here ten minutes after Tom. I have the room next to yours."

Kate reddened, but her face never twitched. "I had to check some emails." She reached for the cream. Tom took a larger gulp of coffee and burned his tongue.

Willie killed off another sausage, then leaned back and grinned. "Hey, okay by me. But you two ought to dig into some of this fine food. From what I heard, you're going to need it to keep up your strength."

"Enough, Willie." Kate was smiling, but her voice held a warning tone.

Tom was happy enough to change the subject. He looked toward Kate. "How do we go about locating the dead burglar's daughter? What was her name again?"

"Branna Fitzpatrick." Kate slipped a folded square of paper from her right shirt pocket and slid it across the table to Tom. "Here's her address. She's in Sligo. Up on the northwest coast of the Republic.

Tom was startled. "How did you figure that out?"

Kate forked a rasher of bacon on Willie's plate and swirled it around in the beans. "Wasn't hard. Branna did an honors project on Yeats. I found a professor at Trinity who said he helped her find a job in Sligo so she could work on some research at a couple of the local libraries. She has ambitions of doing grad work."

"You managed to locate her this morning?" Tom felt deflated. He knew Kate worked like a beaver on speed, but he'd imagined the results of their evening would linger a bit longer.

"Nah. I did it last night." Kate paused to ingest a hardy hunk of bacon. She watched Tom while she chewed.

"But when you called last night, you said . . ." Wrinkles began to appear on Tom's forehead.

Willie broke the silence. "You sure you want to get mixed up with a man this dumb?" He waved his fork toward Tom.

Kate kept her eyes on Tom as she replied. "You think he's worth a try?"

Willie grunted. "Seen worse."

Kate continued staring at Tom. She arched her eyebrows. Obviously, his cue.

Tom knew hesitation would be fatal. "Damned right I am."

*   *   *

Just after nine, the trio climbed into the rental and rolled north toward Shannon. Kate had an early morning flight, and she'd booked a room at the Park Inn by Radisson at the airport. She insisted on driving again, confident she could beat Google Maps' two-hour estimate.

Kate rammed the driver's seat back into Willie's knees for fun, then slid forward and hit the gas. Tom practiced meditation techniques from his martial arts days to keep his stress level down as Kate sped northward. He used the mirror on the sun visor to keep an eye on Willie. His older half-brother wasn't afraid of much, but his eyes stayed closed, and he was looking unusually pale for a New Mexican. At a quarter to eleven, Kate pulled into Shannon airport, and they climbed out. Willie began a stretching routine with his back to the car.

Kate retrieved her bag from the trunk and turned around to face Tom. He put his hands on her hips and pulled her toward him. She stiffened, looked up at him, and squeezed his forearms. "Tommy McNaul, don't kiss me unless you mean it."

"Okay."

He kissed her. They clung to each other for a while, rocking gently. They kissed again. Then Kate grabbed her bag and disappeared into the hotel without looking back.

Tom managed to squeeze himself into the driver's seat, and the McNaul brothers rolled north toward Sligo. Their timetable was upset by a truck accident blocking the highway just north of Athlone. Tom used his phone to plot a detour and roared off into the countryside. The roads narrowed to hilly, winding tracks about a lane and a half wide. There was no shoulder per se, but a strip of grass about a foot wide separated the pavement from high rock walls on both sides. The speed limit was 100 km/hr.

As they breasted a steep hill, Tom stood on the brakes causing the skidding car to fishtail and Willie to bash his head against the window. A tractor with a loaded hay wagon was inching forward, the bales only a foot or so from the rock walls lining the road.

Twenty minutes later, the farmer pulled over at an unusually wide driveway entrance and waved them past. Tom was still picking up speed when he rounded a blind curve and found himself nose to nose with an oncoming tourist bus. He got the car stopped a few meters short of disaster, eased it to within a foot of the rock wall, and tried to pass the bus. The driver shook his head, climbed down from the front door, and ambled over to the car. He bent over and knocked on the driver's window.

Tom rolled down the window and leaned his head out. "What's up?"

The driver pursed his lips. "Yanks, eh? That explains it. Rules of the road here—the bigger vehicle gets the right of way." He walked back to the bus, folded the mirrors flat against its sides, and climbed aboard.

Willie got out and folded both of the car's side mirrors. He directed Tom forward and toward the left rock wall until less than in inch separated the car from the menacing stones. The bus driver did the same, and after twenty minutes' inching forward and back, he waved and rolled past them.

It was three-thirty when they reached the edge of Sligo. Tom pulled into the lot in front of a fish and chips shop, cut the engine, and sent Willie in for takeout. They wolfed down the hot food in ten minutes but spent fifteen more trying to dispose of the refuse and wipe grease off their hands and clothes.

The professor at Trinity either didn't know or wouldn't reveal Branna Fitzpatrick's home address. However, he had told Kate that her part-time job was at the Yeats Memorial Building Visitor's Center. The stately old structure was located on the west bank of the Garavogue River near the Hyde Bridge. Finding a parking spot was hard, even on a Sunday afternoon. It was a balmy day for September in Ireland, and the locals were enjoying the sun and tumbling waters. Unfortunately, being Sunday, the Yeats Visitor's Center was closed.

Tom and Willie decided to join the crowd and settled in at Furey's Pub, just up Bridge Street from the river. A young trio was singing traditional music with enough vigor to rattle the glassware. The redheaded woman was beating a bodhran, and one of the men worked an accordion. All three wore Aran sweaters. The pub was packed, and most of the patrons were assisting the singers.

Whiskey seemed like a possible antidote for the fish and chips, so they began cutting the grease with doubles of Cooley. Midway through the second round, the Clancy Brothers began competing with the amplified trio playing the pub, so Tom took his phone outside. It was Kate.

"Hey, toots. Any news?"

"None of substance. And by the way, I'm fine, thanks." She sounded a bit testy. "Any luck with Ms. Fitzpatrick?"

"Alas, no. The Yeats Visitor's Center is not open this fine Sunday, and we have no other leads. We'll try again in the morning."

"You know, we're good together, Tommy."

Tom recoiled. Kate was prone to rapid changes of subject. He paused as long as he dared, listening to the splashes of river on rocks and the Irish music roiling out of Furey's. "Yeah, we are." He paused, but she was waiting for more. "We'll talk when I get home."

"Not much gilding on your tongue, Tommy McNaul."

"You knew that before you called." That didn't seem like a good place to leave things. He tried for an FBI tone. "I'll call you if we find anything."

"Call me even if you don't. I don't like being in the dark."

"Okay. Hell, we may be starting for home tomorrow morning. We've only got the one lead, and it's likely to expire after the first question. Not very likely this Fitzpatrick woman is going to know much about her dead father. She won't even remember him—she was a baby when he was shot."

"True enough. See ya, creep." Kate clicked off.

Tom decided to look up a hotel while he was still able. He found a nearby place called The Glasshouse. There was only one room left, but it sported a view of the river. He dodged a laughing couple reeling out the door of Furey's and moved past them into the dim interior light. The din ended suddenly as the trio called a set break. Tom collapsed next to Willie, backs to the wall, and they stared at the bustling room of revelers. After a few minutes, Willie rolled his eyes toward Tom without moving his head. "Kate okay?"

Tom shrugged. "No news. Not in much of a mood either."

"What a surprise." Willie rocked his chair onto its back legs and leaned his head and shoulders against the wall. He kept his ropers on the lowest rung of his chair. Spirits were high in the pub, but it wasn't a boots-on-the-table kind of crowd. "You say anything nice to her?"

Tom tilted his chair back parallel to Willie's. "I said I'd call her when we get home."

"Romeo!" Willie leaned his head forward so he could shake it twice each way. "What's the matter with you, Tommy? She seems like an interesting woman, and you've known her awhile. Bit of a hard-ass, but I admire that." He stretched his right arm forward, snagged the glass, and took an unusually small sip. "Nice stuff, this Cooley." Willie worked his lips enough to make his beard shake. "You two keep me up half the night, and you tell her you'll call her someday? You interested or not?"

Tom stared at nothing in particular for a moment. "Yeah. I've always liked Kate. But I kept trying to make things work with Colleen."

"Fair enough, but the witch is gone. She damned near killed you, little brother. Been the better part of a year now. Past time to move your sorry ass on."

"Yeah. Let's talk later, though." Tom tried to change topics with a forced smile. "She's probably too good for me anyway."

"Most any woman is, your exiting wife excepted. You'll be a lonely old man if you stick to that criterion."

The musicians reappeared, but they grabbed pints of Guinness and mingled with a group in a side alcove. Tom shuffled to the bar and obtained another round of the whiskey, singles this time. Back at the table he raised his glass. "Here's to Ireland."

Willie nodded. "Nice place." They tapped glasses, but the clink was lost in the general din. Willie took a slow draw and arched a tangled eyebrow at Tom. "We got a plan for tomorrow?"

"Not really. We'll show up at the Yeats place. Hope the dead burglar's kid is actually there on a Monday. Ask her what she knows about an unsolved crime that happened when she was one. She'll blink at us like an owl caught in a searchlight. We'll find a pub and book flights home. That sound about right to you?"

Willie raised his glass again. "To Ireland."

~ 9 ~

Tom rolled out from the left side of the bed and stood staring at a room barely lit by gray light. Must be dawn. Willie was awake but lay with his face buried in the pillow. As best Tom could recall, the two of them had never before shared a bed. Willie was fifty-nine now, twelve years older than Tom. He had stayed with his mother when their dad ran off with Liz, the ambitious grad student who, three years later, bore Tom. The boys grew close during Tom's childhood, but they had never lived under the same roof.

When the dizziness cleared, Tom ambled to the broad window for a view of Sligo. He yanked open the curtain to face a wall of dull gray. The town was engulfed by dense fog drifting inland from the Atlantic. He grabbed his watch from the dresser top and saw that it was almost eight-thirty. The McNaul boys had slept long past the dawn—the sun being no match for an Irish fog. Tom dragged Willie out of bed, and they agreed to skip breakfast. By the time they were dressed, the fog was beginning to burn off, and Tom noticed low-level clouds heading seaward. The winds had strengthened and backed to offshore.

At nine-twenty, Tom pulled the rental car to the curb just down the block from the Yeats building. It was a handsome red-brick structure with two full stories topped by a complicated third level with gables and something resembling a tower. Tom and Willie headed up the steps and into the front hall. A young man with wild blond curls and a tweed vest sat reading at a table just inside an open door on the right. He looked about eighteen. The room behind him featured exhibits and artifacts focused on Ireland's prize poet, William Butler Yeats. The curly-haired kid was hunched over a small hardback book with a worn green cover. He stared intently at the open pages. Tom couldn't tell if the fellow was in a state of rapture or just waiting for them to go away. It didn't really matter, so he rapped the knuckles of his right hand on the table. Curly looked up. "Oh. Sorry. Can I help you?"

Tom reached for a McNaul Brothers card but thought better of it. It would either confuse or scare the kid. He slipped his hands into his front jeans pockets instead. "Good morning. Is the visitor's center open yet?"

"Yes. Yes it is. You sound American. Have you been here before?"

"You have a sharp ear. No, first time in Sligo."

The kid slipped into performance mode, gave them directions, and offered a tour. Tom offered a relaxed smile. "Thanks, but I think we'll start by looking around." He turned toward the interior of the room, took two steps, then hesitated and looked back at the kid. It was a clumsy move, and he felt a flash of embarrassment. "Oh, is Branna in yet?"

"The kid looked suspicious for a second but shrugged it off. "No, she called in and said she's running a tad late. She should be here soon. Do you know her?"

"No. We were at Trinity last week looking at some of Yeats's papers, and a professor there told us we should talk to Branna if we made it to Sligo."

It wasn't much of a lie, but the kid seemed to buy it. "I'll steer her to you when she gets here." He stood up, put a marker in his book, and headed up the stairs.

Willie nudged Tom's arm and pointed to a cafe across the hall. "Since the kid split for higher floors, we don't have to wander around pretending we like poetry. How about some coffee."

The cafe was only a third full. Willie picked a table with no one sitting close by. It was jammed against a window decorated with a hand-painted sign facing outward. Tom wasn't good at reading reversed text, but he eventually deciphered it as "Lily's and Lolly's," evidently the name of the establishment. Willie acquired a plate of rugged brown bread and jam. The combo paired well enough with the black, no-fooling coffee. As the brothers finished their first mugs, a slender woman with straight black hair, pale skin, and opal eyes behind rectangular, frameless glasses pushed through the door. The eyes quickly focused on Tom, and she strode to their table. "Are you the fellas who were asking Johnny about me?"

Tom scraped his chair back a few inches and stood up. "Yes, assuming you're Branna Fitzpatrick."

Branna squared her shoulders and swelled her chest, though it hardly needed the added emphasis. "I am. What do you fellas want?"

"My name is Tom McNaul, and this is my brother, Willie. If you don't mind, we'd like to ask you a few questions."

She stared into Tom's eyes for a couple of seconds, glanced at Willie, and then decided Tom was the better bet. "This isn't about Yeats, is it?"

Tom abandoned all plans involving bullshit. "No, Miss Fitzpatrick. It isn't."

"Who are you, really? You act like coppers, but you don't sound like you're from this island. Or the one a wee bit east of here, for that matter."

"We're from the U.S., and we're not coppers. We're not crooks either." Branna's eyes flicked to Willie and back, and she sucked in her lower lip. Tom caught Willie's eye and nodded toward the door.

Willie stood up, took his coffee to the counter, and transferred it to a takeaway cup. "I'm going to leave you folks and have a look around town. Nice to meet you, Ms. Fitzpatrick."

When the door closed behind Willie, Tom faced Branna with a tired smile. "I'm sorry to surprise you this way, and I understand why you may be nervous. You're not in any kind of trouble that I know about. I would just like to ask you a couple of questions that might help me recover a lost painting. I know you aren't involved in any way, but a colleague of mine suggested you might know something that would help me."

"And what would you be meaning by colleague? Just what business are you in, Mister McNaul?"

Tom gave up and pulled out his McNaul Brothers card. "I'm a private investigator, and I specialize in missing fine art. My office is in Santa Fe, New Mexico. That's in the United States."

"Yeah?" Branna flashed a wry smile. "I know where it is, Mr. McNaul. Billy the Kid, right?" She pocketed the card.

"That's the place. And I go by Tommy."

"Tommy, then. But the question is: Why should I talk to you? And while we're at it, how would I know anything about a lost painting? I can't even afford to buy a proper poster for my wall."

"I won't be asking you about the painting, Branna. I want to talk about your da."

Branna's smile disappeared. "Jaysus." Her eyes scanned the room, and her voice sank to a low hush. "What you want to talk about him for? I can't even remember the bastard."

"I figured that, but I desperately need to get a couple of facts straight." Branna didn't reply and kept glancing about the cafe. Tom figured she was worried someone might overhear. "How about I buy you a latte and we stroll by the river? Just for a few minutes?"

"And a scone?"

"Done."

Branna led Tom to a walkway along the Garavogue River. They headed east in silence, Brenna munching her blueberry scone, until she pointed to an empty bench facing the river. The bench overlooked a stretch of riffles, and the splashes were audible during lulls in the Monday morning traffic. They sat at opposite ends, sipping coffee and staring at the troubled waters. After two or three minutes, Branna gave a purposeful huff and spoke without turning her head. "What ya want to know, then?"

Tom glanced her way and then followed her lead and gazed at the river. "Did your mother ever tell you the circumstances of your father's death?"

"His murder, you mean?"

"Yes."

Branna ground her teeth for a moment, and lines appeared around her jaw. "Yeah, she did." Tom turned just enough to see Branna. Her face softened, and her eyes seemed unfocused. "Yeah, me ma talked to me about that. Just the once. It was the summer after my first year at Trinity." She lifted her left foot to the bench and hugged the bent leg. "She said I should know. Ma wasn't doing well then. She'd lost her job at the tire plant and couldn't find work." Branna seemed to be waiting for Tom to reply, but he didn't want to interrupt her memories. She took a deep breath. "She said my da told her he was involved in a burglary. That it was up near Armagh, in Northern Ireland."

"Yes, I've been there."

"He and another fella stole a bunch of paintings and other fineries from a manor house. Only it didn't go well. They made off with a lot of loot, but the old lady who lived there and her son came home early. Me da and the other guy killed them both." Branna lowered her foot to the grass and turned her head to face Tom. "Ma didn't know who fired the shots. Maybe it was the other fella."

"Could be. Doesn't really matter, does it?"

"I guess not."

Branna clasped her hands and turned back to stare at the riffles. Tom gave her a moment. "There's more, isn't there?"

"Damn it! Yeah, there's more. Does anyone have to know about this?"

"I'm not the police, Branna. I'm just trying to recover one of the stolen paintings. The rightful owner is a disabled woman in Boston who needs the money." Tom felt like a jerk playing that card, but he needed to keep Branna talking. "The problem is, I've got to follow the trail from that original burglary to find the painting. Look, I'm not out to dredge up your family's past. I'll do everything I can to keep that quiet. But I have to find out who hired your da and the other guy to pull off that burglary?"

"Why should I tell you any more, Tommy McNaul?"

Branna's spirit was returning. It was now or never. "The people your da and his pal murdered were Mr. Sean O'Malley and his mother. Maybe it was just a robbery gone bad, but I doubt it. I think someone hired your da and the other guy to kill the O'-Malleys as part of the job. Murder for hire, and I think you know something about who did the hiring."

Her eyes widened enough for Tom to know he'd guessed right. Fortunately, Branna didn't look like she intended to lie to him. "How did you know?"

"I've been solving crimes for twenty-six years now. I can smell it." Tom felt it was best not to mention that twenty-five of those years had been with the FBI. "So, can you give me anything? A name? Description? Anything at all?" He looked at Branna with pleading eyes. This time they were genuine. She bit her upper lip. "One more thing. I'm betting the guy who hired your da and his pal also hired the men who killed them."

"Don't have a name. I don't think me da knew it, either. But he did tell Ma that the man was an elderly guy who lived some-where near Dublin. Seemed to be well off, and he had a German accent, a heavy one." She searched Tom's eyes. "That's the truth. Or all I know of it, anyway. Is that any help to ya?"

"Yeah, I think so. Twenty years covers a lot of tracks, but at least it's a place to start. If you think of anything else, give me a call tonight. We're staying at The Glasshouse." Tom fished out a card he'd taken from the hotel desk. Branna stuck it in the same pocket where she's stowed his McNaul Brothers card. Tom stared at the strong, young woman. She'd had a hard life already, and it wouldn't be easy to make a living studying dead poets. "Look, it isn't likely we'll find this painting, but if we do, where can I reach you? You'd be due part of the reward." The last sentence was tech-nically a lie, but if Tom cashed in his 20 percent finder's fee, he figured he could share a wee bit with Branna.

She pulled out a pen and wrote her cell number on the Lily's and Lolly's bag. "I can't say it's been a pleasure, but to be honest, it feels good to tell somebody." She handed the bag to Tom and stood up. "I'd best get back to work." She pushed her hair behind her ears and aimed a left-sided smile down at Tom. "Give me a call, Tommy McNaul, even if you don't find the painting. I'd like to know how this ends."

"You can count on that, Branna. And thank you."

"Sure." She turned to go, but hesitated. "What sort of painting is it anyway? Something with foxes and hounds?"

"No, it's by Claude Monet. It's a painting of water lilies."

"Jaysus." Her face stretched into a wide grin. "That's right enough." She looked at Tom for a second, shook her head, and marched back to the Yeats building. She glanced back, and Tom noticed she was still grinning.

Willie was nowhere in sight, and the rental car was missing. Tom's call went straight to voicemail. His brother was a lone wolf at heart and was surely hunting something. Tom didn't want to hang around the Yeats building, so he spent the afternoon exploring Sligo on foot and placing a futile call to Willie at the top of each hour. At three, he collapsed on the bench by the river where he'd questioned Branna, composed a vicious one-liner for his brother, and punched in the usual number. Willie picked up. "Yeah?"

Tom was shocked and forgot his killer line. "Where the hell are you?"

"Doesn't matter. I had an errand to run, and I ran it. Where are you?"

"Bench on the river bank, just down the walk from the Yeats building."

"Stay put. I'll be there in forty-five minutes." The phone went dead.

*   *   *

At a quarter past four, the crisp, offshore wind began gusting with intermittent howls. Tom figured a cold low was passing to the south. The sunken clouds raced out to sea, fleeing the city. He decided to take their hint. Willie was half an hour overdue from whatever alley he'd found to prowl, so he might as well wait in an indoor spot with coffee. He found a bakery with five tables and no customers, ordered two mugs, and sent Willie a text with the new rendezvous target. There weren't many pastries left in the glass cases, but the room was warm and infused with the fragrance of scones and one abandoned donut.

Willie must have been lurking within fifty yards, as he appeared moments later and scowled when he realized the place wasn't a pub. He ferried both coffees to the table and collapsed into a wooden chair that looked like it needed a few buttresses. "Any news from Kate?"

Tom shook his head. He had called Kate just before noon Sligo time, seven in Washington, and of course she answered in her office. Kate was working her connections to see if the Dublin police had any elderly Germans on their lists of usual suspects. He wasn't expecting much. If the man had been elderly twenty-plus years ago, he wasn't too likely to be above ground level now. And if he did happen to be among the living, he might have moved. There wasn't much point in leaving Sligo until Kate finished her search. "We might as well book the room for another night. Sun's going down, and I'm not driving these Irish roads in the dark."

"Good idea, little bro, but let's make it two rooms if they have them."

A few minutes before five, the bakery clerk began placing inverted chairs on tables and giving Tom and Willie the evil eye. They nodded in unison and took to the sidewalk. Kate called as they reached the front door of The Glasshouse. Willie headed for the front desk to check in, while Tom peeled off to a quiet chair in the lobby. "Hey, toots."

"Couldn't you come up with something besides 'toots'? Do you call every woman that?"

"No, just you, toots. Got anything?"

"Not much. There aren't any ancient Germans on Dublin's most wanted list, and nobody came up with any from circa '97 either."

"Figured as much."

"So did I. One thing, though. It's rank speculation, but I talked to one older detective about the German angle. He said there are plenty of Germans living in Ireland, but they don't tend to be prominent in the killer-for-hire trade. However, when I told him the estimated age of your suspect, he got more interested. Seems there was a wave of Germans who moved to Ireland at the end of World War II. A man who was twenty or thirty when the war ended would have been seventy or eighty at the time of the O'Malley murders."

"No offense, but so what? Does it matter when this alleged contract killer decided to move to Ireland?"

"Maybe not." Kate sounded annoyed. "But for what it's worth, that wave of post-war German refugees contained a fair number of characters who weren't welcome just anywhere. Northern Ireland fought with the British during the war, but the Republic stayed neutral. Pissed off the Brits no end. When the war ended, the Republic was a popular haven for Germans with money and a need to disappear. According to my source, the more affluent of these expats often bought protection—from the types of people who would know where to hire a hit man."

Tom frowned at the rug in front of his chair while he thought. "Seems a little far-fetched, Agent Bacon. You suggesting a possible motive?"

"Can't really think of one, McNaul, but I figured you should know."

"Gotta think on this. I'm not sure where it gets us. The Kraut has to be long dead by now, but Willie and I will drive down to Dublin tomorrow. If I see an old guy in lederhosen with a swastika pin on his suspenders, I'll ask a few questions."

"You be careful, Tommy. All told, the odds of your getting anywhere are shorter than I am. But even the proverbial blind squirrel trips over a nut once in a while. If you stumble onto a trail, the guys at the other end will be playing for keeps."

"Point noted, toots."

"Signing off, creep."

*   *   *

Tom briefed Willie on Kate's theory over a dinner of oysters and Guinness. Willie seemed properly dubious. "She wants us to roam the Irish countryside looking for men who've been hiding for seventy years? If they were Nazis on the run, they'd have to be pushing a hundred by now. They wouldn't be alive." Willie began eyeing his last oyster. "It can't be worth driving all the way to Dublin to search graveyards. And to what end? What would we be looking for?"

"I haven't a clue. It seems the epitome of a hopeless case. However, I do think we should drive to Dublin tomorrow."

"Why, may I ask?"

"That's where the airport is."

They finished their dinner in silence. It was only a bit after eight, but they decided to make it an early night. Just one more Guinness. Neither wanted to face the Irish roads with a hangover.

The damp wind whipped at their coats as they walked through the darkness to The Glasshouse. As they entered the lobby, the desk clerk nodded to two clean-shaven men in topcoats and pointed at Tom and Willie. The men intercepted the brothers at the elevator before the doors opened.

The older and shorter man wore the more expensive wool coat and seemed to be in charge. He cleared his throat. "Are either of you gentlemen a Mr. Thomas McNaul?"

"That would be me. What can I do for you?"

The man ignored the question and turned to Willie. "And who might you be?"

"Who's asking?"

The man didn't seem to like answering questions. He reached inside his topcoat and pulled out a badge. Willie didn't act impressed, and the badge disappeared. "Inspector Halloran. Sligo Garda." He nodded toward his taller partner. "Sergeant O'Toole. Now one more time, your name is. . . ?"

Willie still didn't seem impressed. "Willie McNaul, older brother of the gentleman on my left, as well as his business partner."

The cops took turns looking satisfied. The shorter one turned back to Tom. "Let's go up to your room and talk a bit." The group rode in silence until the elevator pinged at the fourth floor. Tom led the group to his room and stood by the window with Willie while the two men browsed the premises. There wasn't much to see. Tom's bag sat unopened on the bed. The two cops stood looking at each other like vaudeville actors who had forgotten their lines. Tom got tired of their act. "Are you guys really cops, or just assholes?"

"Watch your mouth." The younger cop finally got in a line, but his moment died as his boss cut him off.

"We'll let that one pass, laddie, but don't you go thinking you can get by with another."

"Fair enough." Tom glanced at Willie, but his brother looked more bored than interested.

The younger cop took a small notebook and pen out of his pocket as the senior partner stared hard into Tom's eyes. "Where were you fellas during the last few hours?"

Tom glanced at his watch—a few minutes to eight. "We just got back from dinner. That pub right down the street. Great fried oysters and brown bread washed down with Guinness."

"I don't really care about the menu. When did you get there?"

"About six. We had a pint or two first, and another with the oysters."

Halloran nodded, possibly in approval. "And before that?"

"We had coffee in a bakery on the same street as the pub. Left it right at five. Walked back here to check in and clean up. Then straight to the pub. Now suppose you tell us what this is about?"

The Sligo cops looked at each other and shrugged. Halloran relaxed slightly but then resumed his intense focus on Tom's eyes. "Do you know a young woman named Branna Fitzpatrick?"

Tom's eyes widened, and Willie managed to arch one eyebrow as he turned away. "Yes. We just met her this morning at the Yeats

Memorial Building. That was a bit after nine, I think. Say, nine-thirty." He looked over at the younger cop but met only a dead-fish stare.

"It was more like nine-forty-five, but close enough." Inspector Halloran grimaced as Tom looked back his way. "We'll need to check out your story, but it sounds like you're in the clear."

"What is this? And what's it got to do with Branna? Is she in some kind of trouble?"

"Rather a lot. Someone murdered her about an hour ago"

~ 10 ~

Tom's lower jaw sagged until his lips parted an inch. The four stood in silence for several seconds until Willie tilted his head back and his neck cracked. He did a three-sixty neck roll and then stared at Halloran. "The fuck? When?"

The inspector came to life. "Sometime after six, when a neighbor saw her get home from the Yeats Center, and before seven-fifteen, when we got two calls of a shot fired."

Tom frowned. "A single shot?"

"That's what I said."

"Any witnesses?"

The inspector stretched for an extra inch of height, but Tom still had at least eight more on him. "We're not releasing any details, particularly not to you two blokes." He took two steps back from Tom and hooked his thumbs in his front pants pockets. "What was your relationship to Branna Fitzpatrick?"

"We were very close. I met her this morning at the Yeats Center. We sat on a bench by the river and talked for fifteen or twenty minutes, but you know how these things can catch fire. We said goodbye, never suspecting it was forever."

"Fookin' wise guy. Show a bit of respect. The girl's dead."

"Fair enough. How about you show us some? You already said we're not suspects." Tom relaxed his shoulders. "What happened? Branna was healthy enough when she headed back to work. Even had a smile on her face."

Inspector Halloran deflated like a kid who got socks for his birthday. "You being an American detective, you might have figured out she was shot. You don't need to know the details, and we don't know many anyway. It was just over an hour ago."

"How'd you finger us so quickly?"

Halloran retrieved two business cards from an evidence bag in the inside breast pocket of his coat—McNaul Brothers and The Glasshouse. "You left a pretty short trail. You gonna tell us why she had these?"

"I gave them to her in case she wanted to tell me a little more than she spilled on the bench. She wasn't involved in anything, so far as I know. We just wanted some information about her late father. We think he stole a painting that belongs to our client. It was a burglary with murder in County Tyrone more than twenty years ago. Branna's da was himself murdered not long after. She was just a kid, but we figured her ma might have told her something." Tom feigned a whimsical shrug and fed Halloran a few stale details of the original robbery. He avoided any mention of Kate, the FBI, and Branna's reference to the old man with the German accent.

Inspector Halloran got bored in a hurry. "You boys come with us to the Garda station. We'll need statements and some contact information. I'd prefer you stay in Sligo until we've verified all this."

Tom shook his head. "Happy to give you the statements, but we have to drive to Dublin tomorrow morning. We'll keep our phones on, or you could loan us a basket of homing pigeons."

"Piss off, ya fuckin' prick. Get your coats, and we'll decide later whether to lock you up for safekeeping."

The Garda boys fussed and growled en route to the station and for two hours thereafter, but in the end they seemed satisfied with the alibi. Nobody shook hands, and Tom had to call a taxi to get back to The Glasshouse. The driver was a Pakistani immigrant who had lost his construction job when the Celtic Tiger bellied up. He claimed five children, all bound for Cambridge or Harvard. Tom upped his tip on the off chance this was true.

Tom dropped the room key on the dresser and whipped his coat against the wall near the door. He moved to the foot of the bed and turned to face the window. Willie joined him, and they stared without looking into the Sligo night. A moment later,

Willie nudged Tom's arm. The brothers locked eyes, nodded in unison, came to attention, and toppled backward onto the bed. The furniture complained but stood its ground. As the memory-foam mattress adjusted to its dual cargo, Tom stared at a sprinkler lurking overhead. "What the hell's going on here?"

"Murder most foul, little brother. I assume you don't buy it as a coincidence."

"No chance. Shit. She's really dead. Why? She'd had a tough enough life—hard times and harder people, but things were going well for her. She had it together. Good future waiting. He paused, but Willie waited him out. "I don't figure she'd be mixed up in her dad's business. He's been dead twenty years."

"You didn't really know her."

"True dat, bro, but she was a good one. I could tell."

"Oh bullshit, Tommy. How would you know? You haven't a crock of sense to your name when it comes to women. Took you twenty-five years to find out your wife was a murdering bitch."

"Attempted murdering bitch. I'm still alive."

"Splittin' hairs. But let's not argue. We don't know shit about the real Branna Fitzpatrick. What does the timing tell you?" Willie sat up and started untying his shoes.

Tom continued to stare at the sprinkler. "Too fast."

Willie nodded. "Go on."

"Way too fast."

"I was hoping for a few more details."

Tom rolled off the bed and started pacing at quick time in front of the window. "It was only a bit past ten when I finished talking to Branna. She went back to work. Got home at six. Probably killed around seven."

"At the risk of repeating myself . . ."

"Why do I have to do all the thinking?"

"Because, as you've so often told me, you are smart and I am stupid."

Tom stopped, turned to face his brother, and assumed a sloppy parade rest. "We both know better. Look, you agree this was a hit?"

"Uh huh." Willie ran his fingers through his beard. "The Garda boys didn't say anyone reported a fuss. Just one shot. That and the timing. Can't be a walk-in-on-a-burglar. Not a rape attempt either. Agreed?"

"Yep. But why? Come on, Willie. You're on a roll."

Willie seemed to warm to the occasion. "Well, someone was afraid Branna would tell us something. But who? And why?"

"Why is beyond my ken." Tom went back to pacing at the tempo of a soldier on guard duty. "But who—there we might have something. After our conversations in Carrick-on-Suir, there were people who knew we were looking at the O'Malley murders, but the Carrick boys didn't seem to know anything about Branna. We came straight to Sligo, and the only guy we talked to here was. . . ?" Tom made an abrupt stop.

"That book-loving wimp at the Yeats place." Willie pounded his fist into the mattress. "Sonofabitch. What the fuck?"

"You said most of that already."

"Didn't think much of that little pissant, but I can't see him shooting anyone."

"Never can tell. But some folks can kill you with a phone call." Tom folded his arms. "We need to talk to that kid, but not tonight. We don't know where he lives, and someone may be watching us. We'll hit the Yeats building on the way out of town.

*   *   *

At nine-thirty, Tom rolled the hired car to a stop half a block short of the Yeats Center. The gray stratus clouds sank low as if they were pondering whether to sag a bit more and become fog. The brothers unfolded themselves from the front seats, glanced at each other, and nodded. They marched up the sidewalk and hit the stairs harder than bill collectors. The curly blond kid was back at his post, the same book open on the wooden table. As before, he preferred the book to visitors, but Willie slammed his class ring on the table with a report loud enough to jerk the kid's head up. His hands flew apart, and the right one knocked over a steaming cup of Lily's and Lolly's coffee. The coffee sloshed away from the book, but the kid snatched it up anyway and clutched it with both hands. "What are you doing?" He seemed to be searching for enough gumption to feign anger, but he had a ways to go.

Tom eased forward and leaned his thighs against the table while Willie circled around behind. The kid's eyes darted toward Willie, then back to Tom. "You're the American guys who were in here yesterday."

"Not too impressive. You're too young to be sweating short-term memory loss."

"What do you want? Why are you threatening me?"

Tom suppressed a smile. "I don't believe we have threatened you, yet. What's your name?"

The kid started to stand up, but Willie's meaty paws clamped his shoulders and stuffed him back into his wooden library chair. "You heard him. What's your name?"

"Sean Murphy, if it's any business of yours. Why are you guys so hostile?"

Tom ignored the question. "Where's Branna today?"

The kid double-clutched his eyelids, but he looked genuinely puzzled. "I don't know. She should be here by now. What do you want with her?" He blinked two more times. "Is she in some kind of trouble?"

"We've got some questions in need of answers. Let's step outside for a few minutes."

Sean's forehead got wet in a hurry. He was beginning to panic. "I'm not going anywhere with you. Stand away from me, or I'll yell. They'll hear me in Lily's."

"Relax. Nobody's going to hurt you. I just need to ask a couple of sensitive questions. It's important."

Tom looked at Willie and twitched his head toward the door. "Why don't you grab us a couple of coffees next door. Get one for Sean too. We owe him." Willie relaxed his most visible muscles, nodded, and headed for the cafe. When the door closed, Tom turned back to Sean. Sorry we scared you, but we've had a tough trip. Look, nothing dangerous here. We'll sit on that bench by the river. Plain sight. Plenty of witnesses. But we need to do this now. Okay?"

Sean hesitated and looked Tom in the eye. "Yeah, okay." He was trembling slightly, but he didn't seem to be afraid of Tom.

They crossed the street and sat at opposite ends of yesterday's bench. The kid was in Branna's spot. Sean stared into the swirling water, and Tom let him brood a bit. "Okay, Sean. Where's Branna?"

"I really don't know. What's wrong?" Most of his face was twitching. "Is she okay?"

"No. And I think you know that."

The panic returned. "What do you mean? What's happened?" He jerked his head to his left and stared at Tom. The fear seemed genuine.

"She's dead, Sean. Somebody killed her last night, and I'm betting you know who."

"Jaysus! No. I didn't hurt her. I couldn't do anything like that."

Tom was inclined to agree. There wasn't any way this trembling kid could have gunned down a woman in cold blood. Besides, if he'd pulled a gun, Branna seemed the type who'd have come out on top. "I figured that, Sean. But you did something. Branna was barely home from work when someone shot her. It wasn't a robbery. Someone was laying for her. Who was it?"

"How would I know? This is terrible. I didn't . . ."

"Didn't what, Sean?" Tom's voice dropped half an octave, and his lips grew tight. "You called someone. Didn't you?"

"Uh . . ."

"Out with it. Who did you call?"

Sean slumped forward and stared at the grass in front of his feet. He took shallow, rapid breaths and worked his lips for half a minute. Then he gave a sudden sigh and sat up, his eyes shifting back to the river. "You don't want to know."

"Oh, cut the shit, Sean. Branna was a lovely young woman, and now she's a corpse with a hole in her skull. And she got that hole only hours after we happened to show up to talk to her. You can be goddamned sure that I want to know. You told somebody about us talking to her, didn't you? Who was it?"

"A man. I don't know his name. And I mean it . . . you really don't want to know either."

"Spill it kid. We're past playing it safe. My brother and I somehow got Branna killed, and I need to know why?"

"I don't know why. And I really don't know the guy's name. A couple of days after Branna started working here, a man in a leather jacket and a close haircut showed up at my desk. Short and hard kind of guy. He said he was with the military, and they were checking up on Branna. I asked for some ID, and he flashed me something in a wallet, but I didn't get a good look at it. The guy said they were doing some kind of security check."

"What did he want you to do?"

The kid shrugged. "Not much. Just keep an eye on her and give him a call if any strangers showed up looking for her. He was a mean-looking fella. He acted like it was routine but important."

"Interesting. How were you to get in touch with him?"

"He gave me a number."

"Did you ever call him before yesterday?"

"Yeah, once. About three weeks ago. A man in a suit showed up here looking for her, sort of like you guys. Branna was home sick that day. I called the number. The voice I got sounded the same. He just said thanks, told me to keep watching. I found out later the suit was one of Branna's uncles." Sean turned to face Tom with pleading eyes. "I didn't think she was in any danger."

"Yeah? Then why did you say I don't want to know who the hard guy is? What tipped you off?"

"A couple of weeks ago, I saw the guy in a pub down the river a bit. I don't think he saw me. He was at a table with two other men. I recognized one of them, but I'll be damned if I tell you his name."

Tom leaned forward until their noses were almost touching. "Now you do have my attention, lad. Last time, now. Why won't you finger the guy?"

Sean pulled back and craned his neck scanning for people within earshot, but the footpath was clear of passers-by. Satisfied, he moved his lips close to Tom's right ear and whispered. "IRA." He sat upright again and tried staring at a pair of ducks walking along the riverbank.

"The IRA? What the hell? Why would the Irish Republican Army give a damn about some girl who wants to be a Yeats scholar?"

"I don't know. And I don't think the three men noticed me. I'd like to keep it that way."

"Come on, Sean. You've got to be shitting me. I know you Irish haven't really settled who should own the turf up north. *The Rising of the Moon,* and all that. I even saw that movie, Michael Collins. But the truce was twenty years ago. War's over, son. Surely you don't think Branna was some sort of agent for the Ulster paramilitaries?"

"No, I don't. I don't know what to think. But I know that guy in the pub was IRA, and not just a foot soldier. Look, Mr. Mc-Naul. You don't seem to know shit about Ireland. Not really. Sure, the fighting's stopped for now, but there are those on both sides who don't like it that way. People who won't let it rest." Sean made another quick scan for eavesdroppers. "Go home, Mr. Mc-Naul. You think you know what's going on here from books and movies. But this isn't some glorious war of independence. My father fought for that once—a united Ireland. But this isn't my father's IRA. They aren't real soldiers anymore. They're fookin' terrorists. Both sides, Orange and Green. So just go home, back to America, and leave me alone."

Tom was startled by the rebuff, but it was good to see the kid had some fire in him. "Okay, have it your way. Just answer me this. If you knew your contact was connected to the IRA, why did you make that call? Why put Branna in harm's way?"

"I didn't make the connection. Or maybe I didn't want to make it. The men were in the pub drinking ale." Sean paused and looked down. The fire was gone again—he only carried one round in his clip. "Maybe that's all it was. Couple of pints. But if it was IRA business . . . well, I damned well had to make the call."

"Brave fella, aren't you? Throw the girl under the bus, just to be on the safe side. But one more thing before I let you go. Your handler. Did he ever mention an old German man? Lives down Dublin way? I hear he used to do a little business with your grand IRA when he needed to disappear.

"I'm not answering any more of your fookin' questions." Sean leaped to his feet, spun around, and returned to the Yeats building with long, deliberate strides. He didn't look back.

A few seconds later, Willie stepped from behind a dense bush twenty yards away. He carried just two steaming coffees to the bench. "Ran the little bloke off, did you? Figured you would."

"Seemed the thing to do. You catch all of that?"

"Most. Why'd you ask him about the German guy? Seems like you handed him too much information. Could be dangerous."

"That was the point, Watson. We haven't a clue how to find some reclusive German who might have hired some hit men twenty years ago, and who might still live near Dublin, if he's living at all. You figure we'd just visit all the pubs in that part of Ireland?"

"Doesn't sound that bad to me, though I take your point. We'll never pick up a trail that cold one pint at a time." Willie squinted. "You have a better plan?"

"Sure. Yesterday, we asked some questions, and the kid made a phone call, even though he knew it could be bad for Branna. Someone iced her a few hours later. Now we asked more questions, including about the kraut in Dublin. The kid's sure to make another call. If there's anything to our lead, this time they'll be coming after us."

Willie looked too satisfied for a man who just realized he needed more insurance. He grinned at Tom and began nodding his head. "Nice. Didn't see that coming, but I figured you'd get us in trouble somehow. Don't worry, little brother. I've taken precautions."

Tom closed one eye. "Like what?"

"Tell you later. Need to know, and all that. Finish your black lightning, and let's hit the road."

~ 11 ~

An hour east of Sligo, Willie developed a hankering to try driving on the left side of the road. Tom pulled off and switched to shotgun. As they careened into Northern Ireland, the rocks seemed to retreat into the soil and the farms became lush. Gray clouds hugged the treetops, and a light rain began to dampen the windshield as Willie fumbled for the wipers.

Tom pulled a small, spiral notebook out of his left shirt pocket and flipped through the pages. A moment later he punched an address into his phone. "Long as we're passing through Armagh, let's have a look at the O'Malley estate."

Willie managed to shrug using only his lips. "Scene of the crime, eh? Who lives there these days?"

"I don't rightly know." Tom tried to focus on the trees and drizzle to push away the terror of Willie's driving. "Aoife said her grandparents set up some sort of trust to support the estate, and it will eventually go to the national historical trust. Her mother has the right to live there while she's still breathing, but apparently Grace doesn't like the weather."

"She thinks it's better in Boston?"

"Maybe she's a Bruins fan."

"Seems likely. But meanwhile, how do we find out who lives there?"

"I'm planning to knock on the front door if we make it there alive."

Willie smirked and managed to shift the gears of the car and the conversation at the same time. "All Irish roads this bad?"

"They're worse in the Republic. Our dad tried to explain the Irish side of the family tree once when I was home for Christmas.

He had sixty-five first cousins, and it seemed like half the ones he could remember departed the sacred soil via vehicular misfortune." He got through twenty or so. Then we quit and got drunk."

Tom directed Willie onto a narrow strip of damp pavement leading from the highway into a cluster of short, steep hills resembling green sand dunes. The lane twisted between the usual stone walls, and Willie took the curves like a driver going for gold in the two-man bobsled. After five minutes, they breasted a hill and were confronted by a major flock of sheep wedged between the flanking walls. Willie stood on the brakes with both feet, but the car skidded sideways to port, the left rear wheel becoming airborne. The left headlight and its surroundings proved no match for rock as the fender clipped the wall, but the car came to a rest five yards short of the herd.

Tom pushed open the passenger door and collapsed on his knees in front of the terrified sheep. He deposited his breakfast on a mound of fresh sheep-dung pellets as the farmer charged past brandishing a wooden war club, most likely a hurley stick. Tom rolled onto his back and stared, blinking, into the rain. The farmer was flaming Willie with colorful profanity, the Irishman's vocabulary being somewhat more lyrical than Willie's own Marine Corps replies. They drowned out the baaing of the frantic sheep, but there were no sounds of blows, so Tom tuned out the conversation and concentrated on the bouquet emitted by wet sheep, fresh dung, and his own vomit. Rivulets of water trickled through the creases around his eyes. The back of his head felt gooey. He eased the fingers of his right hand through his hair feeling for warm blood, but they encountered only slimy, mashed sheep pellets.

A sudden whack followed by the tinkling of glass shards suggested an escalation in the combat. Tom sat up and struggled to his feet with vague intentions of trying to make peace, but the farmer was already standing a few steps back from the shattered passenger's window. He pointed his club at the mashed front fender. "Fuckin' serves ya right, ya pricks." He spun away and returned to his flock. Willie stared at Tom through the remnants of the window but said nothing.

The road was still blocked, so Tom scouted out a patch of clean grass at the edge of the road, sank to the turf, and lay on his back, eyes closed against the rain. The sheep soon calmed, and he could hear their calls soften as they oozed on down the road. There was a metallic squeak, and he opened one eye to see Willie emerge from the driver's seat to survey the damage. "Not too bad. The insurance company will shit, but it's drivable."

They climbed inside to see if this was true. It was, but cold rain swirled through the missing window. They were soon soaked and shivering. Fifteen minutes later, the girl in the phone said that the destination was on their right. Willie skidded to a stop in front of a massive stone arch enclosing a gate of vertical steel bars with a heart-shaped spear point atop each. It was closed. The gate seemed to stand more for ceremony than security since the white wooden fence attached to either side was missing an unfortunate number of spans. Tom got out and brushed raindrops off his eyelids. Steam fog from the exhaust pipe swirled over him as he searched for a sign or house number. He found only a brass panel with a black button next to a round area of metal mesh. He pushed the button, but nothing happened. He counted to ten and pushed again. The rain increased.

After the seventh or eighth push, a woman's voice crackled out of the mesh. "Who is it?"

"My name is Thomas McNaul, and we are here on behalf of Mrs. Grace O'Malley of Boston." From the corner of his eye, he could see Willie grin at the "Thomas." Tom flipped him the traditional gesture.

"Mrs. O'Malley? What does she want? Is she with you?"

Tom wasn't good at accents, but the voice from the speaker resonated with more brogue than genteel airs. "No, madam. Mrs. O'Malley is at home in Boston, but she sent us here to check out her property."

"She's not supposed to come without warning, ya know. It's part of the agreement."

"I'm sure she's very sorry not to have contacted you, but it's a matter of some urgency that we talk to you."

"We're talkin' now, Mr. McNaul."

"So we are. Would you please wait just a moment, madam?"

Tom walked a few paces to the left of the gate and kicked the only remaining board off one of the spans. The ground seemed firm. He climbed back into the car and pointed toward the manor house. "Home, James."

Willie backed up and then spun the tires on the wet grass as they rolled through the missing fence section. They veered back onto the stone pavers and raced up the steep driveway to the front door. Tom sprang out and took cover under what would have been a front portal in Santa Fe. He had no idea what the Irish called it. He pounded on the door. A second later, it jerked open to reveal a ruddy, largely female face framed by rolls of flesh and wisps of poorly dyed curls. She was short, stout, and could have been the understudy for the cook in "Downton Abbey." Her face was twisted, and she had plenty of loose material to mold it with. "How did you get up here?" Her eyes widened as she looked at Tom's drenched clothes, and then past him at the battered rental car. She twitched her nose as the scent of the sheep dung grabbed her. Sensory overload seemed to throw her brain into a do loop, and her mouth fell open.

"It wasn't too hard. Your horse must have kicked the fence down." Tom produced his McNaul Brothers card and handed it over to the doorkeeper. To his surprise, she became the first known person to take it seriously. "Oh, detectives. Well, you'd better come in then. Did you have an accident?" She flashed a smile but didn't wait for an answer. "I'm Nancy Flaherty. Wait here." Nancy disappeared for a few moments and returned with an armload of towels. Willie joined them in the entryway.

After they answered several questions concerning Grace O'-Malley's health, the weather in Boston, and the nationality of

New Mexico residents, Mrs. Flaherty explained that she and her husband were caretakers. Their quarters were in the former servants' wing, and they were now the only human inhabitants. The estate was open to the public on weekends when volunteers from the Trust led tours.

Tom emoted a few lines of dash and flattery, and soon their hostess agreed to show them the library, the scene of the murders some twenty years back. The boys treaded softly to minimize the squishing sounds from their shoes as Mrs. Flaherty led the way. "A terrible thing, to be sure, but I really don't know much about the details. Jack and I, that's my husband, didn't live here at the time. We're from Belfast. It was a year or so after the crime when the Trust advertised for caretakers, and here we are." She led them into a spacious room furnished with Victorian furniture and worn Persian carpets. Tom spotted tufts of light brown dog hair on both.

"It doesn't bother you, living in the home of the victims?"

"Oh, not really. Kind of exciting, you know." Mrs. Flaherty swept her arm toward the three far walls, only one of which was lined with bookcases. As libraries go, the shelves seemed unusually short of books, but they held a great many photographs, assorted souvenirs, and a few ceramics. A scuffed red cricket ball and a reclining bat had one shelf to themselves, reminding Tom they were in Northern Ireland. The remaining walls were densely populated with paintings.

"Well, what would you like to see, Mr. McNaul?"

"Just the paintings, thanks." There were no empty spaces on the wall. According to Kate, the Irish police thought the burglars had taken somewhere between five and eight paintings in the heist. Obviously, someone had found replacements for the Monet and its fellow victims. Willie peeled off and wandered to a French door that opened onto a rose garden. He seemed to take comfort staring into the rain.

Tom pulled the small spiral notebook from the pocket of his soaked jacket and wrote down terse descriptions of the paintings and the names of their artists. None were familiar to him. His art education was reasonably thorough, and it seemed odd for a Monet to have hung in such low company. He assumed most of the stolen paintings had been replaced with works of similar quality. The Trust could have found lesser replacements to lessen risk and insurance costs, but that isn't the Irish way, he thought. Art theft approaches a way of life in Ireland. Security is lax almost everywhere, even after a heist. Some works had been stolen repeatedly from the same manor house. Quite a game, but one that can turn deadly.

Tom shifted to the bookcases. One shelf featured a cluster of photographs in brown leather frames. A few were clearly studio works—the required wedding portraits and posed family holiday photos. Most, however, were snapshots of family members. The faded sepia images were of young men in the gallant uniforms of the Great War, taken before men and uniforms were shredded in the trenches and no-man's-land. Two open display boxes flanked a black-and-white photo of a beaming young army captain. The left box held some sort of medal—Tom wasn't familiar with British military awards. In the right box, he saw a round tan patch with a green shamrock in the center. A slip of paper identified it as the insignia of the Irish Brigade.

Other frames sported photos of unidentified civilians attired in the varied fashions of the twentieth century, many standing next to the autos of their times. A few of the children managed genuine smiles. Tom was about to turn away when he spotted a photo of a young girl of five or six astride a pony. A stout man in a tweed shooting jacket held the reins. The proud girl looked vaguely familiar. "Who is this?"

"Let me see." Mrs. Flaherty ambled over and moved a pair of reading glasses from her apron pocket to her nose. "Oh, that's Mr. Peter O'Malley. And his daughter, Aoife. I never met him, of course, but Aoife has been here with her mother a few times since the murders. They never stay in the house. Can't say as I blame them."

Tom could see the adult Aoife in her childhood photo. He looked over the collection for other images of her but found none. "Are there any other photos of Aoife, one with her mother perhaps?"

"No, just the one. When Mrs. O'Malley was last here, she collected all the pictures of herself and her husband and took them home. All but the one."

"What about paintings? There seem to be family portraits hanging in hallways and along staircases. Any of them show the last of the O'Malleys? Surely the most recent owner of the manor would want his family on the walls with his ancestral legends."

"Not anymore. There was a fine portrait of Mr. O'Malley, but the Trust put that in storage somewhere. I think there was a smaller painting of the three of them, but Mrs. O'Malley took that along with the photographs."

"Seems unusual. What's the point of a grand estate if you don't let people know who lives there?"

Mrs. Flaherty stiffened. "I'm sure I wouldn't know, Mr. Mc-Naul. Now would you like to see anything else before you leave?"

"I meant no offense, ma'am. And no, thank you, we've seen enough. You were kind to show us around. I do have a last question, though." Tom produced the warm smile that had served him well during his FBI years.

"Yes?"

"Do you or your husband have any idea who killed the O'-Malleys? I've read all the police reports, but I'm interested in the local rumors. The community wisdom, as it were. We're not trying to get anyone in trouble, but it might help us know where to look for Mrs. O'Malley's painting." The last line was an obvious lie, but his smile, like a kiss, could conceal many mistruths.

Nancy exercised most of her facial muscles several times before looking Tom in the eye. She leaned in close, though it was a useless move since Willie was now standing just three feet to her left. "We don't know, really, but we think it was the Orange men."

"Which Orange men?" More than half the population of Northern Ireland still flew the colors of William of Orange, reveling in the memory of his victory over the Catholic King James II at the Battle of the Boyne. Four hundred plus years wasn't time enough to heal much in Ireland.

"We don't know exactly. And we wouldn't tell you if we did. But there are groups of them. Most centered in Belfast, but they have ears everywhere. They're our answer to those murdering cowards in the IRA."

"And these Orange lads, you think they wanted a painting of a bunch of water lilies badly enough to shoot the O'Malleys? It seems a bit extreme."

"Don't try to be smart with me, mister fuckin' detective. I didn't know the O'Malleys personally, but they weren't popular around here. They were a Catholic family that somehow didn't suffer like most after the partition. They kept their lands, and business, and this grand house. They had to be dealing with the Protestants, under the table, you might say."

Tom scratched the back of his head, his fingers slithering through the sheep droppings. "Fair enough, but it would seem to me that would steam off the Catholics, not the Protestants."

"You'd think that, wouldn't you? But here's the thing. The IRA let the O'Malley family be for many years. Decades. And why was that, I ask you?" She leaned in closer but amped up her volume. "The O'Malleys must have been in with the IRA. And we figure some Orange group found out about it and paid them a visit. They probably just took the paintings and such as a cover." Mrs. Flaherty leaned back a bit past vertical and stuck out her jaw in a show of smugness. "Got what was coming to them, most folks think."

"Any group in particular?"

"Time for you to go now. I'll show you out."

There seemed to be nothing left to gain at O'Malley Manor, so Tom and Willie thanked Mrs. Flaherty and returned to the remnants of their rental. The gate swung open as they descended the driveway. Willie sailed through the arch and hung a sharp left toward the road to Dublin. Tom heard a metallic clatter and saw a hubcap rolling into a thicket.

When they reached the N3, Willie pulled into a Topaz station before heading south. He wrinkled his nose at Tom. "You smell riper than a sheep barn. Do something about it. I'll get coffee."

Tom grabbed his bag and lined up for the men's room. Nobody queued up behind him. When he made it inside, he locked the door, stripped off his shirt, and swabbed his torso with wads of soaked paper towels. Water began to pool on the floor. The faucet in the sink was too low to run water onto his head, so he plugged the drain with the towels, filled it to the runoff level, and bent sideways until the right side of his head dipped into the water. He managed to run the fingers of his right hand through his dung-soaked hair for a few seconds. He managed to run his fingers through his dung-soaked hair for a few seconds, then repeated the maneuver for his left side—until his feet slipped and he banged the side of his skull on the sink as he collapsed into the puddle. Tom's head throbbed as he struggled to his feet. The water in the sink was a greenish brown. He pulled a relatively clean shirt out of his bag, tossed the previous one in the trash bin, and bolted for the car.

Willie was behind the wheel sipping coffee. "Jesus, bro. You look like a man who fell off a bridge."

"But better than a man who just fell into a sheep dip tank, so drive."

* * *

When Willie wheeled the sad auto into the Hertz lot at the Dublin airport, it was technically still daylight. The stratus was too dense to reveal the position of the sun, but Tom could read unlighted signs despite the gloom. His plan was to swap the battered car for a new one, but the welcoming smile of the check-in agent crashed to a scowl when she spotted the rolling relic. She demanded to see the nonexistent accident report, rolled her eyes when Tom said he'd left it at their hotel, and impounded the vehicle on the spot. Both brothers found it easy to appear chagrinned as they signed a damage claim form, grabbed their bags, and caught the airport bus to downtown Dublin. Tom figured it would be easier to rent a car somewhere other than the airport given the circumstances. He hoped Grace O'Malley could cover any uninsured damages.

The bus dropped them at a major stop next to a Best Western hotel on Findlater Street. Tom couldn't see the point of staying in a Best Western in Dublin, but Willie insisted on trying for a place that might have a breakfast waffle machine. A young woman named Alice checked them in. "You fellas looking for something Irish to do? You still have time to catch Oscar Wilde's *A Perfect Husband*. It's playing at the Gate Theater just around the corner." Her eagerness suggested she might have kin in the cast.

Tom didn't figure the title applied to him, but he was always game for a Wilde play, and the Gate was one of the great theaters of Ireland. "Sounds good. What you reckon, bro?"

Willie reckoned otherwise, and by seven, Tom was showered, dressed, and alone in the lobby of the Gate sipping his second glass of Black Bush. Willie was back at the hotel booking a new car with Tom's credit card. Willie had owned a credit card once, but his wife, Rosanne, claimed she had fed it to a goat after one of Willie's solo road trips.

Tom was reaching into his left pants pocket to power off his phone when the Clancy Brothers began singing, to the mixed amusement of fellow drinkers. It was Kate. He extracted the phone from his pants and stared at the screen until the first refrain came to a close: ". . . whiskey you're my darlin', drunk or sober." He ached to talk to Kate but didn't have a clue what he should say to her. He turned off the phone, returned it to his pocket, and drained the glass. Just for two hours. All he asked of tonight was a stretch of two hours when he could push his life away. He would call her in the morning.

Tom joined the throng filing into the theater and settled into his seat—second row, extreme left. It wasn't where the purists liked to sit, row twelve center, the target of the director's production. But no, he liked being up front, where he could see the greasepaint and the shortcomings of the costumes. And he belonged on the side, in the shadows, where he could sit unnoticed and watch the actors hurl their lines past him into the heart of the crowd. Tom lived that way, analyzing people from the shadows, seeking out the mistakes and lies in their performances. In most ways, it was a lonely life, and often depressing. But not tonight—this time, the performers would be actors, not thieves or killers. And Wilde's story would be played for humor and biting satire, not for blood.

The curtain rose, and the stage was bathed in light. The performance was close to perfect. Tom snorted a rare, audible laugh when he heard a favorite Wilde line: "When the gods seek to punish us, they answer our prayers."

~ 12 ~

Tom swayed into the Best Western at half past ten and was not surprised to see Willie working a pint of Guinness in the lobby bar. He ordered a fresh round, and they settled into plush leather chairs in an otherwise empty corner. Willie opened the bidding. "I managed to rent us a car. I figured we had to get our hands on one before news gets out about our driving."

"You mean your driving."

"Your name's on the rental form, and there wasn't any police report, so it's your driving."

"Did you hide the car somewhere? They're likely to repossess it in the middle of the night."

"Gave 'em a phony hotel, different part of town. Looked up a posh one in your guide book." They toasted and lowered the stout levels in their glasses.

"Nice work. Sorry you missed the play."

Willie shrugged and stared at the selection of whiskies on the top shelf. "I'm not. Haven't been to a stage play since we went to see Laurie in Oklahoma! back when you two were an item in high school. I can't remember—what was her part?"

"Just a chorus girl. She deserved a better role."

"Well."

Tom's mind rolled back a quarter of a century. Laurie had tried out for the lead role of Laurey Williams, but every class seemed to have one person born for the stage, and that year it was Julie Armstrong. Laurie's folks were out of town on opening night, so she skipped the cast party and took Tom home to drown her sorrows with her dad's liquor and Tom's good lovin'.

"Ahem."

Tom snapped back to Dublin. "Sorry."

"It's okay, little brother, a man's got to dream now and then. Too bad you ditched Laurie for your Irish murderess."

"Attempted murderess."

"Same shit. But let's get back to the plan. Do we just sit here and drink until someone tries to blow up the hotel?"

Willie had a point. Unknown people with violent tendencies objected to the current activities of the McNaul brothers. But presumably, the hostiles had not yet followed them to Dublin. They would have to advertise. "As pleasant as that sounds, I think we need to become more proactive."

"Use fewer words. I've had a few of these." Willie tilted his glass toward Tom.

"Went to Carrick. Asked questions. Found trouble. Went to Sligo. Asked questions. Woman got murdered. Came to Dublin." Tom paused and stared at Willie. "We go to pubs. Ask questions. Wait fifteen minutes and duck."

"My kind of plan, Tommy. My kind of plan. But for tonight, what say we take the beers upstairs and talk in private?"

Tom led the way to their room. As he flipped on the light, he saw most of a bottle of Kilbeggan whisky on the dresser. He wondered if this was what Willie meant by taking precautions. Willie moved his beer to a small table by the window and collapsed into the adjacent stuffed chair. Tom rolled the desk chair to the other side of the table and stared out at the lights of Dublin. He remembered Kate. Why didn't he take her call? He didn't have an answer to that one, or at least not one he was prepared to admit. He'd need to make it up to her somehow. Willie was watching him but seemed content to sip his beer in silence.

Tom's thoughts shifted to Branna Fitzpatrick, and he began to get angry. Branna's cold body was lying in a morgue with a round bullet hole in it. Thankfully, the Garda boys didn't say where she was shot, or whether there was a savage exit wound. The images would only distract him.

Who murdered Branna, and why? What could she have to do with twenty-year-old crimes? Tom didn't buy the idea that she was caught in some sort of terrorist crossfire. The timing was wrong—her death too obviously related to his investigation. Somehow, he had triggered her death, and the killer was in one hell of a hurry. He had to find out why. Not only because Branna needed justice. He needed to get even. Tom felt his mood slipping into a calm, cold fury, and it scared him. He had killed men in such a fury. He leaped from his chair, shoved his beer across the table to Willie, and grabbed a water glass from the dresser. He filled the glass a third with the Kilbeggan and stared into Willie's eyes.

"Talk to me, big brother. Got to clear my head."

Willie gave a slow nod and relaxed his face into a blank mask. "Thinking about Branna?" He chugged the remnants of his beer and wetted the bottom of the pint glass with a splash of whiskey.

"Of course. But get me out of this mood."

"You sure, Tommy? You'll need to get back into it if the bullets fly."

"When they fly, most likely."

"Most likely. Well. How about if we talk about which pubs we hit tomorrow? And while we're at it, here's to Branna Fitzpatrick." Willie raised his glass, and Tom joined in the toast.

Tom set his glass on the table and went back to staring at the Dublin lights. He slipped off his shoes and rested his feet on the windowsill. "You know, I really don't give a damn about the water lilies."

"Me neither, but we've got to pay the bills somehow."

"Granted." Tom was sensitive to his older brother's financial stresses. Tom managed to retain his pension when the FBI forced him into retirement, and he had also inherited a tidy sum from their late father. Willie's entire income came from their struggling detective agency, and their father had left him nothing. When Mark McNaul ditched Willie's mother for one of his grad students at UNM, Willie had stuck with his mother and never forgave his dad, or the floozy. Tom's mother, Frances, was the floozy.

Willie looked relieved. "So how do a couple of swell guys like us get into trouble in Dublin before our expense money gets yanked?"

Tom froze, forced to confront the obvious—he hadn't a clue. "We could Google it."

"Brilliant!" Willie beamed his widest smile of the trip. "But tell me, Sherlock, Google what? Who are we looking to rile up? The IRA? Some yet-to-be-determined Orange neo-Nazi group? Or the grandson of a real Nazi? They might favor different watering holes."

"Likely do." Tom stood up but continued to gaze out the window. His eyes lost focus, and as the specks of Dublin light grew to overlapping circles of fuzz, he looked inward. "Any ideas?"

"Why don't you call Kate? The FBI might be able to round up some names of the local disreputables."

Kate. He needed to call her back, but . . . not yet. "Maybe later. I don't think she has too many bridges left to burn over here, and I'd like to get closer before we play that card." Tom closed his eyes and began a series of slow, deep breaths. As he took the fourth one, he began a slow-motion kata from his years of iaido training—drawing an imagined Japanese sword and sliding his right foot forward while making a controlled horizontal cut. "Ah."

"Bravo, sensei." Willie had seen this a hundred times and was more bored than impressed. "I think you got him."

Tom's eyes snapped open. "The Gardai."

"You nuts? The cops are more likely to lock us up than cooperate."

"Exactly." Tom smiled. "They won't tell us a bloody thing."

Willie sighed. He seemed resigned to a lengthy wait while Tom assembled the details. He was surprised when Tom spun to face him in only five seconds.

"We'll request an audience with a Garda officer or two and ask a few inane questions about terrorist activities in Ireland. Tell them we're working with the *New York Times* or something. Doesn't matter. They'll scowl and give us the run around."

"Yeah, a boot in the ass, we're back in the streets, and then what?"

"It's arse over here."

"The boot will feel the same."

"Allow me to get to the point. The police in Ireland are as corrupt as any."

"My little brother, the master of understatement."

Tom ignored him. "So while we can count on them not telling us the time of day, it's certain that at least one of them will pass on the news of our inquiry. And that, Willie, is all we require."

"Not bad, but pass it on to who?"

Tom forced himself not to correct Willie's grammar. "Don't know. If we did, we wouldn't have to go to this dance."

*　*　*

The sun rousted Tom well before any hour he considered decent. Direct sunlight and blue skies dominated the view from the window. Perhaps last night's clouds were hung over. He rolled his head in a slow circle to test for dizziness and found none. Willie was already up and dressed. By seven, they hit the breakfast room. Not a waffle or pancake in sight, but Willie was a good sport and attacked a tray of rashers. He stuffed a wad of them in one cheek and looked up at Tom. "What now, partner? Seems kind of early to go bothering coppers."

"Agreed. We should put them off until after lunch. Best to approach them when they've already had half a day to get angry."

"Mmm."

"Seems to me we should change hotels."

Willie munched away, but he eventually swallowed the lot. "What for?"

"It's too obvious a place for Americans to be staying."

"I thought that was the idea—alert the locals and sit like ducks on a pond while we wait to see which hunters show up."

Tom tried to stifle a grin. He gave up. "Yeah, that's more or less right, but I'd fancy our chances better if we pulled a discrete diversion."

"Speak English, little brother."

"Subterfuge?"

"Better." Willie forked a half-inch stack of bacon rashers and held the fork a couple of inches from his lips. "You planning on giving the cops a fake address to pass around? What good will that do? We need the bozos to find us."

"Wrong, Watson. We need them to almost find us."

*   *   *

At a quarter past eleven, Tom turned onto a quiet street in Sandymount, a short distance southeast of the city center and near Dublin Bay. He parked their blue Ford Focus a hundred yards down from the Fitzroy Bed and Breakfast. It was housed in a two-story stone building crawling with ivy and exuding a reserved, comfortable charm. More to the point, it possessed two essential assets: a row of three second-story rooms with windows facing the street, and a rival inn called the Black Oak Lodge, also with two stories, directly opposite. Tom dispatched Willie to the Fitzroy with his suitcase and orders to check the two of them into the left corner room of the upstairs lodgings. When Willie disappeared through the front door of the Fitzroy, Tom grabbed his own bag and headed into the Black Oak. Just inside the door, a sign with a red arrow pointing to his left directed him into a lounge room. The only occupant was a lady of generous years who was watching golf on a small television. She rose to meet him. "You must be Mr. McNaul. I'm Annie Makem, the owner."

"I am he." Tom extended his hand and clasped a bony paw. "May I check in now?"

"Certainly. I can handle that. I manage the place. My husband does all the cooking."

"I'll look forward to it. May I see that upstairs room?"

"Yes, but you've had a bit of luck. Shortly after you called, one of my other guests told me she was leaving early. It's a nicer room, with twin beds, and located in the back. No street noise. I can let you have it for the same price, and you wouldn't have to share a double bed with your brother."

"That's quite nice of you, Mrs. Makem, but I'd prefer the upstairs room we discussed. I like having a view."

"Oh, but the downstairs room opens into a small garden area. Nice for sitting out in the evening. I really think you'd prefer that one."

"No, no. The upstairs one if you please."

Mrs. Makem pursed her lips and frowned. "Suit yourself." She gave Tom a wary glance but decided against questioning his motives. "Let's get you settled."

When the room door closed behind Mrs. Makem, Tom removed binoculars from his bag and pulled a chair into a shadowed area well back from the window. He focused on Willie, who was hanging a shirt in the closet of their Fitzroy room. They weren't going to stay in that room, but it needed to look occupied. Tom propped his feet on a second chair and watched Willie scatter items from his shaving kit on the shelf by the water pitcher. Five minutes later, he tapped on Tom's door.

"Ready to rile the Gardai?"

"Soon, Willie, soon. Let's grab lunch."

*   *   *

Tom pulled into the visitor's parking at Garda Headquarters at five after two. It was a massive stone structure set behind a lofty iron fence and located in Phoenix Park, one of the largest urban parks in Europe. The McNaul brothers entered the fortress through the visitors' gate. A ruddy male sergeant gave them a bored smile. Tom handed him a McNaul Brothers card and recited their cover story. It contained elements of truth, but accuracy was not a priority. The desk sergeant scrunched his forehead as Tom rambled on: They were private detectives . . . staying at the Fitzroy B&B . . . trying to recover a stolen painting ... poor old lady needed an operation . . . believed the related murders were connected to a German underworld figure in Dublin . . . would the Gardai have any files that might help them?

The sergeant morphed from puzzled to agitated and decided to kick them upstairs to a detective. The plan was working. Tom gave an encore performance, and the detective passed them up the line to a blonde female inspector with a slender figure and arctic eyes. She showed no trace of emotion as Tom handed her a card and embellished the tale with imagined details of Grace O'Malley's poor health. When he concluded the play with a request for help, the inspector emitted a bored sigh and nodded to her assistant, who shooed the boys onto a slippery wooden bench down the hall. Tom saw the inspector reach for her phone as the door was closing behind them.

After fifteen minutes, the inspector emerged, shook their hands, and said, "No." She added a few terse excuses that struck Tom as made up on the spot, but he didn't argue the point. They tried to look downcast and left. They kept their eyes straight ahead as they walked past the sergeant at the entry gate. Tom unlocked the car. "This won't take long."

"Nope."

They stopped at a convenience store to lay in a supply of stakeout victuals, and Willie directed Tom to pull over at a hardware store. He emerged moments later with a paper bag containing a light timer. Tom parked the car in front of the Fitzroy. The halfbrothers didn't look much alike, but the proprietor didn't question their status as siblings.

Tom led the way up to the room. He partially closed the curtains but left a ten-inch gap. "Mind standing with your back against the door?"

Willie complied. "Okay, now what?"

Tom took hold of the curtains. "Look through the gap and tell me whether you can see the window of our room across the road."

"Almost, but move the right curtain a bit more to the right. Yeah, right there."

The boys settled in and watched the RTE news station. Willie tired as the news cycle began to repeat for the third time. "This isn't shaping up as much of an evening."

Tom shook his head. "Think you're wrong about that, big brother. If the word spreads at all, it will move like a brush fire. If the right people hear the news, they'll have to move fast. They won't know whether we're here for just the one night."

"If you say so, but try another channel."

A few minutes later Tom spotted a black four-door pulling to the curb under a veteran oak tree fifty yards down the street to their left. There were two men in the car, and they had a clear view of the room's window.

Tom nudged Willie. "Check out the two guys under the tree. Let's give them half an hour to see if they're taking up residence."

The men in the car held their ground, and at seven, Tom turned off the television. "Time to make a show of leaving. We'll turn right toward the shops, and once we're down a couple of blocks we'll circle back to the left. We can slip into our other room via the back."

"But our food's still in the car."

"Jesus, Willie. We'll eat later."

The men in the black sedan remained still as mannequins as the McNaul brothers strode down the front steps of the Fitzroy and turned right, away from the car. The road curved slightly to their left, and by the time they covered two blocks, the sedan and its crew were out of view. Tom tapped Willie's elbow and turned down a street to their left. Half a block along, they turned left again down an alley and soon reached a spot behind the Black Oak. There didn't seem to be any dogs or other vocal livestock in the back yard, so Tom unlatched the gate and they eased their way to the rear door. It was unlocked and opened into a well-lit but unoccupied kitchen. As Tom closed the door behind them, he heard Willie opening the refrigerator.

"Damn it, we can eat later."

Willie ignored him and fossicked about for a few moments. He extracted two bottles of Harp Lager and a hunk of local cheddar. "We can fess up in the morning."

Tom snatched the bottles from Willie and stuck them back in the fridge. "Tonight, we need to stay sober."

They left the room lights off and eased the door shut. Willie hopped on the bed, grabbed all the pillows, and propped himself up against the headboard. Tom slid the room's lone, rickety chair to a spot next to his brother. They were about ten feet from the window and would be invisible from outside the building. More to the point, they had clear views of the window of their room at the Fitzroy. Willie broke the block of cheddar into two parts. He retained the larger.

The night closed in. When their room was fully dark, Tom slid his chair closer to the window until he could see the black sedan as well as the Fitzroy room. By nine, Willie was growling for another trip to the fridge, but Tom waved him a halt sign and leaned forward. He motioned for Willie to slide down the bed closer to the window and pointed up the street toward the black sedan. Both occupants climbed out of the car, but the dome light did not turn on. They surveyed the empty street and crossed to the Fitzroy. One of them fetched a key from his pocket and unlocked the front door. There were no lights showing on the lower floor. Willie leaned close to Tom's right ear but kept his voice above a whisper. "This doesn't look right. Why would those two have a key?"

"Exactly."

Less than a minute later, they saw a vertical line of light as the door to their Fitzroy room cracked open. After a short pause, the line widened, and they saw shadows cross the lit doorway. The light narrowed and then disappeared.

Tom bit his lower lip and nodded in the darkness. "Door closed. Pretty sure they're on the inside."

"Yup."

Patterns of faint light began to move along the small, visible portion of the door of their invaded quarters. "Flashlights, Willie."

They came prepared. They saw us leave, but they clearly didn't want to go inside in the daylight. Any idea why?"

"Nope."

The lights continued to flicker off the door, but the men were not working within the narrow field of view. After five minutes the glow of the flashlights disappeared, and a few seconds later the door opened and closed. The men soon emerged from the front door of the Fitzroy, returned to the black four-door, and drove off. Tom rested his hand on Willie's arm. "Let's take five in case they're just looping around the block."

They took ten, then eased their way down the stairs and out the front door of the Black Oak. No moving cars, dog walkers, or stray children were within sight, so they crossed to the Fitzroy and entered. The lights were still out in the common areas of the first floor, but there was a glow emanating from the top of the stairs. Tom could hear muffled sounds of a television coming from somewhere on the second floor. He led the way to the well-lit upstairs hall. They took positions on each side of their door, and Tom slipped the brass key into the lock and gently turned it clockwise. There was a sharp click. He left the key in the door and turned the knob. Willie shrugged, reached across, and pushed the door inward. "No sense standing around. Our company got tired of waiting and bailed." He stepped into the room and flipped on the light switch. Nothing looked out of place, so he strode to the window and scanned the street. "No sign of the car." He pulled the curtains shut.

Tom stepped into the room and closed the door. "Let's give it the once over. Those two were poking around in here for five or six minutes, and there aren't that many places to poke. I don't think they were just looking for loose change."

"Agreed."

The loo was down the hall, so the search area was limited. Willie ransacked the dresser and end tables while Tom checked out the curtains, chairs, and closet. Nothing. Willie started tearing apart the bed, so Tom dropped to the floor and began probing underneath. "Bingo." Willie set down a pillow and lowered himself to the floor on the opposite side of the bed. Tom pointed to a long slit in the fabric covering the bottom of the box spring. "This bed looks too new for a tear like that."

Tom slid his hand through the slit and touched a cold, flat object. Metal or glass. He retrieved his phone from his pants pocket, activated the flashlight, and pointed it through the slit. He saw a glint of glass, a small black mass, and a couple of red wires. "Oh shit."

"Sup, little brother?"

"I've seen something that looked too much like this. Not long ago. It was under a dead man's chair."

~ 13 ~

Tom held his phone in one hand and began to tear gently at the fabric with the other. As the slit widened, both brothers gained a clear view of a cell phone attached by a single wire to an irregular black lump. The lump was a bit larger than a softball and appeared to be covered by black electrical tape. The contraption was bound to a spring by two lengths of red wire. No explanations were necessary. Tom gave Willie a hard look. "You get on out of the room. I'll take it from here." Willie didn't move. "Damn it, get going. I know this design. Looks a whole lot like the one someone left for me in Boston. Only this one is hooked to a cell phone instead of a simple receiver."

"Yeah? I recall that one went off with quite a bang. Maybe you should let me disarm the thing."

Tom's temper flared. "I didn't set it off—the damned cat tripped it. Get a move on. If I do screw up with you still here, Myrna won't have an employer."

"Be my guest." Willie stood up and disappeared out the door. Tom heard the latch click and waited ten seconds. He couldn't hear footsteps, but Willie could move like a ninja, so he went to work. There wasn't anything complicated about the design— nothing that looked like a booby trap. He stared at the ugly device for four or five more seconds, bit the side of his tongue, and unplugged the wire running from the phone's earphone jack to the ominous black blob. He untwisted the ends of the wires holding the phone to the box spring frame. The phone looked cheap and disposable. He stuffed it in his shirt pocket and worked the bomb out of the springs. A few moments later, he opened the door and spotted Willie at the head of the stairs. "All clear."

Willie took the lead as they crept down the stairs into the dark hall. He cracked the front door, eyed the street, and waved for Tom to follow. As they crossed the street to the Black Oak, Willie veered off course and retrieved their bags of food from the car. Three minutes later, they were sitting on their bed downing Oreos, tortilla chips, and beer. The bomb parts lay between them. Tom fingered the phone. "Pretty simple. Someone calls, the ring signal from the mini plug activates the detonator, kaboom."

"Yep."

Tom moved the bomb pieces to the top of the dresser and returned to the bed. "Got a plan?"

"Sure." Willie got up and turned out the lights. "I figure the bozos in the black sedan will be back before long. They aren't going to call the phone at some random time 'cause they wouldn't be sure we were still in the room."

"Not bad. They come back. Then what?"

Willie grimaced. "That's as far as I got. You take over."

Tom leaned against the headboard and finished off another Oreo. "It's time to set up the light timer in the other room. If our visitors stake the place out again, it may keep them looking that direction." He stood up, retrieved the timer, and headed for the door. "Let's roll."

"You go ahead. I'll be down in a bit. Left something in the car."

They separated at the sidewalk. Tom was in and out of their Fitzroy room within four minutes. Willie was waiting for him on the steps of the Black Oak and now had a small blue daypack over his left shoulder. They looked back across the street at the window. The curtains were well lit by the lamp on the left bed table. They headed back to their snacks.

While Tom dug another handful of chips from the super-sized bag, Willie opened the daypack. He reached in and retrieved a thirty-eight special revolver. Tom's eyes widened as Willie set the pistol on the bed. "Where the hell did you get that? You know what Kate said—the gun laws are tough as hell in Ireland. You'll be in deep shit if you get caught toting that."

"Not as deep as I'd be without it if we get down and dirty with those guys in the car. Besides, who says we'll get caught?"

"I'm serious, Willie. We can't shoot it out like cowboys on the streets of Dublin. This isn't New Mexico."

"Oh, pipe down. Here's yours." Willie reached into the blue pack and pulled out a second thirty-eight and a box of bullets. He handed the gun to Tom. "Best load up."

"Bloody hell. Where did you get these anyway?"

"Best you don't know everything. But I did tell you I had to run an errand back in Sligo. I'm good at finding my kind of people."

Tom didn't like it, but he loaded his revolver and grabbed another beer. He adjusted the curtains to give a broader view of the street in case the mad bombers parked in a different spot. They settled in the dark and resumed munching.

The black car returned at eight forty-five and glided to a stop at the curb. Willie grunted. "Same spot. Seldom pays to be a creature of habit."

At ten-thirty, the light in their Fitzroy room went off. Tom put down the bag of chips, but he saw no movement in or around the sedan. At ten-forty-five, the cell phone on the dresser chirped. The boys stared at the faint light from the phone as it chirped another ten times. Tom wasn't surprised that it didn't connect to a voice-mail account. He stared at Willie. Willie stared back. They turned to the window and saw both front doors of the black sedan open. Once again, the dome light did not go on. Two men in dark clothing and stocking caps emerged. They eased the doors of the car shut and crossed the street to the front door of the Fitzroy. One of them turned his head and placed his left ear against the door. A few seconds later, he nodded, took something from his pants pocket, and unlocked the door.

"Back in a flash." Willie leaped from the bed. He grabbed the bomb and the disposable phone from the dresser top. He took a step toward the door but froze, stared at the cheap phone, and tossed it back on the dresser. As he scurried out the door, he whispered over his shoulder, "No questions, Tommy."

Tom was confused. He turned back to the window, but the two men from the car had disappeared into the Fitzroy. He saw Willie emerge from the front door of the Black Oak, leap down the steps, and run to the black sedan. Willie dropped to his knees beside the rear door on the curb side. He opened it. Tom watched as Willie leaned into the back seat area. A ray of light from across the street caught Tom's eye. He glanced toward the curtained window of their Fitzroy room. A second later, the light disappeared. Someone had opened and closed the door. He looked back at the sedan. Tom fidgeted while Willie continued to fiddle with something behind the driver's seat. As Willie backed out of the car and closed the door, Tom saw the light in the Fitzroy window flicker once more. He clenched and un-clenched his fists while his brother jogged back to the front of the Black Oak. Willie slipped through the front door several sec-onds before the two men emerged from the Fitzroy and headed toward their car. Seconds later, he heard a light tap at the door to their room. Tom unlatched it and stepped aside as his winded brother staggered in and threw himself on the bed. "Gotta get back in shape."

"You haven't got that much time. The stakeout twins are driv-ing away."

"I suppose we should join them." Willie's breathing was slow-ing toward normal. "Not a major rush though."

Tom looked sideways at his brother. "You care to explain that? Those guys are already out of sight. How the hell are we going to tail them now? And what did you do with the bomb?" Tom was pretty sure he knew the answer to the last question, but he couldn't understand why Willie would run out with the bomb but not the trigger phone.

"Bomb's under the driver's seat."

"I figured, but why? And how come you left their phone here?"

"Those bastards didn't come here to scare us off. They meant to kill us. I figured I'd like to be in a position to return the favor, if the need arises."

It seemed best not to debate the wisdom of that point, so Tom crossed his arms and waited. Willie rolled off the bed and grabbed his gun and a fresh bag of Oreos. "Let's boogie. Bring your phone, and I'll explain the rest while you drive."

Tom turned their rental around and drove slowly in the direction last taken by their stalkers. Four blocks later, he came to a major intersection. "Okay, now what?"

Willie pointed toward the curb. "Pull over and show me how to get the app working."

"App?"

"Yeah. Give me your phone."

Tom parked under a streetlight and dug his phone out of his left pants pocket. Willie grabbed it and started fumbling with the opening screen. "How do you get to that tracking app?"

"Find my Friends?"

"Something like that. Whatever it was that you set up on our phones so you could keep track of me. It's always turned on in my phone, which is now attached to the bomb."

Tom opened Find My Friends and showed Willie how to keep track of the bomber's car. "Give me what directions you can."

Willie began barking out navigational commands with far more confidence than Tom felt. Within ten minutes, they crossed the M50 heading southwest. Willie missed one turn, but the black car, or at least Willie's phone, wasn't traveling much above the speed limit, so Tom hung a U-turn and caught up to within about a quarter-mile of their target. He matched speeds for another twenty minutes as they rolled out of the Dublin suburbs and turned onto a winding, tree-lined lane.

Tom checked the mirrors, but there were no cars behind them. The lead car was rarely visible because of the lack of straightaways. "No offense, bro, but this seems like a dumb idea. What if someone calls your phone?"

"No chance. I've never given anyone the number. Well, you have it, but your phone is right here."

"Not even Rosanne?" Rosanne Ortega was Willie's woman of

twenty years. She liked technology even less than Willie, and their small ranch southwest of Santa Fe didn't even have internet service.

"Nah. I never told her I got a phone. Stop worrying."

There wasn't much to be done, and maybe Willie was right. Tom had talked Willie into buying a phone that matched his own and helped him with the frustrating setup. Willie had never warmed to its complexities, and only carried it when they worked a case together. Tom knew the number, but he had never passed it on, not even to Myrna. Well, he had given it to Kate, but only for emergencies.

Tom's phone started singing about the joys of whiskey. Willie squinted at the screen. "You've got a call. How do you answer this goddamned thing?"

"Hand it over." Tom grabbed the phone and saw that the call was from Kate. Damn. Forgot to call her back. He started to answer but hesitated just before his thumb touched the screen. Kate would be mad as hell, and she might have news, but she'd have to wait. He handed the phone back to Willie. "Remind me to call her when the car chase is over."

"No way to treat a good woman, Tommy. Or even a not-so-good one. You want me to talk to her?"

"Bloody hell. Get back to navigating."

Two minutes later, Tom's phone dinged. Willie looked puzzled. "What the hell's that mean?"

"Just a text message." That seemed odd to Tom. He didn't get many texts. "See who it is, will you?"

Willie went to the home screen, one of the few things he knew how to do on a smart phone. "It's from Kate."

"Tap on it, just in case it's important."

Willie followed the order. "Says, and I quote: "Answer your goddamned phone, you creep. Possible lead. Need to talk. Will try Willie."

"Shit! Give me the phone." Tom snatched it from Willie's hand and swiped through his contacts while steering with one hand. He hit Kate's number. Agonizing seconds passed. "Come on, come on." The call was routed to voicemail. A flash of light lit the trees and low-slung clouds up ahead. The sound of the blast arrived just over a second later. Tom hit the brakes and pulled off the pavement. They sat in silence for several seconds. Then Tom turned around and steered back toward Dublin.

As the trees thinned and the population density began to rise, Willie gave a mighty sigh. "Okay, maybe it was a dumb idea, but I figured we were in control. Who the hell gave Kate my cell number?"

"Uh, guilty. I figured we could use a third person in the loop if we got separated."

"Mmm."

"Damn it. She wasn't supposed to call unless it was an emergency."

Willie grinned. "Boyfriend doesn't pick up? That's an emergency. But pray, let's move on. What next?"

"From the size of the blast, I think we can assume the two in the car are stiffs."

"Crispy too."

"Somebody sent those guys to do us, and they found themselves in our empty room with no bomb in sight. They didn't dawdle. They came out the door and hurried off in their car, presumably to report in. Agreed?"

"Yep. They didn't sit around in the car playing with their phones, but they might have called someone from the road. Before Kate triggered the bomb."

Tom pondered the consequences. "If they didn't make the call, their boss will figure the guys bungled and blew themselves up. He'll just send another team."

"Yep."

"If they did call in the missing bomb, the big cheese will know we're wise to them. He'll still send another team, but they'll come at us from another angle. Guns drawn."

They stared ahead in silence as several kilometers rolled past. Tom pulled into a gas station and parked in a dark area well away from lights and pumps. He rolled down the window, and damp sea air rolled in carrying odors of dog droppings from an adjacent patch of grass. "Trouble is, Willie, we have to play the part of sitting ducks either way. We still don't know who's after us, let alone how to find them. We'll have to let them try again."

"Not to my taste, little brother. We're in a hell of a mess. How about we quietly skip the country, tap the O'Malley woman for whatever expenses we can, and cut our losses? Back to good IPA and enchiladas in Santa Fe? I know you think art is important and all that, but in the end, we're just chasing a goddamned painting for a reward. No reason to get ourselves killed for one payday. Hell, it probably wouldn't be that easy to collect anyway. Not from a crippled lady who needs cash herself."

"I'm not in this for the cash anymore. Not for recovering an old master for some museum either. Not anymore. Somebody tried to blow me away in Boston. Those two bombers we just exterminated tried to do us both in. And somebody gunned down young Branna Fitzpatrick just because we asked her a few questions in Sligo. I don't know what the hell's going on, but now I take it personally." Tom locked eyes with Willie. "It's okay. I get it. This isn't what you signed on for, and that's fair enough. You go back and report in to the O'Malleys. Hit them up for expenses—no fee. But I've got to stay here."

Tom never saw Willie's jab to his jaw. The back of his head bounced off the driver's window. Willie slugged him again. "Don't you fuckin' ever say something like that to me again, little brother. I think you're dumb as hell to stay here, but you ain't gonna stay alone."

Tom bought some time with deep breaths. When his head was almost clear, he turned back to Willie and grinned. "Sorry. We okay?"

"One more for good luck?"

"Your mother."

They sat in silence for several minutes. Willie began to squirm with impatience. "Tommy, for a couple of small-town detectives, we live interesting lives. When you signed on as my partner, you said you'd handle the art theft. I figured you might starve, but it would keep you out of trouble. Thought we'd be sipping champagne with expensive broads in black micro-dresses and turquoise necklaces. Eating canopies. Now look at us."

"Canapés. And most of the Santa Fe art scene women are too old for micros. But okay. Only . . . if you're sticking around, don't bellyache." Tom started the engine. "We need to get back to the Black Oak before the reinforcements show up."

*   *   *

By eleven-thirty, Tom was bored and staring out the window of their darkened room. Nothing moved on the street or in the windows of the Fitzroy rooms. "We'd better take shifts and get some rest. If the bombers didn't call home before they went up in smoke, their boss won't know his boys are dead. It might be a while before anyone comes looking for them, or us."

"True." Willie paused while he swallowed a mouthful of chips. "Since I'm already on the bed, I'll take the first sleep shift." He swept the remaining bags of food to one side and stretched out with his left forearm covering his eyes. "Wake me at dawn." He was asleep within seconds.

Tom mulled over the less-favorable possibility. If the stalkers had managed to call home, the management would know Tom and Willie had found the bomb. When their guys didn't show up, a team would have been dispatched in a hurry, and not to talk. There wasn't any better place to wait, so Tom crossed his arms and kept scanning the empty street. What the hell was going on? The Monet was worth plenty of dough, enough to kill for, but the bomb and the shooting of Branna didn't smell like simple greed. Somebody must have a more powerful motive.

The quiet ended just short of an hour later when a black Mercedes pulled to the curb fifty yards from the nearest street lamp. As with its cheaper predecessor, the interior lights remained off as both front doors opened. Two men in leather jackets, jeans, and caps climbed out and scanned the street. They looked to be in their 20s. The man on the right side tapped the roof, and a few seconds later, a passenger emerged from the rear seat. He was middle-aged and more formally dressed than his comrades—tall boots and a tweed shooting jacket. The latter seemed appropriate. Tom nudged Willie. "Company calling."

Willie's eyes sprang open, and he rolled off the bed without hesitation. He knelt by the window. "What you reckon?"

"Boss and the B team."

"Uh huh. You come up with a brilliant plan during my nap?"

"Nope. Might as well give them a few minutes to check out the other room." The men in the street exchanged nods. Each of the two in leather slipped his right hand inside his jacket and held it there as they walked to the door of the Fitzroy. Boss Tweed followed, his own hands clasped behind his back. When the lead elements reached the door, the man on the left retrieved something from his right jeans pocket. He scanned the street one more time and then unlocked the door.

Tom watched the three-man war party disappear inside. "When they come back out, we should probably be waiting for them."

"Right here on the street? Seems risky."

"Risky anywhere, but we don't have much choice. We probably couldn't follow them far in our car without being spotted, and we can't plant your phone for tracking again. You blew it up."

"Technically, Kate blew it up, but let's not quibble." Willie stood up and moved to a spot farther from the window. He picked up his pistol, checked the load, and began filling the left pocket of his blue windbreaker with extra bullets.

Tom hesitated for a second, then retrieved his own revolver. "You stay to my left when we face them. I'm quicker shooting cross-body left."

Willie scowled. "So am I."

"Yeah, but I'm faster than you. If it comes to that, I'll take down the first one, and then it's Katie bar the door."

"Speaking of Kate, when are you going to call her back?"

"Damn it, Willie. Not now. Let's get down to the street."

"I think you're wasting a shot at a good woman, kid."

Tom had other shots on his mind, but he let Willie have the last word. They slipped out of the Black Oak and moved to a spot on the sidewalk twenty yards behind the Mercedes and shaded by a grumpy-looking oak. Tom drew his pistol and held it muzzle down alongside his right leg. Willie did the same. They stared at the front door of the Fitzroy and shuffled their feet for two or three minutes. The door opened.

~ 14 ~

A trickle of sweat ran down Tom's gun arm as the three riders of the black Mercedes stepped out of the Fitzroy and headed toward their car. He wiped his wrist on the leg of his jeans. The men appeared to be whispering. When they reached the middle of the street, about seventy feet from Willie and Tom, the man in the tweed jacket spotted the McNaul brothers and froze. The two henchmen followed his gaze, halted, and instinctively eased a couple of steps to each side of their boss. The man farthest to Tom's left began to slide his hand upward.

"Don't." Tom's voice was calm but cold. "Better to talk."

The man's hand stopped at his belt buckle. "Why would we want to talk to old farts like you?" He tilted his head a few degrees to his right and smirked.

Tom glanced at the man on the far right. That one seemed a bit more nervous. He was shifting his weight and didn't appear balanced. The left-side guy would be the first target. The boss was probably armed too, but he'd surely let one of his boys make the first move. Tom relaxed his face and muttered to Willie: "Got left."

"Noted."

The boss took a half step forward and spread his empty hands. "Easy there, lads." He half turned to the snarly man." Let's hear what these fellas have to say. It might be entertaining." He looked back toward Tom. "I'd be feeling more at ease if you'd put your guns away. That okay with you?"

"I think not."

"Well, we can't bloody well talk here in the middle of the street."

"There's a small park around the corner and down a block. How about we all walk down there and have a chat. Nice night for a stroll. Willie, you collect the hardware."

The man on the left sprayed spittle at least six feet. "You're collectin' fuckin' nothin'."

"Then we'll maintain the status quo, but do be careful. Someone gets the hiccups and this could end badly." The man on the left began wagging his jaw. He looked about as stable as a bear on a unicycle.

Tom had only one card to play, and it seemed time. He turned his face toward the boss but kept his eyes on the twitchy man. "See if you can calm down your friend a bit. We've got no motive to take you down. We haven't even got a clue who you are. All we know is that two suspicious-looking guys parked a black car about where yours is now. They staked out our hotel room for most of the evening. Made us nervous, so we slipped out the back and circled the block to this side of the street. The men left a couple of hours ago."

"Yeah? Then what?"

"Then we waited for the boys to come back. Thought we might get up a bridge game, but you three showed up instead, and in a better car. What gives? Pardon the guns, but you don't look like coppers."

The fidgety man on the left set his jaw and seemed to be steeling his nerves. Boss Tweed barked sideways at him: "Stand easy. We'll hear a little more." He smiled, stretched his neck, and slipped his hands into the side pockets of his jacket. Tom raised his pistol a few inches, and the smile disappeared. "You go easy too, fella. We're still three to two." He seemed to waver for a second, but then his voice turned hard. "What happened to those men?"

"Beats me. We watched them from around the side there." Tom tweaked his pistol toward some dense bushes between the Black Oak and a brick house with no lights showing. "They eventually got tired of window peeping and went in the front door of our hotel. The one across the street. The light came on in our room. Behind you—second floor, far left. But then you'd know that, wouldn't you? You three did the same thing, only you didn't stay as long."

"Get on with it, while you still can."

Tom ignored the threat. "They were in there maybe ten minutes. Then they came out and drove away. We thought it wise to stay out of sight in case they came back. After a while, we went out for a bite, but just after we got back, you three showed up." This was the critical moment. If the boss man didn't know Tom and Willie found the bomb, he might figure it was faulty. Maybe his boys were taking it home for repairs. Accidents happen. But if they had called in, the boss would know better, and he'd try to sucker Tom and Willie into relaxing for one fatal second. Best to call the question. "We gonna talk, or shall we play cowboys and Irishmen?"

The twitching man upped his tempo and glanced at the boss, but his hands didn't move. The other sidekick stood still as a pall-bearer waiting for the preacher to finish his eulogy. The boss man looked wary. "You get to the point, don't you, Yank? I'm thinkin' you're worth a few more words. Shall we sit in my fine motorcar, or are you set on a midnight stroll in the park? I'm familiar with the neighborhood."

"Nice car, but it might be kind of cramped for five guys all trying to kill each other. Let's try the park. You guys lead."

"We'll lead, but you holster your guns first."

"Deal." Tom slowly slid the thirty-eight special to his left side. He tucked it into his belt rather than in the holster at the small of his back. Willie scowled but followed. The two wingmen looked uncomfortable as they walked flanking their boss, who led the way to the park with confident strides. Tom and Willie stayed five paces back.

The night air was still fresh from the Irish Sea, and the smell of damp soil reminded Tom of a graveyard. A metal picket fence surrounded the tiny park. Its black vertical bars were just a few inches apart and might have kept out very short dogs had there been a gate. The chief led them to a spot fifty feet in from the road and barely lit by a yellow street light near the entrance. He turned to face Tom and Willie, his hands still in his coat pockets. The henchmen turned with him, their arms down but their fingers flexing. "Okay, Lads. Your turn."

None of the guys looked ready to draw down, so Tom focused on the boss. "Just who are you guys?"

"Next question."

Tom hesitated, but Willie took a half-step forward. "My little brother asked you a fair question. You'd be wise to answer it."

The boss tightened his jaw but didn't reply.

Tom tried to ease the tension. "Okay, we'll come back to that. Here's our story. A lady in Boston hired us to find a painting. It was stolen from her family estate up near Armagh more than twenty years ago, but it was spotted in Boston about a week back. It's worth quite a lot of dough, and she could use some. So she hired me, because that's what I do. I'm an art detective. I get lonesome when I'm away from my dog, so I brought brother Willie here when I came looking for it. You follow so far?"

Nobody spoke up, so Tom pushed on. "We started down in Carrick-on-Suir. That's in County Tipperary."

"We know where the hell Carrick is. Get on with you."

"Got your Irish up, did I? Didn't mean to. As I was saying, we started in Carrick, but people started crawling out of alleys and taking offense at us doing our business. One of them steered us up to Sligo, where we asked a young lady if she knew anything. She said no, but someone shot her anyway. For no reason at all, near as I can tell. You know anything about that?"

"You finish your fairy tale, then I'll get to mine."

"Not much left to tell." Boss Tweed was beginning to rile Tom. "We came to Dublin for lack of a better idea. Next thing we know, a couple of goons are staking out our room. Given what happened to the girl in Sligo, we figured we'd be better off staking them out. It was getting pretty boring, just sitting behind the bushes watching your guys watch our window. Fortunately, they left. That's my story. Your turn."

"Load of bullshit, Yank."

Willie lowered his center of gravity about an inch and interrupted: "Before you say that a second time, Mick, you got a next of kin?"

The boss turned his eyes to Willie and evidently didn't like what he saw. "Calm down, now, okay? We don't give a damn about some fuckin' painting, but word has it you're looking for the men who did the job. Why would that be? The coppers gave up on that case twenty years ago. I don't know who pulled the job, but this is a small island. Could be they're friends of mine." He slowly raised his left hand and scratched his chin with one finger. Tom slowed his breathing and watched for a reaction from either wingman. They didn't budge. Maybe it wasn't a signal. "Sounds fishy to me. If the painting is in Boston, what the hell are you guys doing in Dublin?"

In for a penny. Tom suppressed an urge to grin. "We ran out of leads in Boston when the man trying to sell the painting went up in smoke. It wasn't all bad news, the cat and I survived, but someone got away with the art work." The boss looked quizzical, but then, he wouldn't know about the cat. "We have no idea who has the painting now, so we figured our only chance was to come across the pond to see if we could follow the long, cold trail from Armagh to Boston. You got any better ideas?"

"I don't believe a fuckin' word. What I want to know is what happened to my boys?"

"How the hell should I know? Like I said, they drove off. We figured they were hungry, or maybe they just didn't want to piss in the bushes in such a nice neighborhood. So suppose you fill us in. Who are you guys, and while you're at it, what were you looking for in our room?"

The chief looked uncertain, but he also looked like a man getting ready to clean up loose ends. His eyes flicked to each of his wingmen, and they seemed to tense. Tom readied for a chest shot to the twitchy man, to be followed by a quick side step and crouch as he put another in the boss. Willie wouldn't have any trouble with the slow drone on the right. Shouldn't take a full second. Still, the trail would die with them. Last chance. "I don't know what war you think we're fighting, but damn it, all we want is the bloody painting. We don't work for the IRA, some Orange militia group, or the Boston mob. We've got no scores to settle with crooked Gardai and no yen to solve cold-case murders. All we want is to get Mrs. O'Malley her goddamn painting so we can collect our fee, go home, and pay the rent."

"Mrs. O'Malley?"

"Yes, Grace O'Malley. A widow in a wheelchair in Boston who's running out of money and needs treatment."

"That would be Grace O'Malley from Armagh?"

"I said that already."

The boss smiled and relaxed his shoulders. He turned his head a few degrees toward the twitchy fellow. "Stand down. We'll not be shooting just now." He looked back at Tom. "I know this Grace O'Malley. What's this about her being in a wheelchair?"

Tom was dumbfounded. "Don't know all the details, but she fell off a horse. Dangerous thing to do, ride a horse. You won't catch me on one. But how do you know her?"

"We go way back. Knew her in Armagh before she went to America. Grace is okay, though she was a fool to marry that sleazy O'Malley bastard. You boys go on home and find the painting for her. Tell her Donal says hello."

"Donal who?"

"You know better than that, cowboy. You just be off now, and be quick about it. You said the painting's in Boston. So you two get the next plane out of Dublin and go look for it there. You're messing around in things here you don't want to know about. You follow?"

"I follow, but we're not going anywhere unless you give us something. We came to Ireland because the trail's cold as ashes in Massachusetts. You must know something. How did that painting get from a manor house in Armagh to Boston? And who took it there? We need a lead to have any hope of finding it."

"I'm getting tired of standing in this park. The dew is soaking through my Italian shoes. Suppose you and I go and sit in the back of the car for a bit. My boys and your mad-dog brother can wait down the road and snarl at each other."

Tom nodded and followed the boss back to the Mercedes. They stood on opposite sides of the open back doors, eyeballed each other, then slid inside at the same time. Tom's door closed half a second before the other. The boss didn't seem to be maneuvering for easy access to belt or pocket. "Fairly roomy for a rear seat, don't you think, Yank?"

"Crime seems to pay. And I assume you know my name's Tom."

"I do." The boss glanced up the street to where Willie and the henchmen were flexing their muscles like teenage boys in a locker room. "You'll get no names from me."

"I can live without them, but let's cut to the chase. You're IRA, aren't you? Why do you guys have a stake in this?"

The boss arched his eyebrows and looked impressed. "Not bad for an art shamus. Maybe you deserve something." He leaned his head a few inches closer to Tom's. "Listen well. I'm only saying this once. The story goes back a long time. Back to the '40s, even. Before you or I were born."

"I've got plenty of time."

"Less than you think, so suppose you just sit still and let me tell you a few things before the boys out there get worried." He glanced at the trio fifty yards up the sidewalk, still fluffing feathers. "After the war, a lot of low-level Nazis figured the Emerald Isle was better than a Russian prison camp or a Nuremburg cell. Lots of folks around here were happy to have them if they brought in enough money. Lord knows, we didn't feel any need to turn them over to the damned British."

"I've heard a bit of that. Go on."

"The money was the key. These Germans used it to buy protection, and the IRA was selling for a hefty price. There was peace in the land, but nobody thought it would last. It didn't. There were bitter folks in both Irelands, north and south, and the coming war was bound to be expensive. Me own father was one of those angry folks, down here in the Republic."

"Let me guess. One of these Nazis had a stash of looted art. The rightful owners were likely dead in the camps. Hard to sell but worth a fortune, even at a few cents on the dollar."

"That's close enough."

Tom bit his upper lip. "Was the guy SS?"

"No idea. Does it matter?"

"I suppose not. He's probably dead now anyway."

"So I'm told. Me da would have been a young lad when the German fella came over. Years later, about the time the Troubles flared up, me da told me a story about such a man who lived in the Wicklow Mountains. They're south of Dublin. Fella bought himself quite a pretty hideaway there. Had to have cost a load, even in those times. This German sold a very valuable painting at a very low price to none other than Mr. Robert O'Malley of Armagh, who later became the father of Peter O'Malley—the rich toff who married our mutual friend, Grace."

Tom's eyes betrayed his surprise. "That gets my attention."

"I thought it would. The years went by. The elder O'Malley passed on, and his son, Peter, wasn't much at managing the estate. He ran low on money and got the idea of trying to locate the elderly German man and strong-arm him for cash. To preserve his good name, as it were."

"Blackmail, we call it."

"Aye, we call it the same here. This Peter O'Malley fella wasn't too bright. It was stupid enough to blackmail a Nazi, even an old one, but a Nazi with an IRA insurance policy?" The boss shook his head.

"Might not have known about the IRA connection, but dumb nonetheless. So your old man was IRA, and he drew the job of insurance adjuster, right? I assume your organization was licking its chops over getting their hands on the art work."

"You could die quickly asking questions like that around here, Tommy. I recommend caution. But yes. Manpower was tight, so a lone soldier was sent to Armagh, and he hired a local helper up there."

"Let me guess. The helper was Branna Fitzpatrick's father?"

"Aren't you a clever lad? In other circumstances, I'd share a pint with you, sir." The chief seemed to relax, so Tom doubled his guard. "This Fitzpatrick fella turned out to be a poor choice. The boys pulled off the hit just fine, though sadly, the elder Mrs. O'-Malley, Grace's mother-in-law, went down with her son. The boys took the painting and split."

Tom tugged his left ear while keeping his right hand a foot from his pistol. "How did it go wrong? I heard someone gunned down your hit men and took off with the painting."

"Our soldier was reliable, so it had to be Fitzpatrick. The word is he tipped the constables in Belfast. Probably figured he'd get a fat reward, not a slug in the skull."

"And they decided to clean things up. Then what?"

"Then nothing. That was more than twenty years ago. The Belfast police buried the case in a hurry. The painting never surfaced. Either it was sold, or someone was using it for collateral. You can buy a lot of drugs with that kind of capital."

"Or guns."

"Or guns, yes. But we don't have it, so if it's being used to fund gun-running, look to the Orange bastards. I don't have a name for you. Not that I'd tell you if I did."

Tom was spiraling toward depression, but he kept his eye on the boss's right hand. "Just one more thing. Why did Branna have to die?"

The boss took a long time answering. "'Twas a pity. This is just a guess, mind you. The boys had ordered up the hit on Fitz-patrick, and they were worried he might have told his wife too much. The locals in Sligo kept an eye on her until she died. It should have ended there, but the Sligo captain is a hard-arse. He insisted they keep up a watch on the daughter in case her mother told family tales. When you fellas showed up asking questions, I guess he lost it."

"Sins of the fathers."

"How's that?" The boss looked genuinely puzzled.

"I don't believe in sins of the fathers. Half the troubles in the world result from people carrying their fathers' grudges." Tom clenched his jaw until his teeth hurt. "Why can't you people just let it go? Who cares what someone else's grandfather did to your grandfather?" He began breathing harder. "You've got your Republic down here. The folks up north seem to like the English for some reason. Some of them, anyway. Both sides called a cease-fire years ago. Damn it. The Troubles are over. Life seems good over here even if the Celtic Tiger has a bit of indigestion. Why not live and let live?"

"It's been going on for centuries, Yank. You don't understand."

"Maybe not your politics, but I understand murder."

"Time's up. I've told you too much already. Take your hairy brother and get the hell out of Ireland by tomorrow morning. You're only walking away from this because Grace O'Malley is an old friend of mine. I'm sorry to hear of her condition, and I hope you find her painting, but you've burned up your only credit slip. I'm risking enough letting you boys get on the plane."

Tom nodded in silence and opened the car door. "We'll go. But for the record, Willie and I are the ones letting you walk away tonight."

The boss tossed his head back and laughed. "Aren't we all the generous ones?"

Tom slid out of the back seat. A drizzle had begun, and the chilled air was ripe with the scent raised by fresh rain. Tom joined Willie down the sidewalk and watched as the two henchmen returned to the black Mercedes. The pair glared outward through the windshield and the boss waved from the back seat as their car sped into the night.

~ 15 ~

It didn't seem wise to spend the night at ground zero, so Tom booked a room at a Travelodge west of the city center. He dropped his key at the empty desk of the Black Oak and lugged his bag and an armload of chips and beer to the rental car. Seconds later, Willie sauntered out of the Fitzroy with his gear. After a short drive, they parked the blue Focus next to a small park near the harbor. They walked to a secluded spot on the shore, wiped their pistols clean of prints, and tossed them into the channel. Willie seemed pained. "Hell of a waste of a fine revolver."

"You've got one or two at home."

"Uh huh. You sure the water's deep enough?"

"Doesn't matter if someone finds them. We didn't shoot anyone, and whoever sold you those had filed the serial numbers. But let's get out of here."

The Travelodge only had flimsy plastic cups, but the whiskey didn't seem to mind. They sat side-by-side in straight-backed chairs facing a print of a foxhunt scene while Tom filled Willie in on the conversation in the Mercedes. When he came up for air, he looked sideways at his brother. "Your turn."

"You've got to be shittin' me. Nazis? The IRA? I thought art theft was supposed to be a more genteel way of making a living than my usual divorces and stolen TV sets. I've been misinformed. By you, as I recall."

Tom gave a shrug that fell a hair short of sympathetic. "It was your idea to come along as the other end of a short firing line."

"True enough. You think this guy was telling it straight?"

"In part. I read him as old-line IRA, still dreaming of getting the six counties back. Not one of the current semi-Bolshevik branches. He seemed genuinely sorry about Branna's murder."

Willie cocked his head with suspicion. "You gonna be able to let that go? A mere day ago, you were her avenging angel."

"Yeah, I think so. It stinks, but she seems to have been collateral damage. Nothing to be gained by going back to Sligo and shooting the place up."

"Particularly true since we just tossed our guns in the drink."

Tom nodded in silence and thought of Branna. Killed for nothing, and he had set the hounds on her trail. There was nothing to be done for her. Not even vengeance made sense. But he would always carry the scar. He glanced toward Willie. "You understand the part about the painting being collateral?"

"Not really. Why doesn't the bastard who has the painting just sell it for what he can get? Isn't that what was going on in Boston?"

"Too hard to sell a painting that valuable. Most people think there are a bunch of deranged billionaires, like James Bond villains, who buy stolen Rembrandts and stash them in their castle keeps. There's a bit of that, but for the most part, the real treasures are too hot to market. It's safer to just use them as a shady type of loan collateral. Drug deals, for example. Want to by a planeload of heroin and sell it in New Hampshire? Big bucks are needed up front, and you wouldn't want to trot down to the bank for a loan. So, you put up your Monet to secure a suitcase of fresh Franklins."

"You think we've wandered into a drug deal?" Willie looked dubious.

"Worse. We've stumbled into a four-hundred-year-old war."

"Thought you said the Troubles, as you call them, are over. What gives?"

"Formal hostilities ended in '98 with the Good Friday agreement. But the hard-asses aren't very formal, and my guess is some of them are itching to go another round."

"We live in interesting times, little brother. But the important question is this, what do we do next?"

Tom felt depressed. "We go home."

* * *

The rental agent downtown seemed relieved to see his blue Ford returned in one piece. Tom bought a copy of the *Irish Times* and read it as they rode the shuttle bus to Dublin airport. The bomb made page one, below the fold, but no report of a manhunt for two wily New Mexicans. "Looks like we're good to go, big bro."

The boys hit the airport shops and ended up with a predictable assortment of wool scarves for the usual women. They cleared customs with their prizes before boarding the plane for the long leg to Newark.

Willie grabbed the window seat but crashed a few seconds after takeoff. Tom had booked the aisle for his long legs. A slender Irish girl with a black buzz cut, four visible piercings through lips and nose, and tattoos like a Japanese Yakuza squeezed past him into the middle seat. Surprisingly, she smelled of pungent perfume. Tom felt obligated to say hello, but he was saved when the tattooed woman plunged a hand into her backpack and extracted a mask, neck pillow, and headphones. She soon disappeared into inner space.

Tom closed his eyes and began trolling his memory for details. If Donal, the IRA man, was at all straight, the painting was likely in the possession of a member of the Irish mob in Boston. They were an ecumenical mob, not generally known for letting the bitter Green/Orange divisions of the Troubles get in the way of business. Still, the evidence suggested he should look for an Orangeman first. He couldn't wander around Boston buttonholing mobsters and live very long, but maybe Kate would have some sort of record of Irish hoods who had moved to Beantown within the last couple of decades.

Kate! Forgotten again, and now it was too late to call. They were second in line for takeoff. She'd chew his ass harder than a wolf eating jerky when he finally called. Why was he so afraid to talk to her?

One question continued to nag: Why had Donal let them walk away? Tom figured he and Willie would have been the last men standing if things had gone south, but he was pretty sure the IRA man didn't see it that way. Did the man really have such strong feelings for Grace O'Malley? Didn't seem likely. Grace had been married a long time. Long enough to produce a lovely daughter in her late 20s. Hard to see the IRA man being that sentimental. Still, the guy was genuinely surprised to hear Grace's name. Whatever was cooking in Ireland, it didn't seem she was part of the story. Yet.

* * *

It was approaching midnight when Tom eased his Tacoma down the narrow driveway to his ridge-top condo on Paseo de la Cuma. Willie's place was almost an hour farther on, so he crashed in Tom's downstairs guest room. Tom walked up the half flight to the master bedroom. He flopped on the bed without turning on the lights and stared out at his thirty-degree-wide view of downtown Santa Fe. The town was dead as expected, given the hour. There hadn't been any late-night action in Santa Fe since 1945, when those in the know stayed up for the Trinity test.

Tom could hear Willie sawing logs below, so he took off his shoes before padding downstairs to check on Stella. As he eased back onto the bed, the Clancy Brothers sounded off and alerted him to incoming fire. Sure enough. It was Kate.

"Kate."

"Asshole."

"I've dropped below creep?"

"Long time passing."

"Hey, toots, I'm sorry. Things got busy in Dublin."

"So I've heard. The buzz around the Bureau is that a couple of IRA men in Dublin were blown up by a bomb. The day before you and Willie left Dublin. People are fretting on both sides of the pond about trouble with the Troubles. You should see the headlines in Ireland. Tell me you didn't have anything to do with that."

Tom thought for a moment then gambled on near honesty. "I had no more to do with that bomb going off than you did."

There was a long silence. After at least a minute, he heard Kate sigh. "We need to talk, Tommy. My place. How soon can you make it?"

"How about Saturday? I need to get back to Boston to run down these damned water lilies. I could stop by Washington on the way. That okay?"

"Yeah, but call me tomorrow when you've got a flight time."

"Will do. But at the moment I need sleep more. See ya."

"Goodnight, creep."

Back up to creep? Things were looking up already.

*   *   *

Tom dropped Willie at their Staab Street office just as Myrna began hopscotching up the ruins of their sidewalk avoiding the anthills. When she reached the porch, she paused to catch her breath. She turned toward the boys and assumed an exaggerated slouch. "Nice to see you, fellas. Planning to stay awhile this time?"

Willie grunted. "Ask Tom. I'd like to spend a long weekend with my lady, but if he insists on going to Boston, I'll have to play wing man." He tossed his bag into the bed of an elderly red Dodge pickup with two hubcaps, an empty gun rack, and a layer of dust. "Somebody call me when y'all have some kind of sched-ule." He roared off to the whine of a dying differential and trail-ing an aromatic cloud of half-burned hydrocarbons.

Tom circled through the dead grass and opened the door for Myrna. She rolled her eyes up and brushed his thigh with her hip as she sashayed inside. "Ooh, just the two of us. Sounds marvelous." He could never tell whether she meant it, but it was probably best not to find out. Single mom with two kids, after all. He had enough problems trying to sort out Laurie and Kate, not to mention the divorce proceedings with the treacherous Colleen.

Tom smiled at Myrna. "Sorry, but I've got to hit the road again. Book me a morning flight to Washington." She smirked and twitched her nose as he retreated into his shabby inner office. As the door clicked shut, he considered stretching out on the mangy sofa. The stains and rips were no problem, but there were only a few springs still attached to the frame. He opted for his wheeled desk chair.

With feet on the desk and hands behind his head, Tom realized he had no plan as to what to do next. Kate might be able to come up with a partial list of Irish gangsters who had moved to Boston in the last couple of decades, but she wouldn't have any info linking the guys to the painting. He would have to do the footwork himself, and in Boston. It would be dangerous from the moment he stepped off the plane. If he planned to survive, he'd need to narrow the list. And the only person he could think of who might be able to help him was Grace O'Malley. If Donal the IRA man really knew Grace, she might also know some of the names on Kate's list. Assuming Kate came up with a list. And assuming Tom could get Grace to talk to him. He was pretty sure she'd clam up on the phone, so he'd have to find a way to talk to her in person.

Time to call Aoife. She offered the best chance of breaking through Grace O'Malley's redoubt. As he reached for the phone, he realized he was eager to talk to her. Steady, Tommy. She's too young for you. Tom's hand froze a foot from the phone, but he shook it off. They needed to talk, and besides, there was something vaguely intriguing about her.

"Mr. McNaul?" Aoife's voice was either flirtatious or annoyed. After twenty-five years of marriage, Tom still couldn't read that particular nuance in a woman's voice. Possibly another reason he was about to be single again.

"The very same. Got a minute?"

"Let me check my calendar." There was a long pause during which Tom heard a ceramic clink followed by liquid pouring. Another coffee hound. Add a point. "Your lucky day. What's on your mind?"

Tom was feeling uncomfortable. In truth, Aoife was suddenly on his mind, but that wouldn't do. "Willie and I are back from Ireland. I've got a lot to report, but more importantly, I need to get some face time with your mother, and I need your help to do that. Can you spare a couple of hours? Sometime today? I'm leaving town in the morning, and I'm in bad need of a plan."

"I've got a lab this afternoon until four. If I drive up to Santa Fe, what sort of dinner should I expect?"

"Raise hell with the expectations, but if you don't want to be disappointed, picture enchiladas with some stand-up margaritas."

"Six okay? Text me the address."

*   *   *

Aoife strode in the door of Maria's five minutes late. She wore a dark-blue dress. It showed what it was meant to and didn't evoke lab instructor, so she must have gone home to change. Tom led her to a table in the cantina, and the blue corn enchiladas were slammed on the table within ten minutes. Aoife limited herself to one margarita, which Tom read as intent to drive back to Albuquerque—or at least to have that option. He managed to stop after two. By six-forty-five, the enchiladas were gone, and the ritual wiping up of honey dripped from leaky sopapillas was nearing completion. Aoife leaned back in her chair and flashed a satisfied smile. "Thank you, Tommy. A fine choice."

"Most welcome. We should find a quiet place to talk. My office okay?"

"I've seen your office. How about if we try your place? If you live alone, that is."

Tom tried to hide his shock, but Aoife read him in an instant and laughed. "Sorry, didn't mean to scare you. I just thought you must have chairs with springs at home."

"Can't argue with your logic. Okay, follow me."

Ten minutes later, Tom ushered Aoife into the living room of his condo. She eyed the purple stuffed chair with suspicion, probably triggered by the thick layer of corgi hair poised to pounce on her navy skirt.

"Stella's not here tonight."

Aoife hesitated for half a second. "Is Stella your roommate, or your dog?"

"Both." He pointed to the brown leather sofa. "That's probably safer."

She laughed and insisted on a tour of the premises. In Tom's experience, there was no point in resisting. Every woman he knew treated his quarters like a crime scene, though none of them actually dusted for fingerprints—at least when he was watching. Aoife eventually led the way back to the sofa and slid into the far corner with her feet tucked up and her right elbow atop the back.

Tom considered seizing the other corner but opted for the purple chair instead. He needed the security of his own spot. He cleared his throat. "Let me give you the teaser version of the Mc-Naul brothers' trip to Ireland. If you want the full story, it would take most of the night." He watched for a reaction but saw none. "Short version, then. Willie, Kate, and I flew to Shannon and drove down to Carrick-on-Suir.

"Would this be the FBI Kate? Why did she go along?" Aoife might have arched an eyebrow, but it was too close to call.

"The Art Crime Team has its own agenda. Besides, Kate can open doors in the world of real police. You'd be surprised how few official types will talk to a private investigator, even if they did know me when I was still FBI."

"Mmm hmm."

"Anyway, we wandered the pubs of Carrick looking for the man who was the token Catholic on the Belfast crime team. The team that quickly gave up on the investigation of your family's murders. More to our point, they also quit looking for the missing Monet. It took a while, but we found the guy. Or to be precise, he found us."

"Was this ex-cop willing to talk?"

"Yeah, after a while, he got sympathetic. Put us on the trail of a young woman in Sligo. She was the daughter of one of the pair who murdered your dad and grandma. Both of the girl's parents were dead, but the ex-cop thought the mother might have told her something."

"Sounds like you were down to grasping at straws, Tommy."

"I won't deny it. But those straws attracted a lead. We found the girl in Sligo. Her name was Branna Fitzpatrick." Tom paused, but Aoife just stared at him. "You being a professor, you'll have noted that I used the past tense. Branna didn't have much to say beyond confirming that someone hired her dad to do the theft and hit, but she was gunned down a few hours after I talked to her."

"My god." Aoife's composure disappeared. Her lips parted, and her eyes stared at the dark living room window. "Was she. . . ?"

"Killed might be the word you're fumbling for. Yeah, and it was a hit. Shot in her own apartment a few minutes after she got home from work. I picture a gunman waiting in the dark." Tom's blood was running hot, and he upped the tempo. "Branna was a smart young woman, doing some research on Yeats. And she didn't know much. Not enough to get her killed, but evidently the shooter wasn't taking chances."

Tom paused to let Aoife's mind spiral back toward stability. When her eyes appeared to focus, he leaned forward. "Most of the rest of the trip isn't on your need-to-know list, though I'll forward our expenses to your mother. But what you do need to know is that whatever caused your dad and his mother to get gunned down twenty years ago doesn't seem to be buried very deep. If we keep going after the water lilies, chances are we haven't seen the last corpse." Tom paused again, but this time Aoife was glaring at him. "So here's my question for you. Is it worth that much? Do you and Grace want us to go another round?"

Aoife continued to glare at Tom, though he didn't think the anger was directed at him. "It's my mother who hired you. It's her call. What about you boys? Are you still willing?"

"Maybe. I'll have to talk it over with Willie. But me—I'm all in if you are. I don't like to leave business unfinished, particularly when a fine young Irish girl lies in her native peat because of questions I asked."

Aoife nodded. "Good for you, Tommy McNaul. I don't know how much more my mother can afford to pay you, but she's the one who has to make the call. She owns the painting."

"Says she owns it. That's one of the problems, as you'll recall."

"I stand corrected."

"Look, Aoife . . . if I go on with this, with or without Willie, we'll be playing table stakes. I'm not going to make that decision based on another damned phone call. I'm game if you ladies are, but I'm not going in harm's way for your mother without looking her in the eye. So you need to set up a face-to-face between her and me. None of this cell phone bullshit. Can you do that?"

Aoife looked amused but wary. "I don't know. I'll call her in the morning and try my luck. That sound okay?"

Tom snorted. "We both know that won't work. I figure we're both going to have to go to Boston and kick down the door. You game?"

Aoife flicked her eyebrows and flashed him a crooked smile. "You're a man of action, I see." Tom's face was stone. "Okay, Tommy. I'm game. When do we go?"

"How about Sunday? I'm booked to fly to Washington tomorrow morning to consult with my old FBI colleagues. I'll spend the night there and then meet up with you in Boston. You and Willie could fly east together."

"I could go with you to Washington if you like. We could talk on the plane." Aoife tilted her head a few degrees left.

"Gotta go it alone on the first leg. The FBI wouldn't let you in the door if they found out you were an anthropologist. They'd figure that makes you a communist. And I need to confer with Agent Bacon in private. She's giving us some help that isn't exactly through channels."

"Agent Bacon is Kate?"

Tom gritted his teeth trying to suppress a smile. Maybe it worked. "Yeah."

"Just trying to keep my facts straight." Aoife unfolded from her perch on the sofa and stood up. She searched her skirt and found a few dog hairs to brush off. "I'd best get back to Albuquerque and start making plans. I'll get someone to cover my Monday classes, and I'm off on Tuesdays. Call me as soon as you've got some times and places."

Tom felt a bit flat. He hadn't wanted her to stay over, but he'd have liked the chance to say so. He struggled to his feet and ignored the swirls of fur clinging to his jeans. "Okay. And you call me if you get sudden chills of the spine." He stepped over to Aoife and extended his right paw.

Aoife took his hand and matched his firm grip. After two seconds, she let go, stepped forward, and delivered an air kiss. "I feel like we're partners in crime."

"Let's just hope we're partners in someone else's crime." Tom watched Aoife shoulder her leather bag and leave without looking back. When her car cleared his driveway, he headed to the kitchen cupboard to the left of the tiny sink. It contained nothing but a bottle of Red Breast Irish whiskey, the best in the house, along with two crystal glasses. He shook his head, closed the door, and started a pot of coffee.

16

The direct flight to Baltimore landed just before three. Kate lived about a half hour from BWI, though she had more of a haul to her downtown office. Tom spotted her next to the Southwest baggage claim. She was at ramrod-straight parade rest with only her eyes scanning the arriving passengers. When she spotted Tom, she beamed for a second, then caught herself and marched to confront him.

Tom was almost a foot taller than Kate, but when he leaned over and bent his knees a bit he was able to match her in a proper hug. He nuzzled the top of her head with his nose until she softened. An uncharacteristic waft of perfume drifted up from near her right ear. Neither of them spoke for almost a minute. Eventually, she pushed off and stepped back far enough to avoid craning her neck as she looked into Tom's eyes. "We've clearly got a lot to talk about, creep, but it occurred to me that I've known you for three years and you've never asked me on a proper date."

"Not to be argumentative, but I was married for the first two-and-a-half. Still am until the paperwork clears, though admittedly, it's now a formality."

Kate huffed with her usual accompanying snort. "I never did buy into your asshole art woman's act. Damned if I'll honor any lingering territorial claims." The flash of hatred in Kate's eyes said it all. They both knew Colleen was hoping for Tom's demise when she ratted out their art sting the previous year, but Kate was the one who almost died. Her physical recovery took months. Mentally, it just made her that much tougher. She forced a smile. "Tired of waiting. I'll take you out."

"Yeah? Where we going?"

"Mama Calcagni's. It's Italian."

"No shit?"

"Don't get wise, McNaul. Not polite to dis the hostess's choice."

"My apologies. Food good?"

"Not bad, not crowded. And they've got candles on the tables."

Tom guessed the candles would be the drip kind, stuck in wicker-wrapped Chianti bottles, but that was just fine. He disliked expensive restaurants, preferring to splurge on fine Irish whiskey while confining his meals out to enchiladas or green chile cheeseburgers. Kate's culinary tastes involved different flavors but similar prices.

They reached Kate's apartment around four. It was a modern two-story townhouse in a development strung out along a single winding street. The open space was dominated by a rain catchment basin, but the surrounding grass was mowed and uniformly green. Not a dandelion in sight. Tom had been to Kate's place a couple of times for holiday parties, but that was with Colleen on his arm. Although the interior sported faux colonial trim, Kate's furniture was largely chrome and black leather. On the mantle above a gas fireplace were three photos: one of her parents in wedding attire, a family vacation shot that included her two brothers, and her formal FBI portrait. The lone living-room bookcase was built in and painted the same white as the woodwork. The books on each shelf were of uniform height and consisted mostly of science fiction and military history. A small, round stand on the top shelf supported an autographed baseball. An adjacent Red Sox cap confirmed Kate as a true Bostonian.

"You ever been a baseball fan?"

Tom turned to her voice. "Sort of. My old man liked the Yankees for some reason, but I always figured that was like rooting for General Motors in a soapbox derby race. I did follow the Indians once, but it got depressing."

"Builds character, though." Kate extracted two IPAs from her fridge, and they settled into a pair of matching armchairs consisting of leather suspended from shiny metal frames. Tom was relieved to find his was somewhat comfortable. He glanced at Kate and faced an intense stare. She had cleared the decks for action and wasted no time.

"We've got a couple of hours before dinner. Best to talk shop here. How about you start?"

Tom leaned back and briefed Kate on his time in Sligo, the murder of Branna Fitzpatrick, and the side trip to the O'Malley house near Armagh, leaving out the mashing of the auto and his roll in the sheep droppings. He began to get nervous as the story approached Dublin, so he bought time with a few, slow draws on his beer. He still hadn't decided what details he should withhold.

Kate got tired of waiting. "So you boys got to Dublin with a guilty conscience and no clue who killed the O'Malleys back when, or Ms. Fitzpatrick now, not to mention who might be holding the Monet?"

"That's not quite right. At that point, we had plenty of clues, just no hard answers."

"Explain."

"Well, we were pretty sure the O'Malley murders were planned and hired, with Branna Fitzpatrick's dad being one of the guns. The shootings don't smell like an unfortunate coincidence during an art heist."

"I'll buy that." Kate eyed the label on her beer and slowly spun the bottle as she thought.

Tom moved on. "After talking to the kid who ratted out Branna, Willie and I figured the IRA had to be involved. Trouble is, what about the second murders in Armagh? The killing of the two hired burglar-assassins? Seemed like that had to have been ordered up by someone else. Maybe someone on the other side of the Troubles from the IRA."

Kate nodded assent. "You've still got my attention. Roll on to Dublin. What was your plan?"

"To be brutally frank, we didn't have one. The first night I went to an Oscar Wilde play at the Gate."

"Quit stalling, Tommy."

"Okay. We figured whoever knocked off Branna would probably enjoy doing the same to us. So we decided to make ourselves conspicuous and see who showed up at our door. Easiest way to do that was to spread the word among the Gardai and count on the crooked-cop hotline. I figured there had to be one in Dublin."

"There is, but I'm not going to talk about it. Press on."

"Sure enough, some goons in a little black sedan came after us. Only, Willie and I had taken the precaution of moving to a little hotel across the street. The guys searched our empty room and then drove off. A bit later three guys showed up in a bigger black car. We introduced ourselves to these gentlemen, and I had a pleasant conversation with the boss. He came as close as such guys ever will to pinning the O'Malley murders on the IRA. Motive was blackmail. Did I mention the Nazi? Never mind, he's allegedly dead now."

Kate's eyebrows merged to form a single caterpillar arching down toward her nose. "Are you shitting me?"

"Nope. The boss man figured the second murders were carried out by crooked cops in Belfast, likely connected to one of the Orange paramilitary groups. Said he didn't know for sure. Then he left, and Willie and I split for the high plains of New Mexico."

The rest of Kate's IPA disappeared with one long chug. "He say anything else?"

"Nope."

"What about the two IRA guys who blew up in a car?"

"I was never introduced to the gentlemen, whoever they are. Were."

"That's enough for now. Let's eat." Kate headed upstairs to change.

*   *   *

Calcagni's was ten miles down a highway from Kate's place. It was near the center of a strip mall, squeezed between a fitness center and a laundromat, but the decor was two levels up from Tom's earlier guess. Kate was proudly showing off a slick little black dress designed to stir hormones. Her figure was harder than a model's, with no unwelcome fat in sight, and she looked damned good, even in a ponytail. As she strode behind the hostess to a reserved table in a back room, her mid-altitude heels clacked confidently on the dark wooden floor. Tom hadn't seen heels on her feet since the ill-fated sting operation when she was posing as a wealthy German art buyer, dripping with rented diamonds. Kate slid into a half-moon booth of plush red leather while Tom scooted in from the other side. The candlesticks appeared to be silver.

Tom gulped at the wine menu, but fortunately Kate wasn't an oenophile. He escaped with a mid-priced Sangiovese. He assumed he'd be grilled for details, but Kate stuck to her guns—this was their first date. He relaxed into the plush leather aura. They were still laughing when their waiter cleared dessert, and Kate nabbed the bill with the subtlety of a snapping turtle.

As Tom closed the door of Kate's apartment, he felt her lean softly against his back. He turned slowly into a lingering kiss. She batted her lashes twice and reached for his left hand. "I need to get out of this outfit before we get back to the case. Come on upstairs. You can help."

*　　*　　*

Tom awoke to a ticklish sensation at the back of his left knee. A couple of seconds later, he turned his head far enough to see Kate perched on one elbow and exploring some of his less private parts with a meandering index finger. He rolled onto his back as she leaned away and ran her fingers through her flowing blonde hair.

"Hiya, toots."

Kate smiled. "That's okay, I'll settle for toots at the moment."

"Any idea what time it is?" Tom couldn't see any signs of dawn at the window, though it felt like they'd made love through most of the night.

"Not quite five. When's your flight?" Kate began eyeing some of his other parts.

"Bit after nine. I'd better get started on my coffee ration." Tom couldn't keep both eyes open at the same time until he'd downed at least half a pot.

"Spoilsport. How do you feel?"

Tom forced a sigh. "Exhausted. Exploited. And excited. But if we're supposed to talk deeper meanings, I need coffee."

"Kate smirked. We do need to talk, but before we start arguing about how many kids, we'd best go over your plan of the day. Meet me downstairs in five." She popped off the bed, grabbed a blue sweatsuit with FBI in large white letters from a plastic chair, and disappeared into the bathroom.

Tom used most of his five minutes scrounging about the room for his scattered clothes and shoes. He stumbled to the downstairs guest bath with his armload and did what he could. His carry-on bag was still standing unopened in the living room when he emerged. Kate was back in her ponytail and had added some veteran runners to her Sunday morning outfit. The coffee pot was already gurgling and blowing off aromatic steam. Standard Cuisinart 12-cup, fine for these lower elevations where water boiled at a decent temperature. She glanced at him over her right shoulder while filleting a bagel with what looked like a samurai's short-bladed knife. "Cream cheese okay?"

"Sounds good." Tom collapsed into his chair from the previous evening. "So what do you want to know?"

"Sec." Kate continued her mayhem for another minute and then carried a plate of bagel halves and a plastic container of white stuff to the living room. "Pour your own."

Tom lurched to the kitchen and back with the largest cup in sight filled to the brim with the dark nectar. He blew on the surface several times before sipping off a quarter-inch, then decided to lower the fluid level a bit more before trying to sit down.

Kate bounced into her chair without spilling a drop and assumed a severe slouch. "For the record, I know you left plenty out of your story last night. We'll settle up on that later. What I want to know now is, who do you think has the damned painting, and just how do you expect to go about finding it in Boston without getting shot?"

"Don't know who has it just now, but I think the IRA boss man was circling close to the truth. His story about crooked cops in Belfast lifting the Monet from the first pair of thieves makes sense. And almost all the cops in Belfast were Protestants at that time, so Orange makes more sense than Green. Trouble is . . . the dirty cops would have moved it on in a hurry. Almost certainly to someone in the local underworld. That's where you come in."

Kate's eyebrows shot up. "Me?"

"You. I figure the water lilies disappeared into the land of underworld collateral. We've talked about this before. A major piece like that is too hot to peddle, but it makes nice loan backing."

"Yep. For drugs, usually." Kate set her plate on the coffee table and sat erect.

"And could be in this case, but I've got another hunch this time. Guns."

Kate's eyes sparkled like a prospector eyeing a nougat. "The IRA link!"

"Maybe." Tom was enjoying her sudden fire. "But both sides in the Troubles had mob connections. I'm betting that the Belfast men who ran off with the painting moved it to an underworld boss with Orange leanings. He could have used it to finance some Protestant operations, but then the Good Friday Agreement occurred. Then what?"

"You're on a roll, Tommy. Don't stop."

"You said that several times last night, but I digress. We know the Monet made it to Boston. Lot of Irish mob guys cross the pond, both colors. The Boston mob doesn't discriminate —they accept members of both religious groups. Have you got a list of such immigrants?"

"You know I do. Most of them, anyway."

"Great, but we've got two problems. First, I'm persona non grata in Boston since I shot that congressman's son at the Lexington sting."

"He was a mob boss's nephew."

"That's the point. I was supposed to stay out of town—they would lay off me. I figured the deal was off when they sent a hit man to Santa Fe anyway. The guy Willie left in a wheelchair outside St. Vincent's Hospital with two or three bones intact. They didn't send another, but you saw what happened last time I went back to Boston. I ended up swimming in the harbor, and then trying to outrace a cat after the bomb went off."

"But you're going back."

Tom's blood was warming. "Yeah, I'm going back. I'm going back because I don't like being thrown in the drink, and because someone shot a nice young woman because she talked to me and, finally, because some fuckers tried to blow me up in my bed. I don't want to talk about the latter incident." He paused a few seconds. "Also, Willie and I need the money."

"You don't need the cash, your dad left you plenty. But I'll buy Willie being needy."

"Bottom line—I'm heading to Boston in three hours. Willie's going to meet me there. But that brings me to the second problem. Time. I figure it won't take the bad guys long to find out we're in town. We've got to narrow down the list. So, I need you to give me the names of all the Boston mob immigrants from Northern Ireland who have known Orange leanings. It will narrow things down, and we just might survive long enough to work our way through the short list. Can you get me that?"

"I'll email it to you by noon. And I'm coming with you. I'd elbow my way onto your flight, but I'll need some time to get you the list. Be there sometime this afternoon, though."

"Best not, toots. This is my fight."

Kate stood up, took three steps toward Tom, and punched the left side of his jaw hard enough to stun. When his senses reassembled, he looked up to a fierce glare. "That's for calling me 'toots.' And I'm coming to Boston. Meanwhile, you do what you have to."

"Well."

"Don't be so damned eloquent, Tommy. You'll need a real badge carrier up there." Kate's eyes softened. She took two steps backward and slammed both fists onto her hips. "Told you we work well together. By the way, last night. How many times do you figure?"

"A gentleman would never admit to counting."

"Bet you did, Tommy McNaul."

17

The MTA lurched to a stop at Aquarium just in time for lunch.
It was too early to check into the Harbor View Hotel, but
Tom wanted to ditch his bag before grabbing a bowl of Irish stew,
or perhaps a shepherd's pie, at the pub down the street. As he
rolled his battered suitcase to the unattended front desk, a familiar female emerged from the inner office door. She assumed a coy
smile. Molly!

"Welcome, Mr. McNaul. Back already. I noticed your name on
the arriving guest list." She made a show of scrutinizing a computer screen. "I gather you must have enjoyed your previous visit."

"Parts of it. Uh, nice to see you."

"You might have called." The exaggerated Dublin accent from
their previous encounter was missing. Her smile soon disappeared as well.

"I didn't know I'd be making this trip until Friday. Figured I'd
get in touch if I actually made it here." Tom tried to sound off-
hand but clearly failed.

"I see you're only booked for the one night. I'm not too flat-
tered. I don't usually work Sundays, but when you showed up on
the guest list, I traded off to be here."

"Look, I'm sorry, but can we talk later? I've got some business
at the moment, and I just want to check this bag till my room's
ready."

"It's ready now. Same one as before." She flashed him a one-
arched-eyebrow meaningful stare.

"That's great. I'll drop this off and head out. I'm running a tad
late. Will you be at the desk long?"

"Maybe."

Ten minutes later, Tom was washing down a bowl of Guinness stew with a pint of the famed stout itself. Aoife and Willie were due in a couple of hours, and he hadn't come up with a viable plan. Kate still hadn't emailed the list of names. She would show up sometime that afternoon. The four needed somewhere to start looking, and likewise some idea of where it wasn't safe to look. Someone had it in for him, but who?

Tom thought back to the bomb that nearly finished him on his last trip to Boston. He had been in town for only a day, and setting up that trap would have taken some time. How did the bomber find out about both the would-be Monet seller's identity and Tom's search for the painting so quickly? There had to be a snitch. If he couldn't figure out who it was, sooner or later, he'd end up looking back over the wrong shoulder. He began flipping through the pages of his mental case file, but nothing clicked.

Distant thunder rumbled. The storm must be close to make itself heard above the pub rattle and downtown traffic. His mind wandered back to Molly. How was he going to keep her stable when she got a load of Aoife and Kate? Could he pawn her off on Willie? Didn't seem like a good idea. Besides, though Willie and Rosanne weren't actually married, he was faithful to her. Shouldn't mess with that.

Tom could only recall flashes of that whiskey-soaked romp with Molly. Was it just two weeks ago? He remembered the knock at his door and the arrival of the Black Bush with two glasses. Not much after that until the room phone sounded off a couple of hours before dawn. Then Molly staggering around, drunk as he was. She was fiddling with his soggy belongings on the dresser top when he stumbled out of the bathroom. Tom's eyes widened a millimeter. My spiral notebook was on that dresser. The notebook with the would-be Monet seller's phone number. He'd left it open to that page hoping to dry it before the ink ran into oblivion.

Surely, a random phone number would mean nothing to a drunken desk clerk recovering from a one-night stand. But he'd told Molly about the water lilies, and about the would-be seller. She'd seemed pretty interested. Could she have made a connection? It seemed like a reach, but he needed to find out, and it had to be when they were alone together—before she got spooked by the rest of his team. Tom waved for the check and was back at the Harbor View in six minutes.

Molly was still alone at the desk. She was clearly pleased to see him. "Done already?"

"Yeah, turned out to be simpler than I thought. You got time to come up to my room for a sec? Last time I was here, I had some trouble with the ringer on the phone. Nearly gave me a heart attack when it went off in the night."

"We can't have that." Molly led the way to the elevator. Seven floors later, Tom closed the room door behind them, and as he turned to face her, she took a long step forward and slid her hands behind his neck. He rested his hands on her hips and massaged the curved bones with his thumbs. They played eye tag for several seconds. When Molly pressed forward, he stiffened his arms and stopped her six inches short of a kiss. "Not just yet, babe. Got to talk first."

Molly began to rock slowly from side to side. "What's the matter, Tommy? Lost your nerve?"

"In a way. I was thinking back to two weeks ago, when we were right here."

"As I remember it, we were mostly over there." Molly twitched her head toward the bed.

"True enough. But when the temperature dropped a bit, I noticed you standing over there." Tom nodded toward the dresser. They continued to search each other's eyes, and Molly's turned wary. "And you were staring at my little wet notebook. Looking rather intently at it, as I recall." The last of Molly's smile was gone, and her lips rolled inward. "There wasn't anything on that page of the notebook but a phone number, Molly. What was it to you?"

Molly glared and tried to step away from him, but he held her fast. "Did you recognize that number? Or did you guess why I had it? Who did you call after you left me?" Tom pulled her closer until he felt her warm breath on his lips.

"Are you nuts? I sure can pick 'em." Molly tried to wrench free of his grasp, but Tom pinned her in place.

"I've gotta know, Molly, right now. My life may depend on it. My brother's too." He decided to omit mention of Aoife and Kate.

Molly reduced her squirming to a pro forma level. Her eyes darted around the room. Suddenly, she relaxed. Tom loosened his grip but didn't let go of her hips. Tom watched her suck in her cheeks as she stared at his chest. After a few seconds, she looked up. "What the hell are you talking about? What do you mean about your life being in danger?"

"Two weeks ago, I told you I came to Boston to find a stolen painting. You were all ears. I figured you just thought detectives were sexy. Not many hours after we parted, somebody murdered the guy who was trying to sell it. He tried to kill me too, but the cat and I survived." Molly stopped resisting, so Tom pulled his hands back and nailed them to his own hips. "So spill it, lady."

Molly turned her head sideways to face the window, but her eyes seemed to be roaming. Tom couldn't tell if she was trying to assemble a puzzle or cooking up a tight lie. After a lengthy pause, she looked back his way. "I didn't mean you any harm."

"Go on."

"Look, I wasn't trying to set you up for anything. I got curious to know a little more about the guy I just spent the night with. Your notepad was open, and I took a peek at it."

"Yeah, but you must have recognized the number."

"No, I didn't, but that night you told me you were looking for a really expensive stolen painting. Didn't you say it was by Monet? A picture of some water lilies?"

"I did, much to my regret at the moment."

"Well, my Uncle Tim told me a few weeks ago that a guy he works for was shitting bricks because someone had stolen a painting from him. A really expensive one. I don't know if it was a Monet, but it must have been something in that price range. Uncle Tim said the word was out all over Boston to keep an eye out."

"So you passed on the number in my notepad to your Uncle Tim?"

"Uh huh."

"And you just happened to drop my name into the conversation?"

"Well, yeah. He asked who was looking for it. I didn't think it would matter. Honestly, I didn't have any idea he'd care who was trying to find it. I thought I was just doing my uncle a favor. Might get him in good with his boss, you know?"

"I can imagine. Just what does Uncle Tim do for a living?"

"He's an accountant. His office is in Back Bay. He does taxes and stuff, but he also does books for a guy who does some sort of finance work. I don't know the guy's name. Uncle Tim told me once not to ask that."

Tom decided it probably didn't matter whether Uncle Tim's client was laundering cash or loan sharking. Either way, the guy was probably mob connected. The main question was whether Molly was telling him the whole truth and nothing but. His years as an FBI agent left him with a good feel for spotting lies, but he had a tendency to lose that skill when dealing with women he liked. Molly looked upset. He watched her look down and rub a finger under her left eye. Was she wiping off a tear, or did she touch her eyeball to cause one? He opted to trust her—a little. "It's all right. I'm still standing. But this time, you need to keep your mouth shut about our little conversation. Can you do that?"

Molly chewed her lower lip. "Yeah, I guess I owe you that. I didn't think it through before—I never thought anyone would get hurt."

"Okay, but just between you and me, I'd be careful about telling too much of anything to Uncle Tim from now on."

Molly's face contorted into an artificial pout. "You got time for a bit of makeup sex?"

"Aren't you on duty?"

"Not really, I just asked Maggie to step out the back for lunch when I saw you coming."

So he'd been ambushed. "Not just now. I need some time to get my head straight."

Molly shrugged and started for the door. "Suit yourself, but call me this time. I wouldn't want to be left crying on Uncle Tim's shoulder." She winked and flashed a half-second smile, and then she was gone. Tom felt clueless, as usual.

The thunderstorm roared into town like cowboys at the end of a cattle drive. All afternoon arrivals at Logan were already delayed by at least an hour, and in Boston, that meant the snafu was just beginning. Tom sat with his feet on the desk in his hotel room, watching massive raindrops hurl themselves against the window with low thuds. Occasional hailstones rattled off the glass. None of his missing compadres would show up any time soon. There was a small bar off the lobby, but he didn't want to risk running into Molly if she happened to be hanging around with the desk clerk.

Tom was checking new arrival times on his phone when there was a rap at the door. He opened it to a room service delivery boy carrying a small tray, a bottle of Black Bush, and two glasses. It was the same kid who'd brought Tom the identical load two weeks earlier. He grinned and rolled his eyes a full three-sixty. "No charge."

Tom grinned back and tipped him ten bucks. He poured himself two fingers and raised his glass to the storm. Here's to ya, Molly, whoever the hell you are. Tom needed to think clearly, but he did have a reputation to maintain. He unwrapped two water glasses in the bathroom, filled them with whiskey, and stowed them in the bottom dresser drawer. Then he placed the bottle, now half empty, on the desk by the window to impress the incoming crowd.

* * *

Willie and Aoife called from the lobby just after four. That didn't seem too bad—evidently the tunnel hadn't flooded this time. Or maybe the city had fixed that problem. Tom hadn't spent much time in Boston since his undergraduate days at MIT. Quarter of a century ago—Jesus. Aoife insisted she needed some time to get decent, but Willie came to his room straightaway. He barged past Tom and splashed down into the leather armchair looking as much the drowned rat as Tom had when he'd crawled out of the harbor two weeks earlier. White-water rivers ran from his soaked hair onto a soggy shirt. Like most New Mexicans, Willie didn't travel with rain gear. Tom strode into the bathroom, grabbed all the towels, and threw them onto his brother's lap. Willie growled and brushed them to the floor.

"Hell of a climate, little brother."

"Nobody ever moved to Boston for the weather."

"One reason among many to stay in New Mexico. Well, you got a plan yet?"

Tom couldn't take it anymore. He grabbed a bath towel and wrapped it around Willie's head. After a quick rub, he tossed it back on the floor and resumed his seat by the window. "No."

"Figured."

"We've got two missions here, and we need the two incoming women to accomplish them."

Willie picked up the towel and began wiping off the arms of his chair. "Enlighten me."

"Before we head out into harm's way, I've got to talk to Aoife's mother, man to woman. I have to make sure she's really in this hunt to the bitter end. No way Grace will talk to me one-on-one. Hence, Aoife."

"I guessed that already. But what's Kate coming for? And where the hell is she anyway?"

"She sent a text from Logan an hour ago. Should be here soon.

As to why, she's supposed to show us a list of Irish immigrants with unsavory lifestyles."

"She could have emailed them. But I guess I know why she didn't want to do that." Willie spread his face into a broad grin. His mustache wrapped halfway around his nose.

"Yeah, well."

"Glad to see you're taking that fine woman seriously. Did I mention she seemed like a good fit for you? Couple of hard-asses with fast guns and fancy educations?"

"You did. Now mosey on back to your own room and dry off while I try to salvage that chair."

After Willie left, Tom sopped up as much water as he could and tossed all the towels in the tub. He was wiping his hands on his jeans when he heard a knock at the door. His right hand flinched an inch toward his belt, but his pistol was still in the bag. Easy now. Too early to get jumpy. As soon as he turned the knob, Kate rammed the door inward until it bounced off his left toe. "That might have hurt, lady. Good thing I wasn't barefoot."

"You're never barefoot. I sometimes wonder if you've got a shoe fetish. Glad to see me?" Kate posed with the back of her right hand against one hip and her chest inflated.

Maybe she got that move from Myrna. Tom was polite enough to give her a good looking over. Kate was no femme fatale, but she was attractive when she tried—which wasn't often. She had obviously given it a little effort this time. The ponytail was gone, and there were hints of something that might be makeup in the vicinity of her eyes. No lipstick, though, and her nails looked chewed, not polished. Her zippered boots split the difference between stylish and rugged. Despite Kate's modest stature, she was never shod in anything with more than an inch of heel.

"Lookin' good, toots. Welcome back to Boston. Last time we were here together, it was a hot time in the old town."

Kate feigned a snarl. "It'll go better this time, though it might still be hot."

Tom let that one go. "Willie and Aoife will be back shortly. They didn't arrive quite as dry as you." Kate kept scrupulous track of weather forecasts, and when necessary, she toted a Patagonia rainsuit in her carry-on. The storm must have felt ignored, as it began to pound the glass with increased fury. Tom glanced at the window. The rain streaks were almost horizontal, howling in from the harbor, but the hail shaft seemed to have moved on. His silent forecast was for clearing within the hour. "Care for a shot?"

"You're on. Whatcha got? Not that it matters."

"Black Bush."

"Better than I expected." She spotted the half-empty bottle. "Was that a fresh one? Shit, Tommy. Think of your liver." Kate gave up her pose and strolled over to the window. "Remind me, just who is this Aoife person?"

"Our client's daughter."

"I know the business part, but who is she?"

Tom sensed the first tweak of tension, but he couldn't think of any brilliant diversions. He felt a sinking sensation as he lapsed into matter-of-fact demeanor. It was the best tactic he could think of, but he knew well that it never worked on a woman. "She's a new assistant prof at UNM. Late 20s, I think. Cassidy's in her class this term."

"Seems a bit of a coincidence." Kate was trolling, but she held her fire.

Tom turned away toward the whiskey so she couldn't see the whites of his eyes. After all, Bunker Hill was just across the harbor. He poured two glasses, and they clinked them without words. They took two silent sips each before Kate grabbed both glasses and placed them on the dresser. She leaned into Tom and slipped her arms around him. The kiss began with a rage like the howling storm outside, but it melted as it lingered. Kate eased away, and Tom knew he was expected to say something. "Nice to see you too, toots. Did you bring the list?"

Kate kicked him in the shins. It hurt like hell, and he let out a yelp as his butt hit the bed and bounced. "Yeah, here it is, creep." She dug a folded paper out of her left pants pocket. "I could only find twelve names. That is, twelve who moved from Ireland to Boston after the Armagh murders, were high enough in the mob to have some likelihood of being in possession of a painting worth a hundred mil, and most important, who we knew about. God knows how many others we don't know."

Tom took the paper and nodded. Twelve would be a manageable number if the target didn't know he was in town, but he wasn't going to bet his life on Molly keeping her trap shut for long. Even if she did, too many people on both sides of the pond knew too much. Word of this case seemed to get around in a hurry. Maybe someone in the mob had a Twitter account.

"Twelve is a bit too many. How many of them are of the Orange persuasion?"

Kate shrugged. "Can't tell for sure. Four I know are, and five aren't. The other three don't seem to be particularly religious. You'll note I color coded them."

Sure enough, Kate had located Green and Orange highlight pens. Tom stared at the Orange names. None was familiar, but that wasn't surprising. He didn't expect to see anyone who showed up on the Interpol or FBI lists of suspected art thieves. "Any clues how to rank them?"

"Nope. All four of the alleged Orange types lived in Northern Ireland for at least some years after the Armagh shootings. But from your story, the first round of murders were connected with IRA business, so it's not a sure bet your man is from the north. As to allegiances, they don't put them on their business cards." Kate crossed her arms and waited.

Tom stared at the floor to his left. He couldn't think straight looking at someone's face. Kate had done her best, but she was right—the list wasn't reliable enough to rank with much confidence. The pain in his shin was fading, so he forced a grin and stood up. "Nice work." He paced slow laps in front of the window for a minute. Then he stopped. "How about we show the list to Grace O'Malley?"

"What the hell for? Why would she know the names of any mob boys?"

"No obvious reason, but there might be one that isn't so obvious. I just know that she's the one who had family murdered in a hit. It's her painting we're looking for, and wherever we go looking for it, we run into serious trouble. Her family might be tighter with some of the unsavory types than she lets on. I don't think she's told us everything she knows."

"Women never do, Tommy."

"Amen. But while I'm sitting down with Mrs. O'Malley, I think I'll show her your list and see if her eyes get wider."

"Yeah, worth a try." Kate retrieved the whiskeys and passed the one less full to Tom.

The door thundered like a cheap subwoofer blowing its cone—Willie's characteristic knock. Tom twisted the knob and stepped aside as his brother sailed smartly past him, making a slight course correction once he spotted the whiskey. Aoife trailed in Willie's wake and tossed Tom a curious smile as she brushed past him. Could he actually feel Kate bristle? Surely not.

Willie paused before Kate and leaned into an exaggerated bow. "Madam FBI agent, how nice to see you again." His head still topped out three inches above Kate's.

"Likewise, Bubba." Kate's delivery was friendly, but her eyes were on Aoife as she spoke. "And you must be Tom's client, Mrs. O'Malley."

"No, that would be my mother, Grace. I'm Aoife, her daughter. Miss O'Malley." There was a clear hiss in her 'Miss,' but nobody flinched. "And would you be Miss Bacon, Tommy's assistant on the case?"

Willie guffawed, and even Kate cracked a smile for half a second. She raised her glass toward Aoife. "Something like that. Care for one?"

"Just the thing to cut the fog." Aoife grabbed the bottle of Bush and looked around for a glass. Willie fetched two more from the bathroom and poured them each a serious slug.

Tom decided to get things rolling while they were still sentient. "Now that you're all here, this meeting of the Santa Fe Society for Securing Swiped Water Lilies will come to order."

When the collected eyes of Willie, Aoife, and Kate finished rolling, he sat down on the bed. "Sorry."

"Have a couple of glasses of water, Tommy." Kate was always short on sympathy. "Nobody gives out medals for self-inflicted wounds."

"I'm sober as a judge."

"Judge Roy Bean, maybe."

"I resent that, but let's move on." Tom brought the latecomers up to speed, ending with his plan to show the list to Grace O'-Malley before the search teams hit the streets. When everyone was done nodding and checking out faces, he turned to Aoife. "How big a war party should we take to your mom's place? I wouldn't want you to take the list there without me. She might find it too easy to fib and claim she doesn't know any of them."

Aoife rolled her jaw though two orbits while she pondered. "You're probably right. On the other hand, if we show up with an FBI agent and your shaggy big brother, she'll probably go to ground. So, just the two of us?"

"That's how I see it. We'll call her in the morning."

Willie and Kate fumed for five minutes but begrudgingly agreed to other roles. Willie would provide backup and serve as a lookout in case the bad guys were a step ahead of them. Kate would set up the one-woman command post in her hotel room. She'd keep an open line to her tech assistant in Washington in case they needed to scan databases or make quick calls to Ireland.

Willie called for relocation to the hotel bar. Everyone demurred, so he grumbled off alone to parts unknown. Kate and Aoife took turns waiting for the other to leave, but when it became too obvious, they left together. Neither smiled on the way out.

Tom performed a hardware and ammo check and then searched the TV channels for an old film. Turner Classic Movies was having a Doris Day night, but a local channel planned to screen *Robot Monster* at 10:30. A classic of crummy sci-fi. He chucked the bag of complimentary popcorn into the microwave. The first kernels opened fire just as his phone began singing. It was Kate. Tom noted the time before answering. Quarter past eight. Maybe he could make it back in time for the movie.

~ 18 ~

Darkness still cloaked the city when Tom dragged himself back to his room. Sadly, the *Robot Monster* had long perished. He vowed to order the DVD when he got home. The room was quiet—the storm having split for the North Atlantic—but the place reeked of stale, scorched popcorn with an oily overtone of ant spray. At least the message light on the phone wasn't blinking. Maybe he could catch a bit of sleep. He rolled onto the bed and was gone in seconds.

Tom jerked awake and thrashed his arms as he tried to remember where he was. He seemed to have slept only minutes, but his phone alarm was scolding him at full volume. He shoved it under his pillow and heaved himself to a sitting position. Then he remembered: Boston. Seven a.m. Scheduled to meet Aoife for breakfast at eight. Plenty of time. He silenced the phone and lay down to catch his breath, just for a few moments.

The room telephone was even ruder than his cell. Evidently, Molly still hadn't reset the ring volume. Tom clawed for the receiver and knocked it off the nightstand. He flailed at the floor with his right hand and hit pay dirt on the second try. "Yeah?"

"Morning, Tom."

Aoife! Oh shit. Dozed off.

"Are you standing me up? I'm the only guest hanging around in the lobby, and the desk clerk is looking at me like I'm a hooker."

"Can't wait to see what you're wearing. But no, be right there. Sorry. Had a few things to get straight first. And don't worry, a real Boston hooker would be chewing gum with one side of her mouth open." Tom's plan was to walk Aoife to a place on State

171

Street for breakfast. He was still in last night's clothes, though one shoe had come off. He retrieved it from under the desk, combed his hair, and swiped a razor across his face a few times like a windshield wiper. Although he hit the lobby in five minutes, he was half an hour late.

Aoife's stunned look seemed sincere. "What happened to you?"

"Long story. Uh, I didn't know how to dress for your mother's fancy place, so I thought I'd get your advice on what to wear and change after breakfast."

"That's a pretty lame excuse to try on a professor, but at least it's original. Clean it up a bit and I'll review it tomorrow." Aoife led the way out of the lobby. She stopped a few paces down the sidewalk and faced Tom. "Look, I don't want to spoil breakfast, but I already called my mother this morning." Her tight lips clearly signaled bad news.

"I thought we were going to work on the script first."

"I know, but I would have been too nervous trying to talk to Mom with you sitting there. You and I have reached the mutual sniffing stage, and she'd pick up on that in a tic."

"Why would she disapprove? I know I'm a lot older than you, and my employment is only rumored to be gainful. But on the other hand, I went to college and I carry a swell gun."

"Stow it, Tommy."

"Okay. So what you reckon now?"

"She wavered a bit. Why don't you try calling her one more time?"

"I plan to, but did she leave any kind of opening? Something she was unsure of?"

Aoife looked at the sidewalk and shook her head. "No. I'm just trying to make myself feel better. I messed up."

"Don't think twice. I think Bob Dylan sang that, but we haven't got time to look it up. Let's walk the other direction. Down toward the harbor. We can grab coffee and some donuts and eat by the water. Pretty quiet this early. I'd like to be outside walking around when I talk to Grace."

"Why?"

"I can think okay sitting down, but I talk better on my feet. No idea why."

When Aoife was safely settled on a metal park bench, dipping chunks of bran muffin into her latte, Tom strode about fifty yards down the path, punched in Grace O'Malley's number, and slurped the last of his black coffee. He had time to crumple the cup and toss it in a trash barrel before she answered.

"Mr. McNaul. Somehow, I was expecting you to call. What can I do for you today?"

"You know that well enough, Mrs. O'Malley. You talked to Aoife less than an hour ago. She's sitting just down the sidewalk from me now. Out of earshot, if that matters to you."

"Not particularly. She said you two stayed at the Harbor View last night. Tell me, Tom, you didn't sleep with her, did you? That would seem a bit unprofessional, even for a private eye."

"Not that it's remotely your business, Grace, but as it happens, no. I'm a private investigator, not a lawyer. Suppose we get down to business."

"As you like." Grace made a point of sounding bemused.

There wasn't any point making small talk. "We need to meet, Grace. How about if Aoife and I come over to your place right now? You've obviously been up for a while."

"Try a new subject. We agreed to the terms, and I expect you to live up to them. We'll do our talking on these fancy smart phones."

"No dice. You hired me to find a lost painting, which you may or may not legally own. Said you needed the money. Okay, my kind of work. Fly to Boston, track down an art thief, hand over the painting, and let you figure out how to prove it's yours. But two weeks later, four people are dead, and I'm lucky as hell not to be a fifth. No signs of an impending ceasefire, and I don't know for sure who's firing. There have to be things you're not telling me, and I've had enough. Either we sit down face to face and you fill me in, or you find yourself another clay pigeon."

"Four?" Grace sounded stunned. "Who . . . where? Four?"

It was nice to score a point once in a while, but Tom felt uneasy. Grace seemed more disconcerted by the number of deaths than by the occurrence of any. Had she expected at least one? Maybe his?

"I'll fill you in when I see you. Aoife can hold your hand, if that would make you more comfortable."

Grace paused long enough to make Tom yearn for a coffee refill. "Not today. I'll think about it. Maybe tomorrow. No guarantees." She waited for Tom's reaction. He ground his teeth and waited her out. "Well, we're talking now, so ask what you will."

Grace was digging in, and Tom knew when to cut his losses. He was pissed that she wouldn't see him, but he couldn't afford to lose a day hoping she'd feel sunnier in the morning. "Okay, here's the deal in a nutshell. The two guys who murdered your husband and mother-in-law, and ran off with their water lily painting, were themselves murdered a couple of days later. Neither case was solved, but rumors abound that crooked cops in Belfast had something to do with covering things up. The people I've talked to figure the painting disappeared into the Irish underworld. It's too prominent a painting for a wise crook to sell for a proper price, so I figured it's been used as a very large chip in the old collateral game. We uncovered some evidence that it may be mixed up in Irish politics, maybe with some connection to the Troubles. Who and what the connections might be remain unclear. In any event, we all know the painting somehow ended up in Boston." Tom paused to catch his breath.

"What do you mean by 'the collateral game'? I'm not familiar with the term."

"People who want to borrow large sums of money for unsavory purposes often go to organized crime for the dough. Even hedge fund managers have some scruples. Such people charge usurious rates, and they also demand major collateral. A nice Monet would be just the thing. Usually they want the money for a shipment of drugs, or maybe a major bribe. Even a hit. But sometimes they want weapons, military-grade stuff. The kind you might see at a Texas gun show but can't buy on the street in Ireland. Can't import them either. They have rather tough gun laws over there."

"I think I see." Grace's voice dropped to a worried monotone. "You think maybe someone is using my painting to fund a violent Orange group? That sounds awful."

Tom froze at Grace's mention of an Orange militia. That was a big jump. Moments earlier, she had professed ignorance of art being used as underworld collateral. Now she assumed it was being used by paramilitaries. And why Orange? Why not the IRA? "I don't know for sure, Mrs. O'Malley, but that's a possibility. Whoever these people are, they play rough. If I go wandering through the streets of Boston knocking on doors, I'll end up like Jimmy Hoffa long before I find your painting. I'd prefer a better ending, so I need a bit of help from you."

"Like what?"

"Names. I've got a list of some Irish mob types who moved to Boston sometime after the murders in Armagh. I need to know if you've heard of any of them. I think one of them may have brought the painting here from Ireland."

"Good lord, Mr. McNaul. I should be insulted. How would I know the names of gangsters? That's rude of you."

"I know it's a long shot, but hear me out. The original theft and murders could have been an inside job. Someone might have had connections with both your family and the local mob in Ireland. The guy we're looking for most likely would be fairly high up in some business—not the sort of street hood who gets his hands dirty. A lawyer or businessman maybe. You might recognize the name but not know of his seamy side. Let's give it a try, okay?"

"If you insist. How many names are there?"

"Twelve."

Tom started through Kate's list. The names were in alphabetical order. He kept his voice steady and listened intently for any verbal clues of recognition, silently cursing his inability to watch her face for tells. Grace mulled over each name for several seconds but always replied with some version of no. Her answers all seemed sincere. "Do you want me to read them again?"

"No, I heard them all clearly. I'm sorry, Mr. McNaul, but none of the names sound familiar. I'm not surprised, if they are all criminals."

"Well, thanks for your help. If a bell sounds in the night, call Aoife. Or you can tell me when we visit you in the morning."

"If you visit in the morning. I don't really see any point in that, but I'll let you know." As Grace hung up, Tom kicked the trash barrel hard enough to leave a dent in the steel and a sharp pain in his big toe. He hobbled to the park bench and retrieved Aoife, then led her on a silent lap around the adjacent block to cool off. By the end of the circuit, his toe felt fine.

* * *

Tom watched Aoife disappear into the Harbor View. She was lead scout in case Molly was lurking about the lobby. A few seconds later, Aoife's arm beckoned from the door and then disappeared. When he reached the lobby, she was nowhere to be seen, and the front desk was unmanned. His phone chirped as the elevator cruised past the fourth floor. The text was from Kate and consisted solely of the number 701, presumably a room number. Last night they had thrashed around in 612, but he rerouted the elevator to the seventh floor. Room 701 turned out to be a suite at one end of a long corridor. He knocked once, and a few seconds later Aoife opened the door.

The living room of the suite was at least three times the size of Tom's room and sported a TV the size of the Fenway Park scoreboard. Fortunately, it was off. Willie and Kate slouched in black leather chairs facing a square, marble-topped table. Willie waved. Tom headed for the chair facing the window, but Aoife was closer and cut him off. He settled for a view of the darkened TV screen. No one spoke. They seemed to be waiting for Tom to proceed with opening remarks. He felt annoyed but obliged. "Nice digs. Who's the big spender?"

"Get on with it." Kate straightened the blank pad of paper in front of her and began twirling a ballpoint through her fingers. She glared at each of her three companions in turn and huffed. "If I'm going to be stuck in the command post, I want some space."

"Good idea. We need to get rolling." He paused for a few seconds, but his team members only blinked. "Kate, what remains to be extracted from the data files?"

"Mostly updated status reports. You asked for a list of Irish underworld immigrants to Boston who arrived during the past twenty or so years. I came up with the dozen names, all male. But all I know about each guy is his name, approximate date of arrival, and such random details as I could glean from summary case notes. Some of those notes are mighty old."

Kate glanced at Willie and Aoife. "I was able to finger four of the twelve as probably Orange flavored and five as more likely to wear green ties on Saint Paddy's day. I'm clueless about the other three." She huffed an exaggerated sigh. "I don't have recent addresses or contact info on any of these guys. I'll work on that straightaway. Shouldn't take long. My techie, Annie, will see what INTERPOL knows. I'll stay here and make some calls to Boston's finest to get started."

"You getting any help from the FBI locals?"

"I'm having lunch with a guy I know from my very first posting in Oklahoma: Sam Foley. As you surely know, the local mob managed to infiltrate the Boston FBI office back in the late '90s. The Whitey Bulger case—remember? That was cleaned up a long time back, so I'm told, but no sense taking chances. Fool me once, as the saying goes. I'm staying clear of the Boston office in general, but I trust Sam."

Tom frowned. "There were rumors of an FBI insider impeding the investigation of the Gardner Museum theft. How'd that work out?"

"Don't know. Everything was hushed up." Kate's eyes narrowed. "What's that got to do with this case?"

"Probably nothing, but if the rumors contain a grain of

truth, it would indicate the local Irish mob has a taste for old masters." Tom stared at Aoife and strained not to smile. "You want to help Kate?"

Aoife made no attempt to hide her annoyance. "No. I can't see how I'd be any help to her." Tom saw Kate smirk. "I'm going to visit my mom as soon as we're done here. I should have done that in the first place instead of calling her. Maybe she'll open up if I'm alone."

"You won't be alone. If you're going to Grace's, I'm going in with you if I have to kick her door off the hinges."

Aoife hissed louder than a punctured life raft, and Tom saw sparks in the amber eyes. "She's my mom, and I'm going by myself. I want some time with her before you barge in tomorrow and stir things up."

Tom was dubious, but he couldn't think of a rejoinder. "Well, how about if I at least give you a crash course on reading tells?"

"Oh, shit. Get real! She's my mom. I can read her a hell of a lot better than you can."

"How about if I lurk under a street lamp?"

"Fuck off, Tommy." Eerily, Aoife was beginning to sound much like Kate. Did he affect all women this way?

Tom turned to Willie and faced a silent scowl. "What about you, big brother?"

Willie stared back for a few seconds and then grunted. "I figured to have your back when you shoot it out with whosoever, be they Fenians or Orange mugs, but now it seems a waste of time. You don't seem to be up to much. Not to worry, though. I've got a small mission of my own, and this afternoon will be fine."

"Translate."

"Don't care to. I'll keep my new phone on, Tommy, but you won't need me for a while. As to my business, you're as well not knowing."

Tom knew it would be futile to ask more. "Okay, let's roll. Kate, call me when you've got anything. Or even if you don't.

Aoife, let's have lunch somewhere quiet after you get back from Grace's place. I need to hear how many times her nose twitched. I'll hang out here with Kate in the meantime. And Willie, call me when they set bail."

Willie finally grinned. "They'll have to catch me first."

The four sat in silence for a few moments, scanning faces and hiding thoughts. Willie was the first to stand. He nodded toward no one in particular and left without a word. Aoife and Kate tried to steal unnoticed glances at each other but found themselves staring into each other's eyes. Aoife seemed to realize Kate wasn't going anywhere, so she stood up, flashed a "don't you dare" at Kate, and stalked out.

As the door clicked shut, Tom surveyed the details of Kate's suite. His eyes paused on the bed, which was high enough to need guardrails. What was the point of a mattress that thick? As they flicked back to Kate, she smirked.

"Keep your pants on, Tommy. We've got work to do first." She swiveled her chair and reached for her phone.

Incorrigible. Tom felt a need for space that bordered on panic. He jumped to his feet and headed back to the safety of his own room. Besides, he wanted to call Paddy McGrath in Carrick-on-Suir, and he didn't want anyone listening in. The former Ulster cop had worked homicide for years, and he might well recognize some of the names on Kate's list.

~ 19 ~

It was a bit past ten in Boston, so just after three in Ireland. Tom didn't have a personal number for Paddy McGrath, but he hoped the barkeep at Tommy's pub would pass the word again. The phone rang eleven times before a woman with a lyrical brogue and a smoker's wheeze picked it up. She claimed not to have heard of Tom but soon confessed to knowing Paddy. He was expected to make his daily appearance momentarily. Tom didn't figure the barmaid would call an American number if he left one, so he said he'd call back in twenty minutes.

An hour and four calls later, Tom heard Paddy hawker like a coffee grinder full of glass. Tom managed not to gag and eventually heard a serious spit. "The fuck you want this time, Yank?"

"I'd like you to play a game called name that goon, Mick. Here's how it works. I'll read you some names. You tell me where they hang their hat."

"You figure I'm daft? Word gets out I'm giving names, I'd be lucky to finish this pint."

"You're not giving names, I am. And I'm not asking you what they've done, or for anyone's address. I don't care about that stuff. The guys on my list are Irish gentlemen who moved to Boston sometime during the past twenty years. All I want to know from you is whether any of them got homesick for the green and moved back. Must be public knowledge over there, but I'm not part of your public. Seems safe enough for you. Deal?"

"Some deal, sure. I give. You get. Seems a tiny bit unbalanced, wouldn't you be agreein'?"

"Buy you a pint next time I come over? Come on, McGrath. We were cops once."

"Aye, once. Long time ago for me." Paddy lapsed into near silence, but Tom could hear a slight rattle in his slow breathing. "Read your damned list, but don't ever call me again unless you've got something I want to hear."

Tom started through Kate's dangerous dozen. He paused for ten seconds after each name but heard only the troubled breathing. When he finished them all, he sat in silence for a full minute. He gave up. "You still living, Paddy?"

"Barely. Fuckin' bronchitis." His next hawker sounded like someone had added a bottle cap to the coffee grinder. "Ian Shea."

Shea was the seventh name on Kate's list. More to the point, he was one of the four with Orange leanings. "Yeah?"

"Yeah. Only stayed in the states a couple of years. Been working the Dublin to Belfast trade ever since. Rest of those bums, no idea where they're living. Or if. You're welcome to keep them on your side of the pond, one way or the other."

"Just the one?"

"One's enough." Paddy's voice softened. "When do I get me pint?"

"Sometime after I sort out the other eleven. But you'll get it. Thanks, Paddy."

"Sure. Anything else before we call it a life, Tommy?"

Tom's thoughts flashed back to Dublin. "Well, I hate to ask, but . . ."

"Shite."

"My brother and I met a fellow in Dublin recently. Important enough to have a couple of midlevel guns to drive his Mercedes. Name of Donal. Said he knew Grace O'Malley."

"So?"

"He IRA or Orange militia? Got to be one or the other."

"You really want to get out of buying me a pint, don't ya? I'd rather go on livin', if you please." This time, the pause was silent. Tom began to worry that he'd lost the connection, but eventually, he heard a resigned sigh. "IRA. But don't you go fuckin' around with them, Tommy McNaul. You won't last long, sure. They're not glorious rebels anymore. Terrorists more like. This isn't my father's IRA. You follow?"

"Understood, Paddy. The case is on me now. Call you when I close it."

*　*　*

Tom propped his feet on the windowsill of his room and watched a squadron of ragged cumulus clouds swarm in from the harbor. They didn't appear to have much of a future. Neither did his case. The call to Carrick only crossed one name off the list, and time was getting short. He was pondering his next move when Aoife called. "Hey, Tommy. Talked to my mom. Are you free for lunch?"

Fifteen minutes later, they were seated in a dark corner of The Quiet Man. The lunch crowd was still mustering, so they were due a few minutes of privacy. Aoife was flushed, but whether from success or despair was beyond Tom's ken. She planted both elbows on the table and began to lean forward, the amber eyes boring into his, her perfume battling the background odors of stale Guinness and boiled cabbage. She stopped just within the range for light kissing, but Tom figured she might just be striving for confidential talk. Either way, he knew he was supposed to say something.

"How'd it go?"

Evidently, she expected better. Aoife froze for a few seconds, then withdrew a few inches. "No luck. Sorry."

"That's it? How about a curious inference or something?"

Aoife sighed and leaned back to fully upright. "We chatted about my new job for five minutes. Then Mom steered me into a girl-to-girl, really more of a mom-to-daughter, about the evils of older men, with various specific examples matching all of your personal attributes. She went on for half an hour despite my best attempts at avoidance. I finally pulled out my phone and stared at it. That always scares her—she figures I'm about to leave. And she's usually right."

"So you left?"

"No, dummy. I just got her to pause the lecture long enough to ask her about the names on Kate's list. I had her a bit off balance, and I knew that door would slam quickly, so I just read the names of the four guys you thought were Orange."

"And?"

"At first, she denied knowing them, like before. But her eyes flicked at mine when she heard Liam Collins. I didn't press her on those four names, but then I asked her if she knew your fellow, Donal. She stayed silent at first. Just stared at me. But a few seconds later, her eyes lost focus. She said: 'I did know a lad named Donal back in County Tyrone. A bit sweet on me, he was. It's a common enough name, though.' She smiled, and I said he'd asked about her. The smile grew a bit wider as she poured the tea. I'll bet the pot your Dublin man is her Donal."

"Maybe. She say anything else?"

"Nothing I'd repeat."

"Ya did good, Aoife. An eye flick isn't much, and even if your mom did recognize Liam Collins, it doesn't mean he's our man. It's something, though. Meanwhile, let's eat."

Tom managed to talk Aoife out of ordering a salad, and they washed down bowls of mutton stew with a couple of pints each. The latter sent her on a mission to the ladies room. After she disappeared from view, he called Kate.

"Yo, Tommy. Keep it short, will you? I'm in the middle of a hot lunch date."

Tom refused to take the bait. "You got news?"

"Of a sort, creep. One of our four Orange guys, Jimmy McElroy, is spending some time out west. In California, to be exact."

"How much time? Is he on vacation?"

"Twenty to life in Folsom. First degree—shot a woman. I didn't bother with the details. He's been inside for five years now, so I don't think he set your bomb in Boston. You got anything?"

"Yeah, actually I do. I called Paddy McGrath back in Carrick-on-Suir. He says one of our four Orange mugs, Ian Shea, moved back to Ireland some time ago. Still alive and up to no good, making mischief somewhere near Dublin."

Tom heard a whistling exhale. He could picture Kate's nostrils flaring. "Nice, Tommy." Her voice was monotone and down half an octave from normal. "Only two now."

"Yeah, if our man is really one of the people on your list, and if he's one of our four suspected Orange types. But wait, there's more."

"You sound like a late-night TV ad for a tearless onion peeler. What more?"

Tom made her wait a few seconds while he pretended to clear his throat. "Aoife talked to her mother. She said Grace flicked her eyes when she heard the name Liam Collins."

"Pretty thin. Did she still deny knowing him?"

"Yeah. She did admit knowing Dublin Donal, though."

"Interesting. Collins is on our short list. Let's gather the clan at three. My place.

"Any word from Willie?

"No, and I don't know how to reach him. He doesn't seem to answer that new phone you got him."

"Odd. He answered the old one once. Sort of."

*   *   *

The sun had not quite reached the yardarm when Willie reached Paddy's Oyster House. He hadn't a bloody clue what a yardarm was, but once someone had told him it meant 11 a.m., or maybe noon. Screw it. There was a family score to settle. He stared up at a sign marred by long strips of peeling paint. To the right of Paddy's name, two eyes peered out from a half-open oyster shell. He considered shooting out the eyeballs but decided he had nothing against oysters.

Willie scanned the parking lot and the short stretch of pier between the restaurant and the shore. No pedestrians in sight. He shoved open the front door and was met by a backdraft reeking of stale beer. There were four or five male patrons scattered about at tables, probably hiding from the women of their fears. The long bar was manned by a slouching young fellow in a collarless shirt, a single loop earring, and a lopsided leer. The kid was polishing glasses while trying to make time with a blonde waitress with three visible tattoos and a stud in her lower lip. She glanced Willie's way as if she was looking to be rescued. The barkeep matched Tom's description from his earlier visit to the pretentious dump. Willie sidled up to the couple and leaned on the bar, his forearms remaining dry because of the early hour. The tattooed lady made her escape and flashed Willie a wink over her right shoulder. He winked back, then turned to the scowling kid. "Whiskey!"

The bar kid smirked and craned his neck to stare up at the clock above the shelves of booze. "Bit early for you isn't it, old timer."

Willie smiled. His left hand shot forward, hooked behind the kid's neck, and slammed the smirk onto the bar. Even the deafest of the patrons would have heard the crack of a breaking nose. "Try again, little boy. I want a glass of whiskey. Irish. Bush if you've got it. I don't much like Catholic whiskey."

The kid staggered through a door to an inner room, so Willie flipped open the hinged bar top, helped himself to a bottle of low-shelf Bushmills, popped off the pouring spout, and drained a long pull from the bottle. He set the bottle on its side. The precious fluid spread along the top of the bar as he wiped his mouth with his sleeve. "Aah." He swallowed a couple of gulps of air, then let out a slow, controlled belch. "Mighty fine." He grinned at the moon-eyed waitress and walked out the front door.

Once outside, Willie hustled to a spot behind a van in the parking lot. He crouched low enough to keep his eye level at the bottom of the van's windows. Still no foot traffic in view. His knees didn't like the stance, but in less than a minute, two men burst through the front door and scanned the street. One was a young, skinny guy in a tweed vest. The other was a muscular fat guy wearing either a Hawaiian shirt or a muu-muu. Willie couldn't tell. They were clearly the pair that had tossed Tom in the drink. Bingo.

The two bar bozos walked up the pier toward downtown. They looked behind cars and around the corners of buildings but only glanced back a couple of times. When they seemed to tire of looking over their shoulders, Willie sprinted after them, keeping low. He sapped the fat man on the back of his head with a sock full of lead shot. The hulk went down face first and lay like a sack of flour.

The kid in the vest was quicker. He spun to his left and crouched, a knife in his right hand. Too late. Willie's boot hit him in the nuts with enough force to endanger his chances for progeny. The kid crumpled, his Irish cap landing upside down on the pier. Willie grabbed the kid by his hair, yanked him up to his knees, and kicked his crotch again. The kid groaned as Willie dragged him to the edge of the pier and cast him into the harbor. The fat guy was a bit more trouble. He was too heavy to drag easily, so Willie rolled the guy to the edge and shoved him under the lowest rail. A quick glance satisfied him that both guys were conscious, though floundering. Good enough. They'd make it to shore. Willie double-timed to the land end of the pier and ducked into an alley. Three turns and four blocks later, he stepped into a recessed doorway and watched the street. He could detect no pursuit but laid a slow zigzag course back to base like a fleet dodging submarines.

As Willie strolled into the lobby of the Harbor View, he found himself contemplating the shapely backside of a young woman who was leaning inward over the front desk and whispering to the tall young man manning the station. The desk clerk spotted Willie and seemed startled. "May I help you, Mr. McNaul?"

The young woman rotated her neck like an owl and spotted Willie over her right shoulder. "Mr. McNaul? Are you Tom's rascal older brother? Your reputation precedes you."

"I am. You must be the infamous Molly." Willie waved off the clerk as Molly turned the rest of her body toward him and smiled.

She seemed like the kind of woman who was incapable of an innocent smile. "Just stopping by the room on my way to lunch. You on duty?"

Molly arched her eyebrows for a second, but the surprise quickly turned to interest. "No, I'm off today. Want some company?"

"Lead on, madam."

*   *   *

When Tom reached Room 701, Kate and Aoife were back in their earlier seats and exchanging stiff platitudes. Willie was nowhere in sight. Tom grabbed the chair across from Kate. "Sorry I'm late."

"You're not." Kate glanced at the door and sniffed. "No sign of your brother, but let's get started. He's probably out shopping for assault rifles."

"He doesn't use rifles in a city, but he could be low on hollow points." Tom glanced sideways at Aoife. Her lips were tight, and she was staring at her clenched hands. Seemed a little nervous. "I'll lead off."

Tom related his morning adventures. Kate summarized what she'd told Tom on the phone and then turned to Aoife. "How'd it go with your mother?"

"She was guarded, but she didn't stonewall. I got the impression she recognized one of the names on your list: Liam Collins. But I'm really not sure. She flinched ever so slightly, but she often does that when I talk to her."

Kate leaned back and stared at Tom. "I've got one more other thing. My lunch companion thinks the Boston FBI office is clean now. Has been for some time. I still don't want to bring them up to speed on our case, but I think it should be safe to ask for their help on tracking down locations of known hoods."

Tom pursed his lips and nodded approval. "That'll help. Okay, here's where we stand. We have no way of knowing whether our target is really one of the four guys on Kate's original short list, but we'll proceed as if he is. If we bust on that and live to tell about it, we'll come up with a Plan B. Agreed?"

He was met with two rumbling grunts. "Right. The good news is that the short list is now down to two. Grace O'Malley's flinch suggests Liam Collins, but that's not enough to anoint him as prime suspect. We'll need to keep after Ian Shea as well." Kate and Aoife glanced at each other, probably to see if the other was nodding. Neither was.

Tom bounced to his feet and began his usual patrol. "Kate, see if the local office can get us possible addresses for Collins and Shea. Also a list of their known associates."

Kate snorted. "You mean the roster of the whole Irish mob?"

"No, only close associates. And family. I'm fishing here, but we need to get some sort of idea as to where the painting might be stashed. I doubt it's in a commercial storage locker, and it won't be in their homes or offices."

"Shouldn't be too hard." Kate gnawed on her upper lip. "I'll have a first cut sometime tomorrow morning."

"Good. Aoife? I think we should let your mother ponder life for a while—at least until tomorrow. Let her stew a bit."

"I think that's best." Aoife slumped and sounded relieved.

Tom figured she was worried he would storm the ramparts of O'Malley Castle at dawn, but that could wait. "Okay. Anyone have an idea as to Willie's whereabouts?"

Kate looked at him with obvious disgust. "Of course not. He's not much of a team player."

"Do remember, you and I were FBI trained. Willie's a private eye. He likes to work alone."

Kate barked a sarcastic laugh. "Fair enough, defend your brother. Maybe he's gone undercover somewhere."

*　　*　　*

Willie pulled the sheet and blanket up from the floor and spread them across the bed until he and Molly were covered to their chins. She blinked her eyes a few times, tickling his neck with the lashes, and began to purr. "This is cozy. Let's stay right here under the covers and work up an appetite for dinner."

Willie figured he'd like nothing better. "Good plan, Miss Molly, but let's take a short breather before round two. Plenty of time till dark."

She answered by snuggling in until their skin contact area reached its theoretical maximum. "Mmm. Glad you came to town, big fella. You're more my type than your kid brother."

"Half-kid-brother, but why quibble? I'm glad we haven't found that damned painting yet. I thought this kind of activity was illegal in Boston."

"Used to be. The Pilgrims would have burned us for sure."

Willie grunted. "Still might. I take it you're not married?"

"Little late to ask but no. You?"

"Nope." Technically true. Willie and Rosanne didn't have a certificate, but he felt married. Still, a man was expected to lie under these circumstances. Molly didn't seem to have much patience. She began licking his neck. Maybe she needed salt. In any event, he wanted to slow her down. "Any idea where we might go looking for the lost painting? All of a sudden, I'm in no hurry to leave town, but Tom figures someone's like to shoot us if we hang around too long."

Molly stopped licking and slid on top of him. She planted her elbows on his shoulders and arched her back, staring down at him with a bemused grin. "You mean you're just playing detective with me?" She leaned on the points of her elbows until his shoulders hurt.

"Nope." Willie gritted his teeth. "Just stalling for time. I'm a bit older than y'all."

She giggled. "Not that old, Mister Willie. But honestly, I don't know who has it, or where it might be. I may be a crooked arrow, but my dad isn't in the mob."

"Didn't think otherwise. Forget I asked."

"My Uncle Tim is a bit shady, though. I mean, he isn't a gangster or anything, but he works with some guys who probably don't pay taxes." Molly cocked her head to the left until she was staring down at him with one eye like a bird considering a worm. "He knows a guy who was looking for the painting last time Tommy was in town."

And you tipped him off, little rat. Willie was trying to look nonchalant but felt he was failing. He opted for distraction and began tracing the curves of her breasts with his left index finger. She lightened the pressure on his left shoulder so he had freer range. "You suppose this guy might have the painting in his garage?"

"Mmm. Don't stop now." She rolled her head in a slow circle. "I don't even know the guy's name, but he wouldn't keep it in his house."

"Too dangerous?"

"Uh huh. Uncle Tim says the cops are always raiding guys like that. He says they tend to park money and hot stuff somewhere else. Some place where it's harder to get a warrant. Maybe with family who aren't in the business? I don't really know."

"Speaking of hot stuff . . ."

~ 20 ~

Willie was presumed missing in action at a quarter past seven, so Tom led the surviving party of three out of the Harbor View and up State Street. Kate whipped out her phone and booked a table at the Atlantic Seafood House before Tom could drag them into another Irish place. They were seated at a quiet table well away from windows and more respectable patrons. Tom suggested a house wine, but Kate treated his bid as an ante and raised like a woman holding a full house. After they ordered, he alternated small talk between the two women, who studiously ignored each other until their food came. The arrival of the dishes melted the frost. Tom felt stunned as the ladies oohed over a variety of pale fish and aahed at the paler sauces. He munched fried oysters in silence and wished he had ordered a Guinness.

The dessert menu converged the female heads to within three inches as they negotiated a pact and whispered the results to the bemused waiter. He soon returned and flourished two plates of irregularly shaped chocolate masses teased with a dark goo the color of spent motor oil. One plate sported two wedges of an unknown bonsai citrus fruit, while the other was sprinkled with pine nuts and flanked by something that resembled a radish. Their arrival set off a flurry of raw passion. Tom looked on in shock as Kate and Aoife took turns stabbing each other's concoction with perfect aim. Nary a drop of blood was drawn.

When the feeding frenzy drew to a close, Kate pushed the tab toward Tom and led Aoife deeper into the interior and out of sight. The ladies returned while the waiter was still frowning at the tip. Tom trailed the chatting women by three paces while they ambled back to the Harbor View. He was pretty sure he'd never quite understand the terms of their armistice. When the group was ten feet from the hotel door, Molly emerged, smiled at Tom for half a second, and then strode past him with a dismissive toss of her hair. Tom felt he wasn't likely to figure that out either.

Kate watched Molly sashay to the MTA entrance and skip down the stairs. When Molly's head sank below street level, Kate exhaled with a mighty huff. "I'm not gonna ask." She looked up at Tom for the first time since dessert. "I've gotta call some people. Give me an hour. Okay?"

"Sure. I'll be nearby." Tom glanced at the pub across the street.

Kate rolled her eyes. Tom got the point. He was spared the full dose of her scorn as she spun on her left toe and disappeared inside. He watched the door swing shut and sniffed a waft of perfume. Aoife had either edged closer to him or moved upwind. He looked her way and found both were true. She assumed a playful expression. "How 'bout I buy you a drink at yon pub, sailor?"

"Mighty kind of you, pretty lady. You're on." Tom rested his right hand on Aoife's waist, but she didn't seem to need steering. Five minutes later, he leaned over the table and clinked her glass. "Here's looking at you, kid."

"Not very original, but I like the tone."

"Glad you young folks are into the classics. Films, not me. I may be older than you, but I'm not yet in need of digital restoration."

"We'll see." She took a healthy draw of the amber fluid. It was just a hair lighter than her eyes.

"Tell me about your mom. She seems quite the fascinating woman."

"What a mood killer. You really aren't much good at flirting, are you Tommy?"

Tom didn't quite get her point, but he decided to plead guilty. "Not really. Sorry."

Aoife emitted an unconvincing trill of carefree laughter. "It's okay. There isn't that much to tell. I've told you some of the history. She became a single mom when I was born, and she's never been willing to talk about that. I know she met my dad when I was one. He was a good father, but I was just seven when he was killed. My mom didn't tell me he wasn't my biological father until I was twelve."

Tom twirled his glass enough to tickle the ice. "Any siblings?"

"No, and I'm not sure why. My folks were good Irish Catholics. I assume it was some problem with my dad. Mom was a proven breeder." She drained her glass and knocked it on the table with just enough force to make sure he noticed. She stared at the glass and rotated it slowly.

Tom waved two fingers at the barmaid, who nodded. "And she never remarried?"

"No. I think she decided two men were enough. She had enough inheritance and insurance money for us to live comfortably when I was little, but over the years, the costs of maintaining the estate in Armagh must have drained her. That's why she's so intent on finding the painting."

"Must have been rough. Did you and Grace get along?"

Aoife glanced up from her empty glass. "About as well as mothers and daughters do, I suppose. We didn't share deep secrets, and we rarely talked about men. Never about sex." She grinned. "The Irish way."

"I suppose, but most of my Catholic Irish friends have ten siblings. They must have figured things out."

"Everyone does." The second round arrived, and they took their first sips in silence.

Tom didn't feel Aoife was going to reveal anything useful from her mother's past, so he tacked toward the present. "Any idea why Grace is so dead set against meeting with me?"

Aoife looked away. She'd clearly been anticipating the question. Her head was turned to the right, and her eyes were drifting and unfocussed. "No."

"Uh, could you be a little more specific?"

"What's more specific than no?" Aoife seemed to relax. "Really, I don't know. I've wondered about it. I know she's sensitive about being in the wheelchair. The accident was only about a year ago, and she's not sure she'll get better." Aoife looked back to Tom and forced what she probably thought was a smile. "I think the shyness is real, but I haven't spent much time with her since the accident. Just a few short visits since she got out of the hospital." She paused and nipped her lower lip before proceeding. "She has a caregiver who comes three days a week to help out. A nice Polish woman named Anna. She doesn't talk much about Mom, but she told me there are a few regular visitors. Mostly men, but I don't have a clue who they are."

Aoife slouched with an elbow over the back of her chair and flashed a genuine grin. "Maybe it's something about you. She does seem bent on advising me to stay away from hypothetical men of your type."

"Interesting. It can't be my cheap haircut—she's never seen it."

"Well, you are from the wrong part of Ireland. County Tyrone, didn't you say?"

"I did."

"That might be enough. She doesn't say much about politics, Irish or American, but it's clear she doesn't think much of Ulstermen. Or Brits, for that matter."

Tom wondered just how bitter Grace might be toward the men with orange sashes, but it was clear the inquest was over. He raised his glass and rattled the remnants of two ice cubes. "Another round?"

Aoife pushed her chair back from the table. "Better not. Kate's hour is about up. She'd come looking for a row soon. Tomorrow night?"

Aoife was adept at arching just one eyebrow. Tom wondered if she practiced with a mirror. "Yeah, you're on, crime and the tide permitting. Hey, I do have one unrelated question—just for curiosity."

"Shoot."

"A tough guy in Ireland started laughing when I told him I was working for Grace O'Malley. Said nobody there would name their daughter after an Irish pirate queen. That true?"

"Ah yes, Granualle." A soft smile slowly spread to the edges of Aoife's face as she looked inward. "She ran a string of pirate ships off the west coast of Ireland in the sixteenth century. Quite a woman. Once she even negotiated a deal with Queen Elizabeth, face to face, and came out pretty well. Head still attached and license to put her fleet back to sea. You need to be careful with Irish women, you know. We're hardly demure."

"I wish I'd have known. I might not have married Colleen. It was almost the death of me."

"You shouldn't let that put you off. Nothing ventured, as they say. In my mom's case, she married into the O'Malley name, but it wasn't such a burden. Nobody's heard of Grace O'Malley in the states."

They were crossing the street to the hotel when Tom's phone began singing. It was Kate. "Yeah, toots?"

"Back from your date yet? I've got some interesting news."

"From your Bureau friend?"

"Uh huh. Hurry on up here. And come alone."

"Sounds dangerous. Should I bring my gun?"

"Sure. You may need it."

When the elevator stopped at the fourth floor, Aoife air-kissed Tom but rubbed her cheek firmly along his own. Her scent remained strong after the door closed behind her. Tom figured she was marking her territory. At least she didn't pee on his shoe.

Kate didn't stretch up to sniff his collar, but he saw her nose wrinkle. "Whiskey and perfume. You're a fast worker, McNaul. But let's get to it."

Tom followed her to the table and grabbed the chair with the best view of harbor lights. "Okay, we were down to two favorites for top perp. Whatcha got?"

Kate sat opposite and pulled a handful of papers out of a manila folder. She fanned them on the table like a poker player claiming the pot and selected two. "This shouldn't take long. Ian Shea is bad as they come, but he's something of a loner. Hasn't got any family living in New England, and his girlfriend's a live-in."

Tom scratched the right side of his jaw. "No close friends?"

"Nobody he'd be fool enough to leave a Monet with. Or so our source says. He could be wrong. But Liam Collins is another story." Kate puffed up a bit and waited for Tom to ask her why?

It was best to let Kate win the early rounds. "Why?"

She flashed a smug grin as she picked up one of the papers. "Liam's more prolific."

"A proper Irishman, you say."

"Not quite, but he does have three kids. The two oldest are grown sons, mid- to late 20s. The daughter is eighteen and living on campus at UConn. I think we can rule her out."

Tom nodded. "Can't stash many paintings in a dorm room."

"The oldest boy is married, two little kids, lives in Boston, and he's working with his old man in the mob. The younger one is single, in the army, and stationed in Texas. Did a tour overseas. I don't see the soldier running a lone-star safe house for his dad's loot. Of the three kids, only the older boy makes any sense as the keeper of the loot."

"Yup. Any nephews or nieces? First cousins?"

"Still waiting on those—I wanted stats on the immediate family first. Could get a call any time now." Kate arched her eyebrows at Tom. "Might be a while." She stood up and sidled toward the bed. There was a loud clack as she made a point of dropping her cell phone six inches onto the left bedside table. It didn't bounce, but within a second, it rang. "Shit." Kate snatched the phone and barked her name. She tossed her head back and sighed. "Yeah, come on up." She somehow wedged the phone into her tight back pocket and rolled her head toward Tom. "Willie."

Tom was relieved but worked hard not to show it. A few minutes later, Willie pulled a third chair up to the table. "Fine night. What are you brainy types up to?"

Kate growled some indecipherable syllables that Tom translated as "not enough." Willie's grin suggested he had the same take. He tugged his tangled beard. "How's about you two experts get an old detective up to date?

Kate gave him the one-minute version and then planted her fists on her hips. "So we figure the eldest son is our best shot. Sound right?"

Willie paused, probably pretending to think it over. He had lectured Tom many times that if you plan to tell a woman she's wrong, it's crucial to at least act like you're taking her seriously. After several eye rolls and chin scratches, he slowly shook his head. "Maybe. But I'd say no."

Kate's eyes narrowed and Tom could see her jaw muscles tense. "Why not?"

"Too close a connection. I consulted an expert of my own this afternoon, and she said a mob man stashing his swag wouldn't leave it with that close a relative—too easy for the cops to get a warrant."

"She?" Kate was clearly poised for counterattack. "Where did you find this mystery woman?"

Willie tilted his chair back far enough to leave his ultimate safety in doubt. "It was here at the Harbor View. Can't recall the room number exactly."

Kate's eyes widened. Tom scored a point for Willie and decided to intervene. "You're quite the rascal, bro, but who was she?"

"Shouldn't say. Wouldn't be gentlemanly."

"Wrong rule book for your lifestyle. Come on, Willie, we gotta know."

Willie eased the front legs of his chair back onto the carpet. "Molly. And that's all I'm sayin'."

Eyes roamed and lips twitched in silence for a full minute. Tom was still trying to think of something to say when Kate's phone went off again. "Shit." She stood up, expertly extracted the phone from its snug lair, and turned her back on the McNauls. She spent several minutes growling and muttering uh-huh before ending the call with a huff. After treating herself to a pair of long, deep breaths, she turned back toward the table. Her eyes narrowed, and she spoke barely above a whisper. "There's a niece. Annie Collins."

Tom felt uneasy at Kate's shift in mood. "Just one lousy niece? That's not much of an extended family. Are these guys Presbyterians?"

"Oh shut up, Tommy. Liam Collins has plenty of cousins, and nephews, but the FBI locals thought one stood out like dog balls." Kate stared through the window into the Boston night, her eyes focused on nothing in particular. "The niece is thirty-six. She, her husband, and their high school daughter recently moved into a house in Wellesley. The niece teaches second grade there. Must be a modern girl—she kept her family name."

Tom felt uneasy. "Okay, sounds like a normal lady. What makes her stand out?"

Kate sucked in her stomach, and in a flash, her demeanor returned to FBI mode. "Her husband sold real estate. As far as anyone knows, they were a straight and law-abiding couple. No mob connections. They didn't seem to see Uncle Liam except at holiday gatherings."

"But then . . ."

"But then the husband ran up a gambling debt. Tried to pay it off with some risky housing investments. Went broke. Was in danger of being literally broke, as in arms and legs."

Tom was all-the-way uneasy now. "And he made a foolish move?"

"Apparently. He didn't come home one evening. Turns out someone shot him, stuck a bomb under his body, and nearly blew up you, the corpse, and some damned cat."

"Jesus!"

"There's one more thing." Kate's stare bored into Tom's eyes. "The niece and her family had only been in the Wellesley house a few months when he was killed."

"So?"

"Their previous home was in Lexington." Kate paused to let that sink in. "The house where we went for the sting operation, looking for the stolen Vermeer. The house where we both got shot."

"And you nearly died."

"Nearly."

"I remember it was for sale but still furnished." Tom's emotions were outrunning his mind. "Gotta think." He hunched over, clasped his hands between his knees, and studied the green rug. Kate went back to staring out the window. When Tom flicked a glance at Willie, his brother's mouth was hanging open as he watched the back of Kate's head. A silent minute passed. Then another.

Kate spun around. "Willie, I need to talk to Tom. Catch you in the morning."

"Sure." Willie lurched to his feet, nodded to Tom, and shuffled out the door.

When he was gone, Kate softened. "Tommy, let's go."

"Okay. Anywhere in particular?"

Kate snarled. "You know damned well. I lost a lot more than blood that night. And I still have nightmares. Gunshots. Blood seeping through my clothes. You yelling. I want to go back to that place, just for a few minutes. I don't really know why. Maybe just to see it's not really hell."

"You sure? I don't believe in closure. It's usually better to just suck it up and move on."

"Closure? No, I don't believe in that either. Just strength. But do this for me, Tommy. Just drive me by the place."

*   *   *

It was almost midnight by the time Tom turned the rented car onto a quiet road in the outskirts of Lexington. He stopped at the end of a curved driveway and killed the lights. The long porch was partially lit from a single fixture. There was a Big Wheels tricycle on the porch instead of a gunman lurking in the shadows. The lawn was newly mowed, and a plastic play structure was just to the right of the driveway. The last time he'd seen the yard it was awash in flashing red and blue lights, cruisers and unmarked sedans askew on the lawn, two young officers still stringing yellow crime scene tape, the receding wail as Kate's ambulance sped away. He wondered if the current owners had a clue what had gone down here. He rolled the window halfway open and smelled the cut grass as the damp air drifted in. The night seemed to rest easy.

Kate startled him. "Let's go."

"You okay?"

"Yeah. Easier than I thought. Drive on." But she leaned her head against the door and closed her eyes. They didn't open until he pulled to a stop in front of the Harbor View. "Thanks, Tommy." She leaned across the center console as if to kiss him but stopped short. "Don't come up, okay? I need to be alone tonight. And I have to head back to Washington early tomorrow. We got a tip on a Jackson Pollack in North Dakota."

"No sweat. I think I'll hang onto the car another day, but I need to find a place to park it overnight. I'll drive around a bit first. Give me some time to think."

Tom watched Kate disappear into the hotel. She kept her chin up, but she didn't look back.

~ 21 ~

Tom's eyes were burning for sleep. He was beyond the help of a coffee as he wobbled around his room trying to think, afraid he'd crash in a second if he sat on the bed. No time for that. He called Willie. "Gotta talk, bro. My place, now."

Willie just grunted, but he was at Tom's door in less than a minute. They sat side by side, all four feet on the windowsill, and stared into the Boston night. A low overcast now reigned, ominously lit from below by the city lights and what was left of the traffic. Tom checked his watch. One minute till midnight. He waited for the minute to expire. At the witching hour, he sniffed once and began briefing Willie on the latest from Kate. Willie occasionally blinked. After five minutes, Tom glanced at their reflections in the window and saw Willie's eyes were closed. He stopped talking and listened for slowed breathing, but his brother wasn't asleep.

"Keep talkin', bro. I'm thinkin'."

Tom finished his monologue with the rationale for suspecting Annie Collins as the most likely keeper of the contraband. "As our mutual friend, Molly, says, if Ms. Collins does have the painting, it's probably in her house. We've got no direct evidence, but it smells right."

"And it's the only decent lead we've got."

"That too. Well?"

"I like it. It'd be thin as hell if it weren't for the connection to the Lexington house, but that's enough for me. Tell me, though, where's Kate? Not like her to get a lead like that and then hit the sack. Why aren't we all sitting in the war room?"

"She was spooked by seeing the shootout house again. Wanted to cozy up by herself tonight. And she's flying back to Boston tomorrow at oh-dark-thirty. Said the Art Crime Team got a tip on a hot Jackson Pollack. In North Dakota, of all places."

Willie opened his eyes and aimed them at Tom. "Oh please. She made the Jackson who-the-fuck part up. You just left her? Your woman's got post-traumatic, and you just wave her off to be alone? Jesus, Tommy, you're dumb as a stump about women. She deserves better."

"I'm too tired to deny it, but I'll be damned if I'll sashay up to Kate's room and tell her what she needs now is a good roll with me. I might get shot. So what say we two come up with a plan?"

Willie dropped both feet to the floor with a muffled thud. "Somehow, I suspect you've already made the plan. If so, spill it."

"Grand theft, canvas. This Collins woman is a teacher, and tomorrow is Tuesday. She'll be at school most of the day. So will her kid. I figure we pull a B and E, toss the place, and if we find the Monet, take it with us. I know it'll be a rush, but this case leaks like my first Chevy's oil pan. Molly, in particular, knows way too much."

"Whoa. I may be dumb, but neither of us is stupid enough to dash into the place without casing it. We need some recon. And even if we do get in and out clean, as soon as Ms. Annie finds out the painting's missing, she'll call her uncle. Our asses will be grasses. We'll end up at the bottom of the outer harbor with our feet in concrete."

Tom approached full-alert status as adrenaline kicked in. He shoved back from the window and bounced to his feet. "You can get us in and out, Willie. I've seen you do it before. Take the car and do a drive by tonight to get the lay of the place, then do what you have to. We should go in around midday. Might take us a while to find the Monet."

"If it's there. And if it's not sealed inside a wall, or in some steel vault in the basement."

Tom clasped his hands behind his head. "I'm betting it won't be. Uncle Liam would want to get his painting out of there in a hurry if things get hot. By stashing the painting with a niece, he might buy a little warning time. The cops would need a search warrant, and they'd probably have trouble showing probable cause for a niece with a clean record. It would take a while, and the local constabulary isn't good at keeping that kind of news under their service caps. Some dirty cop tips Collins, and he moves the goods before the judge signs off on the search."

"Lot of assumptions, Tommy. But you haven't said how we keep the hounds off our asses when they find out we've made off with their painting. Dare I ask?"

"Elementary, Wilhelm. We make sure they don't know it's missing. Leave that to me. Meanwhile, you take the rental car, mosey out to Wellesley, and go figure out how to break into Mrs. Collins' castle. I've got some shopping to do tomorrow morning, but I can take the MTA. Find me at noon tomorrow. Come alone, and don't say a word to the others."

"Find you? Where should I look?"

"My room, I hope, but I'll have to dodge Aoife. If her temper goes off, I might be up a tree somewhere. If I'm not at the hotel, try my cell. You can use a phone, I've seen you do that before too. And Willie, not a word. This is our operation. If it works, we'll figure out who gets to know what, and when. If it flops, we've bought it alone. Okay?"

Willie chewed his upper lip for a moment but nodded.

* * *

By noon, Tom had turned off his phone, stood Aoife up for breakfast, and completed his shopping trip. There would be hell to pay, but time was short. A single deep thud shook the room. It was louder than Aoife's best effort, so Tom checked his watch. Noon on the dot. He peered through the peephole, saw only a tangle of gray beard, and unlatched the door.

Willie seemed ready to collapse onto Tom's bed, but he saw it was occupied by a large, flat package wrapped in brown paper. He shoved his fingers into the side pockets of his jeans and hooked each thumb over his belt. "The Collins place shouldn't be much of a problem. It's a dormered Cape Cod in an older part of the town. Lots of trees and overgrown bushes, but the lawns are trim. The back yard has a six-foot solid wood fence with a gate on the driveway side and another in the back. Once we're in the back yard, nobody will see us. I got up close enough to check out a few downstairs windows. Didn't see any signs they were wired. I hate casing a place that late at night. If anyone sees you, they aren't going to believe you're checking the meter."

"You're my hero. So how do we get into the yard in broad daylight?"

"I propose the brass balls approach. The driveway is lined on one side with a dense hedge. If we pull our car in, and nobody's watching, maybe we can slip out on the hedge side and crawl around to the back."

"What if Miss Marple across the street is watering her window plants?"

"Then we're toast." Willie shrugged.

"Too dangerous. Damn. We haven't got time to go steal a delivery truck and some overalls. Even if we did, we need too much time in the house. Someone would get wise. We're cooked." Tom bit the inside of his left cheek a little too hard and tasted blood.

"Of course, there's also an alley."

"Bastard!" Tom cocked his fist for a punch to Willie's midsection but thought better of it. He'd had a lifetime of coming out second best with his ex-Marine brother.

"The alley's lined by fences on both sides. It's narrow, and we wouldn't want to park the car in there. Might get hemmed in. I figure we go in on foot, one at a time. Maybe five minutes apart and from opposite ends."

"That'll have to do."

Willie flicked his head toward the package on the bed. "That looks suspiciously like you snarfed the painting already. What's the deal?"

"That's our ticket home." Tom paused for effect, but Willie just looked annoyed. "The Sotheby's agent who started this lily hunt saw photos of the Monet. It was unframed, just under four feet wide, and slightly rectangular. He said it was sitting on brown wrapping paper with bits of masking tape. So I went to an art supply store this morning, purchased a decent quality canvas of roughly those dimensions, and wrapped it up with brown paper and tape. That's it lying on the bed."

"So you're gonna . . ."

"Switch them out." Tom picked up the package. "I'll carry this to the house, via the alley. When I leave, I'll carry out the water lilies in the same wrapper. I cut the paper extra large in case we're a bit off on the measurements."

Willie couldn't suppress a grin. "And this canvas goes into the Monet's wrapping."

"Sherlock. I've got a few extra pieces of wood and some cotton padding in my package to adjust the size and weight."

"And you figure she won't notice?"

"Uh huh. I doubt Annie Collins knows exactly what's in the package, and she probably doesn't handle it. And I doubt that Uncle Liam will come around to play with it. From all accounts, he steers clear of her home. So if we're lucky, it could be years before anyone knows the painting's gone missing. By then, there could be plenty of suspects."

"Tommy, you think too much. Someday you're gonna come to grief because of it. But it seems like a plan. Let's do it." Willie suddenly looked worried and stared at the painting. "Why the sudden secrecy? I can understand why you might not want Aoife blabbing to anyone, but are we really gonna pull this off without telling Kate? Why?"

"We are, but I'll explain that later. We good?"

Willie just nodded, but Tom could see the corners of his mouth twitch.

* * *

At a quarter past one, Tom watched Willie stroll past his car and turn south into the alley abutting the rear of the Collins place. When he disappeared, Tom counted to ten, started the car, and drove to a shady spot two blocks from the other end of the alley. He waited ten minutes. No calls, no passing cars. No one was visible along the street. He climbed out of the car and retrieved the canvas in its plain brown wrapper. He felt conspicuous as hell, but he tucked it under his right arm and headed for the south end of the alley. He tried to scan the street without turning his head. Only branches were moving, stirred by an ominous north wind.

Most of the homes Tom passed had tall, solid board fences screening their back yards from view. All the gates were closed, but only one had a visible lock. A few lots had single garages opening to the alley. He passed two yards with chain link fences, the second of which contained a ferocious squirrel sitting erect with its dukes up. It chattered and gave mighty flicks of its tail, evidently guarding the acorn crop. A sudden gust of wind rustled the oak leaves, and the feisty beast shut up. The sixth yard on the left had a tall wooden fence much like the others. The wood looked old, but the boards were tight and recently painted a forest green. The gate was slightly ajar. Tom gave it a gentle push, and it swung open with a slight rasp from the lower hinge. He glanced both ways in the alley, but there were no signs of a witness, so he slipped into the yard and latched the gate. The lawn was mowed and free of dandelions. The shrubs looked ancient and appeared to be randomly trimmed. There were none of the usual hunks of garish, molded plastic typical of a house with young children. Tom strode to the back door. It opened before his hand could close on the knob, and he stepped into a small kitchen. The sink was clear of dishes, as were the counters. A scrawny spider plant hung from a hook over the lone window, possibly depressed by its limited view of the sky.

"About time, little brother. Let's boogie. I'll start in the basement."

Tom frowned. "Not the most likely spot for stashing a painting this pricey. We're not in New Mexico. A Massachusetts basement can be damned damp."

"I sniffed from the top of the stairs. Didn't smell moldy. How about you start on the top floor, and we'll meet in the middle?" Willie pulled a small bag of latex gloves from his jacket pocket and handed a pair to Tom. They each performed a brief samurai bow and split up.

Tom took the stairs two at a time and started with the left rear room. As he opened the door, a streak of white fur shot between his legs and bounded down the stairs. Apparently the speedy Persian shared the master bedroom with Mrs. Collins. A stiff whiff of cat byproducts drifted from the attached bathroom, attacking Tom's sinuses and causing him to gag. Otherwise, the room was tidy to a fault. The bed was made, all surfaces were free of dust, and the only object not aligned with the edges of the furniture was a book lying slightly askew on the lone bedside table. It was a well-worn trade paperback of *Pride and Prejudice*.

Tom examined the furniture. None of the cabinets or dressers was large enough to house the Monet. He searched under the bed and behind the bookcase, and he scoured the orderly closet. No painting, and no sign of secret panels. The bath contained nothing out of order other than the cat box.

The daughter's bedroom was diagonally opposite. Tom was shocked to find a bed as tightly made as a drill sergeant's. The floor was free of discarded clothing. All the photos and posters were neatly framed. There were enough of them to abate the unfortunate print wallpaper, which must have dated to the girl's infancy. Evidently, this teenage daughter was a different breed of cat from Tom's own. He performed another futile search and moved on to the left-front room, which appeared to be the mother's office. The desk was tidy and bare except for three colored pens next to a blank notepad. It supported an aging Dell computer attached to a bulging CRT monitor and an ancient printer. A card table in one corner held two piles of homework papers, one with brief comments in green ink. The closet was classic teacher—stacks of cardboard storage boxes from Home Depot labeled by year and course name. Tom lugged enough of them out to make sure no masterpieces were hidden behind. He hoped he put them back in the correct order.

The door to the fourth room could only be opened halfway. Tom squeezed through and found a rowing machine obstructing the door. The walls were lined with built-in bookcases that had obviously proven insufficient. Stacks of cardboard liquor boxes were piled five feet high in closely spaced rows. The boxes were closed but not sealed, so Tom dug through half a dozen. All contained books ranging from thrillers and bodice rippers to a full set of Encyclopedia Britannica. The bodice rippers showed the most signs of wear. Fortunately, none of the boxes was large enough to house the framed Monet.

The closet held more boxes of books, but it also had a short plywood door giving access to an eave closet. The closet was empty save for three sprung mousetraps, each covered with a grim layer of dust. One still held a sliver of hardened cheese and a tiny, petrified mouse foot. Tom retreated to the hall and noticed a cord hanging from the ceiling. He pulled down a set of folding stairs and climbed until his head and shoulders were within a dim attic. A string brushed his cheek, and he saw a bare bulb light fixture attached to a roof joist just above his head. There was a click when he pulled the string, but no light was forthcoming. Nobody ever changes bulbs in the attic. He pulled out his phone and switched on the flashlight. The glow revealed a small wooden platform directly in front of him. It was empty. Beyond the platform lay rows of pink insulation looking like a warehouse of cotton candy. He couldn't see into all the corners from his perch, but he wasn't about to go stepping from joist to joist and risk putting his foot through a ceiling. It didn't matter. No one would store art in this un-insulated space.

Tom heard a muffled clang, followed by a burst of obscenities. He descended the stairs to the ground floor just as Willie emerged from the basement shaking his head. "Lots of junk down there. The furnace room, a bike with one wheel, boxes of Christmas ornaments. Even a kayak with two paddles. But no closets or doors, and no boxes more than about two feet square. What about you?"

"Nada. Let's do this floor together."

The neatness of the Collins women extended throughout the main living areas. Within five minutes, the living room, TV room, coat closet, and dining area were cleared. Tom's hopes were sinking as they poked through cupboards in the kitchen to no avail. Willie leaned back against the counter and crossed his arms. "Looks like we're busted. Time to go?"

Tom didn't reply. He made another slow circuit of the ground floor. What had he missed? Willie cleared his throat as Tom returned to the kitchen. "Ready? You go first with your package. I'll lock up."

"Gotta find the cat first and toss him back in the master bedroom. You see it?"

"Yeah, under the table in the dining room. I'll get her."

"You sure it's a her?"

"Don't care."

As Willie left for the dining room, Tom struck a spark. Cape Cods almost always have a storage closet under the central stairway. He'd made several laps around the house core, but he hadn't noticed a closet door. He tried another lap. Still no sign of a door. The stairs opened on one side, and the two adjoining walls were adorned with paintings. On the side opposite the stairs, just outside the door to the kitchen, there was a built-in set of shelves holding rows of spices and bottles. The shelves looked relatively new, and the wood did not quite match the kitchen cabinets. He glanced around the kitchen. There was no pantry. Tom examined the spice shelves and found a small handle just above a tin of bay leaves. He grasped it and gave a gentle tug. The shelf unit swung outward.

The central closet had been converted to a pantry. It was only three feet deep, and the sides were lined with shelves. The ceiling sloped downward following the angle of the stairs, so the rear of the space was only five feet high. The back surface was made of stained pine, and it sported a row of iron hooks along the top from which hung colorful aprons, dishtowels, and a wok. More important, it also had two hinges and a doorknob.

A screeching yowl, followed by a string of Marine Corps profanity, caused Tom to smash his right elbow against a side shelf. He retreated to the kitchen and listened to Willie stomp up the stairs. The swearing faded, a door slammed, and his brother descended the stairs with a lighter tread. He strode into the kitchen looking like he'd been in a bar fight. Blood trickled from a deep scratch over his left eye, and the latex gloves were shredded. "Goddamn cat is tougher than it looks. Female for sure."

"You okay?"

"I'll live. Ready to blow this hole?"

"Come see something first." Tom led the way to the pantry and pointed at the rear door leading to the space under the stairs. "Mind if I try this?"

The hinges barely squeaked as Tom pulled open the inner closet door. There was no light for the space under the stairwell, but enough leaked from the hall to confirm the contents. The cramped space with the descending ceiling held a collection of rectangular packages, all wrapped in brown paper and sealed with masking tape. Tom stepped into the pantry, leaned forward, and counted six. They varied in size, but the one leaning on the right wall matched the dimensions estimated from the photos of the Monet. Tom lifted it gently and carried it to the dining room table. Willie picked up a second package, the smallest in the collection, and followed.

Tom took his time peeling masking tape from the prize, as he planned to return the wrappings to the closet hideaway. He managed to undo the tape without tearing the cheap paper, and he stood back treating himself to a moment of dramatic effect. "Ta da." He peeled back the last fold of paper covering the painting and found himself in a garden, staring at a cluster of lilies floating on an algae-free pond. "My god, Willie. We've got it." He quickly lifted the painting and leaned it against the hutch.

"My turn." Willie stepped forward and laid his smaller packet on top of the lily wrappings.

Tom eased his brother aside. "Let me do the tape work." He didn't trust Willie's blunt approach. When the tape was peeled back, he stepped back. "Your shot."

Willie knew nothing of art, but he was a kid on Christmas morning as he leaned over the table and slowly lifted the paper. His expression changed from excited greed to bewilderment. "What the fuck?"

Tom leaned in for a closer look and grinned. "Picasso. I win." Willie was dismayed, but Tom wasn't interested. "It's a good piece, Wilhelm, but we've got to leave it. If anything's found to be missing, they'll let loose the dogs of war." Tom felt a twang as he began rewrapping the Picasso. There were four more pieces in the closet, so they'd be leaving five paintings behind. Probably major pieces. Best not to know the identities of the other four. Always best to hood the victim before hanging. And the Picasso he could bear to leave. It was valuable but not rare. Besides, he didn't like cubism.

While Willie returned the Picasso to the closet, Tom unwrapped his own package and taped several of the enclosed wooden strips to the edges of his blank canvas until it matched the dimensions of the Monet. He hefted both paintings and decided to tape a few more strips to the inner edges of the frame to equalize the weights. The replacement canvas now fit perfectly into the original wrappings of the Monet, and Tom placed the package back in the closet while Willie hastily wrapped the water lilies in the new paper. They did a quick walk-through looking for anything left out of order and rendezvoused at the kitchen door. Willie clapped Tom on his left shoulder, scanned the backyard, and slipped out.

Tom began shifting his weight while staring at his watch. He was to wait five minutes while Willie exited the north end of the alley and walked to a pickup point four blocks from where Tom had dropped him off. Two minutes later, the kitchen phone rang.

Tom began to sweat. After five rings, he heard several clicks and a cheery voice requesting a message. He assumed it was the voice of Annie Collins, and a wave of guilt made him shiver. He felt very much the intruder. A gruff baritone voice followed. The man didn't bother to introduce himself, so it had to belong to someone Annie knew well. The voice requested a call back as soon as possible and didn't bother to leave a number. The voice of Liam Collins? He shook it off. One minute to go.

Tom spent the minute at the kitchen window scanning the back yard and watching for danger in the alley. Nothing moved. After a final glance, he eased his way out the door and wiped the knob with a clean bandana. He did the same to the latch on the rear gate and then removed his latex gloves. All quiet in the alley, so he turned southward and tried to act as nonchalant as any man with a stolen masterpiece in his arms. As he was passing the third house down, he heard a motorcycle turn into the alley behind him. The deep growl sounded like a Harley, and though the engine was grumbling just above idle, it was getting louder. Tom weighed his options. He had a thirty-eight special under his jacket in the small of his back, but that was a last resort. He might out-shoot the Hog rider, but so what? Once Uncle Liam found out, he'd be dead before he had time to top up his life insurance. Keep on strolling.

Tom didn't look back, but the bike was closing on him. He was a hundred feet from the end of the alley when the engine sound dropped to a steady idle, then died. He tensed for the sound of running footsteps but heard only a faint scuffle followed by the sound of a garage door opening. As he reached the street and turned left, he glanced back down the alley. The Harley was disappearing into a single garage two lots down from the Collins house. Tom was still breathing heavily when he reached the rental car.

~ 22 ~

The McNaul boys rode in silence as Tom maneuvered the car toward downtown. Willie looked bored as he stared out the side window; Tom was trying to stave off an anxiety attack. He replayed their heist, wondering what they'd overlooked, as he dodged through angry Boston traffic with the stolen Monet propped up in the back seat. His attempt at Zen breathing ended with the blare of a horn and screeching tires behind him. He didn't look in the mirror. Got to get off these goddamn streets and think.

There wasn't much point in driving back to the Harbor View. He might run into Aoife. Or Molly. Or even Kate if she'd changed her mind and scheduled a later flight. Instead, he decided to head for familiar grounds to hole up awhile. He crossed the Charles River into Cambridge via the Boston University Bridge and headed east on Memorial Drive. The power steering bawled like a lost calf as he steered the rental car into a parking garage at MIT. His alumni card earned him a laugh from the mousy blonde attendant. He tried a smile and showed her the brass rat on his right hand. She rolled her eyes, handed him a ticket, and pointed toward the visitor's section. Tom found a spot not visible from the entry booth, backed in, and killed the motor.

"What the hell are we doing here, little brother?"

"We're thinking, Watson. Or at least I am."

"That's swell. We got anything to eat?"

Tom ignored him. He narrowed his eyelids to a slit and slowed his breathing. After a couple of minutes, he heard Willie open and slam the door. Fifteen more minutes passed before the door opened again and Willie scrunched into the passenger seat. Tom smelled cheeseburger. His eyes shot open as he snatched a fry.

"You're alive!" Willie smiled but moved the cardboard tray with the fries out of reach.

"Where'd you get that?"

"You don't need to know. Think of anything?"

"Yep. Behold." Tom pulled out his phone and called Kate's FBI office number in Washington. She picked up midway through the first ring. "Tommy."

"Kate."

"Creep."

"You got anything new?"

"Hell no. You're the one who's supposed to be working. Give me something."

"Nothing to report yet. I just wanted to make sure you got home safely."

"What bullshit. You just wanted to make sure I'm out of the way. Got a hot date tonight?"

"Give me a break. Look, things are moving fast here. I'm just trying to figure out where everyone is. Gotta hang up now. I'll call you when it's over."

"The fuck, Tommy! I'm coming back up there with a team."

"Don't do that. It would end badly. Trust me this time." He hung up.

Willie leaned against the car door. "Always the lady's man."

"Guess I shouldn't have called." Tom dialed Aoife. She answered after three rings.

"Hi, Tom." Her voice was guarded, with a hint of disguised eagerness.

"Hiya. How about dinner tonight? Say, seven?"

"You get right to the point. How big a party this time? I assume you know Kate's left town."

"Table for two. Willie's got some business elsewhere."

"Ooh, sounds cozy." Aoife's version of Mae West was lame compared with Myrna's, but Tom gave her a B for effort.

"Meet you at the hotel. You pick the spot."

"You're on." Aoife clicked off.

Willie was shaking his head with an expression somewhere between disgusted and resigned. "She seems a bit young for you. I still recommend Kate."

"I need to face down Grace O'Malley tomorrow, and I can't get through that door without Aoife. So lighten up. This isn't a date."

"Clueless as ever, little brother."

*   *   *

Tom stopped in a loading zone a block down the street from the Harbor View and evicted Willie. "Get your stuff and meet me right here . . . thirty minutes sharp."

"No problem, but I might be a little late if Molly's working the front desk."

Tom snorted and drove off. The power steering noise had ebbed to intermittent burps. He pulled into a parking garage that offered fifteen free minutes and made a phone call. Then he took a slow route back to the hotel. Willie and his weathered duffel bag were waiting. He stuffed the bag on the floor of the back seat, laid the Monet over it, and climbed in front. "Where in hell am I going? And how come you're not going there with me?"

"Just a few blocks." Moments later, Tom pulled up in front of the Hyatt Regency. "You're staying here tonight. When you get checked in, stroll over to South Station. It's just a few minutes' walk. Go to the Amtrak office and pick up your ticket. It's paid for. Tomorrow, you and Monsieur Monet's masterpiece are leaving town on the Lake Shore Limited. Change in Chicago to the Southwest Chief. Should be in Lamy sometime Friday afternoon."

"What the hell, Tommy? Two days on the train? For what?"

"Don't bellyache. I got you a private sleeper each night. You'll have a swell time. Just lock the room when you head down to the dining car. Or the bar."

"You gonna tell me why?"

"The painting has to disappear. Without a trace."

Willie crossed his arms and stared out the window. "Disappear? That's nuts! How we gonna get paid? Do you figure on charging the widow O'Malley for our trip to Ireland and then running back to Santa Fe with her painting? That's cold."

"Think it through, Willie. We give Aoife the painting, she takes it to her ma, and they try to sell it. Uncle Liam will get wind of it by nightfall and, thanks to dear Molly, he'll be damned sure we took it. Grace O'Malley will end up dead within twenty-four hours. Maybe Aoife too. Then they'll come after us."

Willie snorted hard enough to bounce his head off the headrest. "Great. But why not give it to Kate and let her deal with Uncle Liam. Be nice to have the FBI sitting between us and the Irish mob, no?" He suddenly grinned. "Say, that works. Kate could put together a raid of that Wellesley house. They charge in with a warrant, snatch the fake piece we left, but they don't unwrap it. Kate makes the switch back at the ranch, and we're in the clear. The O'Malleys end up with their painting. Maybe we even get paid."

"Good try, Willie, but it won't work. First, Kate is too much of a straight arrow to set up a fake raid when she's sitting there with the painting in her office. Second, no way the Boston FBI could keep a secret like that from the mob for more than an hour. And once the word got back to Liam Collins that Kate already had the painting when the team charged in, we'd end up just as dead as in option one."

"I think you're selling Kate short. She can't be that straight an arrow if she's mixed up with a desperado like you. But if you're right about the leaks in the FBI office, we'd be fucked anyway."

"So we have to make the painting disappear. Think about it. Uncle Liam thinks his painting is safely in long-term storage, albeit not in an archival environment. With luck, he won't actually try to retrieve it from the closet for years. It may be used as collateral in any number of shady deals, but possession will just change on paper. At least I hope that's how it works. I figure that if Uncle Liam doesn't unwrap his painting for a few years, he won't finger us for the job when he does. After all, if we'd stolen the water lilies for Grace, she would have tried to sell it. I figure he'll suspect an inside job."

Willie grunted. "We still don't get paid. How does it end?"

"Couple of years from now, maybe longer, the FBI receives an anonymous Christmas present from Switzerland. Or better yet, Ireland. Once their dogs get done sniffing it for bombs, they'll find they have a lost Monet on their hands. Grace O'Malley will put in a claim. Maybe she gets it. If she loses, it'll at least end up in a museum somewhere."

"Bugger." Willie rolled out of the car, retrieved the painting and his duffel from the back seat, and disappeared into the Hyatt Regency.

Tom turned in the car and hid out in his room. He lay on the bed until seven contemplating the many ways his plan could run awry, but no better scheme came to him. His mind drifted to Grace O'Malley. At every turn in this case, he seemed to feel her shadow. Yet she still refused to meet with him. He wanted to do right by the struggling widow, but how far could he trust her?

* * *

"Holy shit." Aoife's version of the little black dress fit her like a tattoo. Instead of her usual aura of sensible-young-professor, she cut a figure that would drive a priest to purgatory. Tom had never figured out the subtleties of women's makeup, but somehow the glow of Aoife's eyes reminded him of a jaguar. He swallowed hard as his right hand made an involuntary swipe to ensure his wallet was still in place.

"How eloquent. Are you ready to eat?" Her eyes twitched just enough to suggest the issue was in doubt.

"Starved. Where we heading?"

"Mario's, in the North End. I feel like Italian tonight."

"Beats herring. I'll call a cab."

"No need. Uber will be here in four minutes."

Two hours later, Tom gave a slight shake to the bottle of San-giovese in a vain attempt to extract a final dram. Aoife's spoon was clattering like castanets as she gleaned a few final scrapes of tiramisu, a spot of which clung to her left cheek. He tried not to stare as he leaned back in his chair with both hands on the table. "Splendid choice, my dear. Okay if we discuss tomorrow morning before we go?"

Aoife set down her spoon and tilted her head to what she must assume was her best viewing angle. "Morning seems a long time off."

"Maybe so, but we need to talk now."

She shrugged with an overtone of annoyance. "Shoot."

"I'm going to your ma's place tomorrow. Early and unan-nounced. You have to go too. She'll never let me in without you."

Aoife's smile sank but didn't quite reach a frown. "I knew that was coming. I don't want to shock you . . . but okay."

"I expected more of a fight."

"I don't want to fight you, Tommy. You need to take your shot. I can't promise I can get you in, but I'll try." She arched her right eyebrow. "Anything in it for me?"

"I'll pick up the tab." Tom reached for the check. He tried not to wince as he glanced at the total.

"Some hero." But she smiled as she said it. "Actually, we might be in luck. I think my mom is getting a bit worried about you. You know, predatory older male with dubious career prospects. She might invite us in so she can run you off." Aoife's phone pinged to announce the arrival of the Uber car.

As they waited for the elevator in the Harbor View lobby, Tom saw Aoife studying his reflection in the gleaming brass of the outer doors. She twitched her nose. "This is our first date. You need to escort me as far as my door."

She led him to her door, slipped the key card from her bag, and spun to face him. "I had a lovely time, Mr. McNaul. Will I see you again?"

"Well, seven tomorrow morning for starters."

Aoife stared into his eyes and pursed her lips in annoyance, but she eased forward until her breasts just touched his chest. There are times when a man must not think. He slipped his arms around her waist and pulled her tight. They kissed gently, lingering just long enough. She eased away, her smile was back. "That's better. Night." She turned, flashed the lock card like a blackjack dealer, and disappeared inside. Tom sighed and drifted back to his own room.

~ 23 ~

In the morning, Aoife was back to standard front-of-the-classroom attire. Tom rarely noticed women's clothes unless they were unusually shy of fabric, but he was struck by the change from her previous evening's vamp look. "Dressed for Mom, I see."

Aoife stuck out her tongue. "I'm not hungry, so why don't we grab a coffee and go? If we get there while she's still groggy, even you might be allowed inside."

Tom picked a cramped deli a half-block toward the harbor. There was just room for a counter and two tables covered with stained, checkered oilcloths, perhaps red and white. The dump's most obvious virtue was that both tables were available. The tray of pastries looked fresh, and a few were missing, suggesting there were surviving customers on the streets. At the far end of the counter stood a teenage shop girl with spiked blue hair and enough tattoos to leave her racial background in question. She stared downward at a worn Glamour magazine as she rubbed what looked like a mechanic's rag over the countertop. Tom shuffled his feet for a few seconds, but the girl read on. He drummed his fingers on the glass. "How about a couple of blue-corn donuts, a side of red chile, and two mochas?"

The girl kept reading, but she flailed one hand toward the pastry tray. "That's all we got."

Tom settled for two maple bars and a black coffee. Aoife ordered only coffee, black with two sugars. She poached half of one maple bar, and Tom enjoyed watching her lick the frosting off her fingers. She wiped her hands on her pants, shoved her chair back a few inches, and failed to appear nonchalant. "Could I ask you something a bit personal? I realize it's none of my business."

But of course, she was making it her business. Tom knew what was coming. He'd been here before with women, but he'd never found a good way out. "Sure, why not?"

"Kate."

"Kate who?"

Aoife's eyes focused into amber laser beams for about half a second, but he saw her lips twitch toward a smile as she relaxed. "FBI agent Katherine Bacon would be the one."

"Oh, that Kate. What about her?"

"Come on, Tommy. Are you guys a couple, or are you still in play?"

Tom stared at the harbor through the grimy window. "To be honest, I don't really know."

Aoife thought for a moment and then assumed a twisted grin. "Well then . . ." She stood up and nodded her head toward the door. "I think I'll take you home to meet my mother."

It was eight-fifteen when they hit the sidewalk. Aoife stepped just out of earshot and made a thirty-second phone call. When she returned, Tom pointed to a subway entrance across the street. "Can the MTA get us there, or do we need a car?"

"Neither. Let's walk."

"Beg pardon? Not to sound frantic, but time is somewhat of the essence. I'd prefer not to traipse around a town full of people who seem to dislike me."

Aoife pursed her lips. "Fastest way. Trust me."

"Trusting women hasn't worked out for me lately. How far are you proposing we hike?" Given the prices of condos in Boston, Tom couldn't imagine the widow O'Malley living within an hour's forced march.

"Just yonder." Aoife waved a finger toward the harbor, her eyes twinkling in the morning light.

Tom's gaze followed her finger. His eyes focused first on the glass pillars of Revere Towers. The twin towers jutted skyward from their base along the waterfront as they shielded the Boston citizenry from a possible view of the harbor. Their gleaming glass

and puzzling curves announced a refuge for the wealthy and sig-
nified a clear disdain for the aristocratic aura of old Boston.
Couldn't be those—much too ritzy. He scanned neighboring
buildings for telltale signs of condos more suitable for a widow
of limited means, but he couldn't see any. "I haven't a clue. Where
away, captain?"

"Two points to starboard. Follow me." Aoife set a brisk pace
as she wove through foot and auto traffic, and within five minutes, they stood at the entrance to Revere Towers. The doorman
exuded professional disgust at Tom's appearance but smiled and
stepped aside as he recognized Aoife. "Nice morning, Miss O'-
Malley."

"It is that, Johnny. We're heading up to my mom's place. Got
to show off a new beau."

Johnny just smiled like he'd seen it all. He probably had. Tom
nodded as they walked past him into the lobby.

When they reached the fourteenth floor, Aoife turned left and
led him to the end unit. It didn't strike Tom as a likely spot for
an entry-level condo. The door was an inch ajar. Evidently,
Aoife's sidewalk call had been to Grace. She stepped aside as Tom
took a cleansing breath and pushed the door open. The pirate
queen awaits.

The entry hall was dim and long enough to build suspense,
but the tunnel ended in a blaze of light. Tom surveyed an ex-
pansive living room with floor-to-ceiling glass on the north and
east walls. The morning sun glared through a slit in the Boston
cloud deck. A woman was seated in a wheelchair a few feet from
the east windows. Her back was toward Tom. She appeared to
be staring at the harbor, though Tom couldn't see her eyes. The
chair was a sturdy manual model, free of motors, batteries, and
play stations. A folded Pendleton blanket was draped across her
lap. Tom spotted a few modern paintings on the two interior
walls. He thought he recognized one of the artists—expensive
but not master class. There was a Lichtenstein print of a bub-
ble-gum cartoon. Worth fifty grand, easy. In the center of the

room, a leather seating group with two stuffed chairs and a love seat surrounded a coffee table hand fashioned from a slab of dark, tropical wood. Nothing about the place suggested a struggling widow. He felt uneasy.

Tom's eyes returned to the back of the silent woman's head. Although her hair was streaked with a few gray lines, it still shone a fiery Irish crimson. Tom stood still, waiting, tapping his toes inside his shoes. He felt Aoife's breath on the back of his neck, but she didn't touch him.

"Come in, Mr. McNaul. You are expected."

"And welcome?"

"That remains to be seen, but please have a seat. I assume you realize I'm Grace O'Malley." Grace continued to stare at the harbor, as if waiting for her pirate fleet to emerge from the mist.

Tom eased into a single armchair facing the coffee table and the south wall with the Lichtenstein. He didn't want the sun in his eyes. Aoife seemed annoyed by his choice but settled alone into the love seat facing her mother's back.

Grace waited a few seconds more, then sighed and rolled her chair back from the window. She turned until she was facing Aoife and gave her daughter a snap inspection. Apparently she approved. She turned her head to examine Tom. Grace's eyes were sparkling green and every bit as unsettling as her daughter's amber ones. They probed every inch of him, and when they returned to his face, she tilted her head slightly and stared at him for at least ten seconds. He stared back. Sooner or later, she was bound to start talking.

Grace grimaced, rolled her chair back an inch or two for effect, and shook her head. "Amazing. Not bad looking for your age, but you really are the ultimate clueless man."

Tom had no idea what she was getting at. It was hardly the first time he'd been called clueless. "Why, thank you kindly, Mrs. O'Malley."

"Spare me, Mr. McNaul. Is it okay if I call you Tom? Aoife likes to refer to you as Tommy, but you and I seem a bit old for that."

"That'll do."

"Well?" Grace crossed her arms. "You got your wish. You're here. What do you want?"

There was something unsettling about Grace O'Malley. Something more than just Tom's suspicions of her true motives. He shrugged. "What I've said many times before. I need to know just how badly you want this damnable Monet? And why? Do you really want this painting enough to continue the case?"

Grace managed to purse her lips and twist them at the same time. "Badly enough. As to why, the details aren't really your concern. As I've told you before, I need the money." She paused and glanced at Aoife, who was squirming on the love seat. "Steady, dear. I'll get to you in a moment."

"Bullshit."

Grace's attention snapped back to Tom. "Beggin' your pardon, shamus, but remember who's employing ya." Grace's exaggerated brogue seemed more amused than angry.

"Spare me, lady. Look at this palace. You're not some starving widow trying to stay out of the poor house. What's your game?"

"It's hardly a game." Grace smirked and stared at Tom again. She seemed to be both annoyed and enjoying herself. "I don't like your tone, Tom. Explain yourself or get out and I'll find a better investigator."

"There aren't any. And yeah, game. You clearly don't need the dough, and I don't buy you as some sort of obsessed art collector. So either you're in this for pure, ordinary greed, or you've got something else up your sleeve. Which is it?"

"As you might recall, my husband and his mother were murdered for that painting. It's only fair that our family gets it back. I believe 'closure' is the trendy word these days."

Tom barked a laugh. "Oh, please. You don't lie well for an Irish woman. Four people are dead already, and I've only been on the case a couple of weeks. They're the ones who found closure. Four dead, maybe more coming, but you're still hot for me to trot. Closure my ass."

"I didn't plan on anyone getting killed. I'm sorry that happened." She didn't look all that sorry.

"Go on."

"There isn't any more. I need the money, I want the money, what's the difference? I hired you to get my painting back. I never thought anyone would get hurt." Her tone softened, and suddenly, she looked hopeful. "Do you still think you can get it?"

"I don't know." Tom felt uncomfortable with the lie and was afraid Grace might spot a tell. He stood, walked to the north wall, and turned his back to her. He folded his arms and stared at Boston's North End for a moment, then checked Grace's reflection in the glass. She was watching his reflection as well. He turned back to face her. "What do you want the money for, Grace? What's worth all these lives?"

"Simple enough. It's my painting, it's worth a lot, and I want it back. It's a straightforward business deal, and the deaths were not in the reckoning. If you think there's some darker motive, you figure it out and then tell me. You're the detective. Meanwhile, how about some kind of report? What the hell have you been doing for my money?"

"Yeah, that's fair enough. But since you haven't paid us yet, I'll give you the Cliff Notes version." Tom clasped his hands behind his back. He felt the bulge of the revolver under his jacket. "Your husband and mother-in-law were killed in a hit. I can't prove much of this, but it looks like they were blackmailing a Nazi, who probably stole the Monet in France during the war, moved it to Ireland, and sold it to your father-in-law."

"A Nazi?" Grace looked surprised, but she might be faking it.

"Yeah, but don't upgrade your security because of him. I'm pretty sure he's dead by now. To continue, the two hit men were then gunned down by someone else. The painting went missing, probably carted off by the shooters."

This time she looked genuinely surprised. "How did you figure all this out?"

"You don't need to know."

"All right, but do you know who was behind these killings?"

Tom shrugged. "No hard evidence, but I think your husband was mixed up in Irish politics. My guess is that the IRA had something to do with the first murders, and some Orange paramilitary boys paid them back, taking the painting while they were at it."

Grace nodded slowly. She seemed to be accepting all this a little too easily. "That's quite a tale. So how did the painting get to Boston?"

"I figure it disappeared into the Irish underworld, and some mob guy brought it with him when he moved to Massachusetts. I don't know who or when." Tom again eased further from the truth. "All we know for sure is that someone in Boston got their hands on the painting and tried to sell it at Sotheby's. Not a smart move. He was killed before he could unload it, and he almost took me and the cat with him."

"The cat?"

"Big orange one. Didn't get his name."

Grace began tapping the fingers of her right hand on the armrest. "Well, does that mean the painting is still in Boston?"

"Most likely, but I haven't figured out who's got it, and it's dangerous to keep looking. I think we should call off the search before someone else gets snuffed." The lies were flowing more easily now. Maybe he'd learned the art from Colleen. "Even Aoife might be in the line of fire if we keep at this."

Grace's face hardened. "Had enough, have you, Tom? I'm not too surprised. You seem the type to cut and run from trouble."

"You've got no call to say that. When you get down to it, your painting is just a goddamned picture. Paint on canvas. Nice piece of art, to be sure, but it's just an image with shady provenance. Mr. Monet painted it and sold it to pay his grocery bill. Now a lot of greedy folks with too much cash will pay a fortune to own it. But these days you can get a high-res image of the water lilies online and stare at it till your eyes cross. The painted version would be nice to have, but it's not worth dying for. Or killing for."

"I think otherwise, Tom, but have it your way. I'll find a braver man to get my painting back."

Tom stiffened and let his arms drop to his sides. "As you please, Mrs. O'Malley. But I'd advise against it. Even if you get your hands on the painting, you won't be able to sell it. Some tough local guys would take offense, and you'd be the one ending up on the bottom of the harbor. Maybe Aoife too. So take my advice, and let it be."

"Not my style, Tom. Perhaps it's time for you to leave."

"Okay. But you still haven't told me why you want the money so badly?"

Grace smiled like a snake. "And I won't. You'll just have to figure that out by yourself."

Tom felt a sudden calm as the last piece fell into place. It had to be. He smiled. "I just did."

"Oh, so?" For the first time Grace appeared wary.

"Yeah. I should have figured it out when Aoife told me you got starry-eyed at the mention of Dublin Donal's name. You're IRA, aren't you? Same as him. You're not greedy, and you don't give a shit about the damned painting. You want the money so you bastards can buy guns. Maybe even stir up the Troubles again."

Grace's right hand disappeared under the blanket on her lap. Tom slid his hands behind his back until he could feel the revolver. She must have recognized his move, as she nodded and pulled her hand back empty. "You talk too much, Tom, and you're in over your head. You better trot on back to New Mexico while you still can. Leave the politics to we Irish."

"It doesn't qualify as politics anymore. You aren't fighting the noble war for independence. That's over. You're just murderers now. You and the Orange militias. Just a bunch of goddamned terrorists on both sides. Fuck the lot of you. I'm glad I didn't find your damned painting."

"You sure you didn't?" Grace cocked her head to her right and closed one eye.

Tom ignored her. "Like I said, leave it be. You hire some other P.I. and you'll all end up dead."

"I can look after myself. And if your wild speculation is any-where near the truth, you know I would have stout-hearted friends. Out with you now, Tommy McNaul." Grace nodded to-ward the entry hall. "Aoife, you stay here with me."

Aoife stood up and walked to Tom. She slipped her left arm around his waist and leaned against his side. "I'm a little old to take orders from you, Ma. I happen to like this one." She stretched her face upward and kissed Tom's cheek.

"Quite a daring little display. Please tell me, you haven't slept with this cheap detective?"

"Not yet, as a matter of fact, but it's still early in the day." Aoife's face twisted in defiance as she glared at her mother, their eyes flashing like fire opals.

Grace rolled her chair back a few feet. She looked at Tom for a moment, shook her head in resignation, and turned back to Aoife. "You really shouldn't."

"And just why not, Ma? What the hell business is it of yours?"

"For starters, he's your Da."

Aoife's mind clearly didn't compute. She let go of Tom, and he saw her mouth sag as her eyebrows pinched together. She stared at Grace like an android with a dead battery. Tom felt an image stirring in the far reaches of his memory, but it wouldn't focus. He was still searching when Grace tossed her lap blanket on the floor. She smoothly stood up, took two steps forward, and slapped Tom on his right ear with enough force to trigger flashing lights in his head.

~ 24 ~

When the stars flickered out, the image in Tom's head tightened into focus. The hardest lines of Grace's face seemed to melt away, leaving the features of a much younger woman. Suddenly, he knew. "Annie?"

Grace folded her arms, and her nose rose about twenty degrees. She worked her lips into a satisfied smile. "Keep going."

"Annie O'Sullivan? From Simmons?" Tom stumbled a step backward and bounced off the wall. "And County Cork, as I recall?"

"What do you know, Aoife? The rat remembers." Grace lunged toward him and launched another vicious slap at his right ear.

This time, Tom was ready for her and jerked his head back. As her hand passed just short of his nose, he felt the breeze in his eyes. "Bit slow, Annie. I remember now, you're a lefty."

Grace seethed as she whirled and strode back to her wheelchair. Tom spotted a small black revolver on the empty seat. She snatched the gun and spun to face him, but Tom was quicker. She stared down the bore of his revolver for a few seconds, then let her own gun drop to the floor. "Not bad, Tommy. You don't mind if I go back to Tommy now? It's what I used to call you."

Tom heard shuffling feet followed by a thud as Aoife collapsed onto the love seat and stared out the east windows toward the harbor. Her mouth still hung open, and she didn't seem much interested in the view. Tom kept his eyes on Grace as he retrieved her gun and slid it across the floor. It thumped against the baseboard beneath the Lichtenstein. "How about you behave so I can put this away?" Grace hesitated but nodded assent, and Tom slipped his thirty-eight into the belt holster in the small of his back. "That's better. Suppose we both sit down, and you can tell me what the hell you're talking about? And while you're at it, you've still got rather nice legs. They seem to work a lot better than I was led to believe."

Tom returned to the chair facing the south wall while Grace settled into the one opposite. She leaned back and crossed her stocking feet on the coffee table. They resumed their glaring contest.

"For God's sake, somebody say something." Aoife slammed both feet on the floor. "Mom? How come you can walk? And what the hell are you two talking about?"

Tom nodded toward Grace. "After you. I don't understand much more than Aoife does. What the hell?"

Grace snorted, but she softened as she turned to her daughter. "I've been able to walk just fine for two months now. I'm truly sorry I didn't tell you, but I found it convenient to play the invalid awhile longer. It puts some of the hard men I deal with a bit off their guard. But it's the history you'll be wondering about." She dropped her feet to the floor and leaned closer to Aoife. "Twenty-nine years ago, I was a first-term freshman at Simmons. Grace Anne O'Sullivan—I liked going by my middle name in those days. All of seventeen years old. Our dorm had a mixer, fishing for guys, and a group of MIT sophomores came hunting. Most of them were geeks, but I kind of liked one tall guy with a wry sense of humor. He even had a bit of Irish in him. He came from the Orange counties, but I figured why not? We started dating. I fell pretty hard."

"So did I, you'll recall." Tom raised his eyebrows.

"Yes, I suppose you did. For a while. I arrived in Boston as a good Catholic virgin. I planned to major in English, become a famous writer, and raise a brood of kids. But by the end of October, I was drinking cheap whiskey and thrashing around in this bum's bed. He shared a dingy apartment with a couple of guys with thick glasses, but he had his own room. Bay State Road, wasn't it?" She didn't wait for an answer. "There was only room for a single bed, but we managed."

"Jesus, Ma. TMI."

Grace smirked. "Yes, I suppose it is too much information. But we were intimate, and our only birth control was . . ."

"Ma!"

"Okay, but you get the point. We were in love, or at least I was." Grace swung her eyes over to Tom, but he decided to hold his tongue. "It was torture going home for the holidays. Tommy stayed in Boston, but he called me every day. Up until New Year's Eve, that is. Then he stopped. Cold. I thought maybe something had happened to him, so I tried calling his apartment, but his roommates said he'd left town for a few days."

Tom could feel her anger simmering. "They weren't lying—I was away." He sensed at once that he'd said the wrong thing, as usual.

"Damn you to hell, Tommy McNaul! You went away with her!"

Aoife was obviously confused. "Who's her?"

"That bitch, Colleen. Another Irish girl, no less. Fancy art student. The woman he married, by the way."

Aoife wrinkled her nose and looked at Tom. "Colleen? The one who tried to kill you?"

It was Grace's turn to look stunned. "Did she now? And sure, I'm feeling sorry she didn't. How could you do that to me, Tommy? How could you just walk away from me and say nothing?"

"I thought it might be easier that way. Look, I didn't plan to fool around, but there was a New Year's party at one of the frats, and Colleen was there, and well. . . ."

"Easier. You heartless, clueless, son of a bitch. When I got back to Boston, I had to come knocking on your door like a beggar. You mumbled and stuttered until I couldn't take it anymore. I just went home and cried all night. It was a couple of weeks later I found out I was pregnant."

Tom sagged and tried to disappear into his chair's enveloping leather. "You're sayin'?"

"Yeah, I'm sayin'."

"But, why didn't you . . . are you sure?"

"There weren't any other contenders, if that's what you mean. As for why, what choice did I have? You didn't even want to talk to me. I couldn't tell anyone at school, so I howled in my pillow for a few days and went home." Grace paused and glanced at Aoife, who was staring at Tom like he'd just crawled out of a grave. "The result was our lovely daughter." Grace smiled and turned back to Tom. "My folks were horrified, but they came around. Good Catholics, but so was I in those days. I dropped out of Simmons and lived at home. They helped me take care of Aoife when I started taking classes again."

Tom felt like he should say something nice, but intuition or cowardice kept him silent. Probably both. Grace ignored him and returned her attention to Aoife. "You know most of the rest. I met Peter about a year after you were born. I was surprised he'd take on a fallen woman, but he was a good husband and father. His folks were a bit stiff at first, but they warmed up in time. Our life was pretty damned decent while it lasted."

Grace began to twitch all over. She popped out of her chair and strode to the window, her back to Tom and Aoife. "And then some bastards shot my man. It had to be one of the Protestant groups. Those fuckers couldn't stand to see a Catholic family making a go of it in their stolen Orange counties." Her voice lowered. "The O'Malley family did right by Aoife and me, and I inherited quite a bit from Peter outright. We got along okay, and when the crooked Orange cops never got anywhere, I moved on. But when I heard about some asshole trying to sell my family's painting, I had to get even. Those bastards. There has to be a reckoning, and I'll do it my way."

"You might be right, but my money's on the IRA as the boys who did in your husband and his mom. I figure they were providing protection for the Nazi, and your old man pissed them off. Best you let it go."

Grace whirled to face Tom. He could sense her cold fury, and the glowing green eyes turned dead as a shark's. "You don't have a fucking clue about what goes on in Ireland. What do you know about the Troubles? About five hundred years of oppression? Somebody tell you stories in a pub while you were running up my tab over there?"

"I know terrorism when I see it, and I'm not about to help you fund another round."

"Leave it, Tommy. Talking politics just ruins dinner parties, or in this case our little family reunion. It really isn't your business where I make my donations."

"You're right. But if you're planning to drop big checks in the IRA coffers instead of a Salvation Army kettle, you won't do it with my help."

"That's your problem." Grace settled next to Aoife on the love seat and grasped her daughter's hand. "I'm sorry you had to hear the story this way, but I couldn't hide it any longer. I hadn't figured you'd find this asshole attractive."

Aoife's color was almost back to normal. She squeezed her mother's hand but then pulled her own away. "I need to get out of here." She sprang to her feet and fled down the hall.

Tom rose to follow, but Grace stopped him with a hand on his right forearm. He heard the door slam.

"Don't, Tommy. She needs some privacy and a whiskey night. I'll call her tomorrow."

He hesitated, but settled back into his chair. "We've got a lot to talk about."

"I've said my piece. Suppose you start."

Tom scratched the back of his head. "Seems like you know a lot already. Colleen took me off to an inn in Maine for a few days, and I sort of got lost."

"Oh spare me that part. I'm sure she was a lot more experienced than I was." Grace snorted. "Hell, anyone was. I think Aoife said you had a daughter?"

"Yes, Cassidy. She's nineteen, I think."

"You think? Some dad. Maybe I dodged a bullet."

"I wouldn't deny it. A few years ago, I worked a transfer to the Art Crime Team in Washington. Colleen and Cassidy stayed in New York. I drove up from D.C. as often as I could."

"How come just the one kid?"

"Colleen didn't want any more."

"Protestant?"

"No, certified lapsed papist. Just didn't want any others. Anyway, that's about it."

"Not quite." Grace drew her feet up under her rump and propped her chin on her left palm, her elbow digging into the arm of her chair. "I want to hear how she tried to kill you. You owe me that at least."

"Colleen was sleeping with her gallery owner. Apparently, everyone knew it but me."

Grace rolled her eyes but remained silent.

"We got a tip that someone in Boston was trying to sell a painting. Vermeer's *The Concert,* the main event in the Gardner Museum heist in 1990. Worth as much as 200 million. Kate Bacon was in charge of the sting, and I was her partner for the event. We flew up to Boston, led an FBI team to a house in Lexington, and all hell broke loose. Kate was shot in the chest and almost died. I took a flesh wound but killed both of the assholes on the premises. Unfortunately, I shot one of them in the back, and I had a couple of priors. They tossed me out of the FBI. Later, I figured out that Colleen was the one who blew our cover."

"Ooh, nasty. I'm almost sympathetic. Then what?"

"I moved home to New Mexico. Joined my brother's private investigator firm in Santa Fe. When Cassidy heard the details about her mother ratting out the sting, she came to live with me. Right now, she's a freshman at UNM. You know she's in Aoife's anthro class?"

"She told me."

"Before I go, out of all the gin joints, in all the world, etc., etc., why did you call me to find your goddamned water lilies? I haven't seen you in twenty-nine years."

"I couldn't resist. When I got the call from Agent Bacon about my Monet, well, McNaul is hardly a common name, is it? Seemed like too big a coincidence. I chose to regard it as fate."

"Maybe so, but it's not quite as surprising as you might think. The art theft world is pretty small in this country. There's the

FBI Art Crime Team, one or two police investigators in L.A., and a handful of us specialized detectives. That's it."

"So I learned. Actually, Ms. Bacon recommended three P.I.s, but I couldn't resist choosing you."

"Normally, I'd be grateful for the business. In this case, I'm just grateful to be still breathing. Though my gratitude is tempered by the fact that I'm not getting paid."

"I'll pay you for your time, as well as the expenses. No percentage bounty, though. You didn't deliver."

"Fair enough. I'd still feel better about things if you'd just write off the painting and get on with life. You're well off, and you've got a lovely daughter. That seems like enough."

Grace tried to look angry, but this time her heart wasn't in it. "Let's agree not to talk about the water lilies anymore. Okay?"

"Yeah."

Grace got up and glided to a cabinet uncomfortably close to the pistol lying on the floor. Tom tensed, but she ignored her gun and extracted two crystal glasses and a barely touched bottle of Red Breast whiskey. The glasses were elegant, and Grace poured a fair measure. She dipped her left index finger into one glass and touched it to her tongue. "You'll like this one, Tommy. Single pot still." She handed him a glass and eased back into her chair.

"I'm familiar with it. If I was looking at a big payday, I'd stock my own cupboard with the stuff." They raised their glasses and savored long, slow pulls.

"Almost seems like old times, Tommy."

"Almost, but the whiskey is better."

"What happens now? I'm going to find another investigator to look for my Monet, but are you going to keep quiet about it?"

"Yeah, I will. Not my business anymore." He figured Grace and Aoife would probably stay out of harm's way since they wouldn't ever get their hands on the painting. Grace could afford to blow some P.I. money digging holes in the sand.

"Before you go, you and Aoife didn't, did you?"

Tom squirmed despite his best efforts. "No, and that's all I'm going to say about it."

Grace uttered a deep growl. "Thank God for that, but I'll bet you can still taste your daughter's lipstick." She eased back in the soft leather. "Believe it or not, I'm sorry. I didn't dream you'd make a play for Aoife, or vice versa. I couldn't resist having her be the one who contacted you, but I didn't mean for it to get awkward."

"Thanks, but we'll survive. Maybe it would be best if Cassidy transferred to another section though."

"Whatever's best for our girls . . ." Tom flinched, which triggered a pensive smile from Grace. "I was thinking of visiting Aoife at Christmas this year. I hear that Santa Fe really puts on the traditional dog for the holidays. Perhaps we could all have dinner somewhere? See how the sisters are adjusting?"

The idea scared Tom shitless, but he couldn't think of any reason to say no. "That would be nice, but let me see how Cassidy takes the news she has a sibling before I commit to anything."

"Splendid idea." Grace stood up, clearly signifying it was time for him to leave. "I have some things to attend to now, Tommy, but we'll meet again, one way or another. I'll see you in Santa Fe . . . or I'll see you in hell."

~ 25 ~

The Southwest Chief crept into view as it rounded third for a whistle stop in Lamy. The train was two hours late, and given its speed, Tom was in no hurry to leave his bench on the platform. He glanced around at the sparse vegetation and scattered houses. Lamy, New Mexico, sat twenty miles south of Santa Fe and was a town only by the most generous definition, but it served as the lone passenger stop for the capital city. Air brakes hissed defiance as the wheels squealed to a stop. A shaggy bear of a man with a black duffel bag strapped to his back and a large, flat box in his arms trotted down the steps and squinted at Tom.

"Yeah, Willie. It's me. Enjoy the trip?"

"Not bad, actually. Nice views from the club car. I hope Mrs. O'Malley will be picking up the bar tab."

"Not bloody likely." Tom took the package and led the way to his Tacoma pickup in a corner of the empty gravel parking lot. There were no people visible in any direction. He secured the painting in the small cargo space behind the front seats while Willie tossed his duffel in the bed. It was only about forty-five degrees, but the sun was shining and the wind was taking a break. He lowered the windows as Willie climbed in.

After half a minute, Willie began drumming his fingers on the center console. "I agree it's a fine day, Tommy, but if you're planning to wait here for the next train, I think I'll walk to town." Tom continued to stare at the empty tracks. "Or, you could fill me in on just what our brilliant plan might be. Seems to me we've got a painting in a plain brown wrapper that's worth a king's ransom, only there ain't no king to ransom it."

Tom continued to stare down the rail line, but he let a smile show. "Not going to try. As far as we know, you and I are the only ones who know the painting has been recovered."

"You mean stolen, from an Irish mobster no less."

"Let's not quibble. As long as said mobster thinks the painting is still in his niece's closet, he won't send out a war party. Our job is to make sure the Monet stays missing. The chances are quite good he won't discover it's gone for a long time, months at least. Maybe years. After all the furor in Boston last week, it's too hot for him to try moving it."

"It'll cool off sometime." Willie scowled and spit through the open window.

"True, but by then our trail will be cold. There won't be anything to suggest we have it. After all, the lilies have been stolen and recovered once already, and that was a local job."

"Maybe so, but your plan only works if the painting doesn't surface. It belongs to Grace O'Malley, not us. Are you proposing we steal it from her? What then? We wait five years and try to sell it in Shanghai?" Willie shook his head. "No way I'm doing that."

"You won't have to. We won't sell it, now or later."

"So what else can we do? You said we can't hand it over to Kate. . . ."

"Correct. Nobody but you and I can know. I've got part of a plan, but it still needs work. We'll talk."

Half an hour later, Tom pulled to the curb in front of their Staab Street office. As he followed Willie and the painting up the ruins of their sidewalk, a bare arm began frantically gyrating out the window of the back room. It seemed to be waving them away, but that didn't compute, so he shrugged and opened the door.

Myrna's desk was empty. However, a short woman occupied the sturdiest of the sprung visitor's chairs, her back to the door. Tom dropped his keys as she exploded to her feet and spun to face him.

"Kate. What the hell?"

Myrna emerged from the back room. "Tried to warn ya." She plopped into her rolling desk chair and looked eager for the show to start.

Kate squinted and glanced sideways at Myrna, but her eyes snapped back to Tom. "Nice to see you, too, Tommy." She folded her arms across her breasts and began rhythmically tapping the toes of her right foot. "What's in the goddamned box?"

Willie caught Tom's eye and made a slight, questioning nod toward the door. Tom shook his head. "How did you get here?"

"A plane, stupid. I repeat—what's in that box?"

Willie stepped forward. "We stopped for some pizzas. Family size. Thought we might have an office party after we close up. You're welcome to join us, but we need to check our emails first. Why don't you wait out here?" He edged toward the door to the inner office.

"Fat chance. I'll go with you and we can have some now." Kate grabbed Willie's elbow and steered him into the back room.

Tom followed. Myrna flamed him a parting glare as he shut the door in her face.

Willie set the box flat on their rickety worktable. "The microwave's busted, so maybe we should wait and take this back to Tom's condo."

"Stop bullshitting me. Pizza my ass." Kate set her bag on Tom's desk, reached inside, and pulled out a stubby, serrated knife. She brandished the weapon in her right hand and pushed Willie back a step with her left. "You gonna do this, or do I have to? I don't know how it's packed. It would be a shame if I accidentally cut the lily stems too short for your vase."

Willie never reacted well to being pushed. He slipped his right hand inside his jacket. It emerged gripping a combat knife a good deal meaner than Kate's. "You set that little toy down right now, Kate. Before you get hurt. Then how about you go pick up a side salad and a bottle of wine? Meet us back at Tom's condo in an hour."

Kate exploded with rage, as Willie must have planned. Tom stared as she lunged at Willie with a feint followed by a practiced sideways cut, but he dodged, grabbed her right wrist, and twisted. Kate's knife clattered on the wooden floor as she groaned, dropped to one knee, and cradled her wrist with her left hand.

Willie kicked her knife under the sprung sofa. He frowned concern. "Sorry. Didn't mean to break anything."

Kate stared at the floor. "You didn't, but it's at least sprained. Should have let the anger cool first. You suckered me."

Willie shrugged. "Yeah. Bet I'll catch hell next time, though. What say we call out for a pizza. Screw the salad, and we've each got a bottle of whiskey in our desks. Goes pretty well with pepperoni."

Kate snorted. "You'd know."

Tom was less shaken by the one-second knife fight than by the increased number of conspirators. Kate and Myrna made four. No way to shut them out now. He called for Myrna, and she burst through the door like the lead cop on a SWAT team. Tom grabbed her right arm to steady her. "See if you can find our first aid kit, and have a go at Kate's wrist. I'll hop over to the Allsup's and get some ice for it. Willie, you order two pizzas, large, any kind you like. We'll set up in here.

* * *

When Tom returned with the ice, Kate was sitting in Tom's chair with her right arm lying on his desk. Myrna was gently rubbing Kate's wrist, which looked relatively straight. There didn't seem to be much swelling yet, but that wouldn't take long. Tom fashioned an ice pack using plastic trash bags and duct tape, and Myrna wrapped it around Kate's right wrist and hand. She looked up at Tom. "Best I can do for now. Where's the whiskey?"

Tom assembled four battered coffee mugs, retrieved a bottle of Jameson from the file drawer of his desk, and poured a round. They drank in silence, eyes shifting as they each assessed degrees of blame. Tom was considering another round when the pizza man arrived. One of them actually had green peppers and sun-dried tomatoes on it—Willie's apology to Kate, perhaps.

The wolf pack finished off the last bits of crust within fifteen minutes. Tom crushed the pizza boxes into his trashcan, effectively ending the ceasefire. "Who wants to go first?"

The question was rhetorical—everyone turned to Kate. She started to stand but winced as she pushed off and eased back into Tom's chair. Her eyes bored into Tom's and dared him to look away. "Is anyone going to deny that the water lilies are in there?" She waved her left arm toward the box, still resting on the work table, without breaking eye contact with Tom.

Myrna broke the silence. "Actually, I don't know what the hell's inside. But I'm dyin' to find out. It sounds excitin'."

Kate snorted. "That's the first honest thing anyone's said since I got here. Seeing no objections, suppose someone tell me just how you got your hands on it? And then, Thomas McNaul, explain why you didn't tell me about it?"

Tom spent several minutes describing the Wellesley burglary and Willie's train journey west. He lacked the courage to explain why he'd kept Kate in the dark, so he just spread his arms, palms up. "We figure nobody will miss it."

Myrna looked like a woman trying to figure out how Sherlock Holmes solved the murder of the bishop's cat. Willie was sliding his right hand slowly toward the bottle of Jameson, and Kate looked either puzzled or hurt—Tom couldn't tell. She stared at the box and took a deep breath. "You're not done yet. This was a team effort. You and me. How come you decided to ditch me at the end? We were in bed together all the way." Willie tried to stifle a guffaw, but he'd had too much whiskey, and he lapsed into a coughing fit. Kate cut him down with a three-second glare.

"Had to, toots. You're FBI. You have to go through channels. If you'd set up a bust through the Boston office, the news would have leaked in hours, way before you could get a team into that Wellesley house. Bye, bye Monet. And if you'd risked going rogue with Willie and me, and it had flamed out, you'd have gone down with us. Career over. No need to put you to that risk."

"But there's more, isn't there? Don't bullshit me, Tommy. You know I'm a big girl, and I call my own shots. What's your real reason?"

Tom clenched his teeth, and he began to get angry. "Because you can't have the painting."

"Huh?" Kate looked surprised, but it didn't last long. "What the hell are you talking about? That Monet is an international art treasure, and it was stolen from Grace O'Malley's family, who were murdered in the process. Of course I'm taking the painting. If Grace can prove ownership, it's hers. If not, it belongs to the world, and I'll see what I can do to find it an appropriate home. Maybe even the Louvre." For a moment Kate appeared to have stars in her eyes.

"She doesn't own it. The Nazi who fled to Ireland with it sure as hell didn't buy it legally. It probably belongs to the heirs of someone who died in one of their camps. That is, if their heirs weren't killed too. And anyway, what if you did give it to Grace? She'd just try to use it to buy more bombs and stir up the Troubles. I won't let that happen."

"Not your call, Tommy. This is FBI business now. I'll do what I can to get the water lilies in a museum, but I can't promise that. Has to go through channels, like you said."

"You can't have it."

Kate stood up and fished her phone from her coat pocket. "Don't make me call for backup."

"Don't try it, toots. There's another reason that painting has to stay hidden. As soon as it surfaces, people will start dying. The mob will go after Grace, and me, and Willie. Maybe even Aoife. Payback time. I don't care how much the water lilies might bring at Sotheby's, or how many art students might get to gawk at it. It wouldn't be enough. So sit your butt down, and let's work out a plan."

Kate shook her head and turned on her phone. She set it on Tom's desk so she could use her good hand. "Law's the law,

Tommy. I'll do my best to get some protection for you guys, but you know how that goes."

Tom saw Willie slide open the top-right drawer of his desk, the one where he kept his forty-five. He paused and arched his eyebrows. Tom shook his head and walked to the supply closet. He rummaged through the cleaning shelf for a moment and returned with an open bottle of alcohol and a roll of paper towels. "Better this way." He soaked a paper towel, rubbed alcohol on the outside of the plastic bottle, and laid the soggy towel on top of the box with the painting. Next, he twisted a second towel into a makeshift fuse and stuffed it halfway into the bottle. "Lighter?"

Willie retrieved a brass Zippo from his right jeans pocket and tossed it to Tom, who caught it, flipped open the top, and clicked up a steady blue flame. "Last call, Kate. You phone, it burns."

"You haven't got the balls!"

"Leave my balls out of this."

As Kate started punching in numbers, Tom lit the paper towel and set the bottle on the alcohol-soaked paper towel. Kate emitted a primal yelp and lunged for the bottle, but Tom blocked her easily. The paper towel burned slowly at first, as Tom hadn't soaked the top part with alcohol. Kate tried to wrench free, but with only one good arm, she was stuck. Tom leaned down to make eye contact. "Deal?"

"Fuck you, Tommy."

"Maybe later, but deal?"

Kate's eyes widened as the flame flared. "Deal."

Tom spun and snatched at the flame. He felt his skin singe as he hurled the burning paper to the floor and stomped it out.

Kate collapsed back into Tom's desk chair. "You crazy asshole. You'd have let it burn."

"Maybe. I didn't really think that far ahead." Tom shook his burned hand, but it only made the pain worse. "Look, toots, I don't really want to burn the Monet. Hell, we could have done that in Boston. But it has to disappear. Maybe forever."

"Just how is that better than destroying it?"

"I don't know exactly, but at least it will still exist."

Kate looked at the floor and shook her head. "What is it with you and art? You make your living trying to find stolen treasures, then you want to close the case by giving the masterpiece a Viking funeral." She looked up at Tom and folded her arms. "Look, why don't we leave it wrapped and put it in an evidence locker? I could make up some cover story, and we could let it sit there for a few years. Then pretend we found it in a dumpster. These things happen in the art theft world."

"Yes, they do. But I don't want to spend those years worrying that one of us will slip up." Or that you might rat us out. "My offer is, the painting lives, but we find it a good home and say goodbye."

"Five years, Tommy." Kate regained her composure more rapidly than was decent. "The Monet disappears, and I'll hold my peace for five years. That's long enough to cool things off in Boston. Then we'll talk again. Okay?"

Tom didn't like it, but he knew it was the best he could hope for from Kate. "Deal, but I get to decide where it goes." Kate just looked away.

Willie closed his desk drawer, stood up, and shuffled over to Kate. "Sorry about your wrist. I didn't mean to do damage."

"It's okay, big guy. My fault for losing my cool."

Willie nodded and begged a ride back to his ranch from Myrna. When they were out the door, Kate flashed Tom a smile and eased to her feet. "Enough art business for one day. Since we're supposed to find other things to talk about for five years, let's amble over to Maria's and get started over some blue corn enchiladas. I've got an oh-six-thirty flight home tomorrow, so I'll be spending the night in Albuquerque. Alone."

~ 26 ~

Saturday morning meant Rosie's for another round of huevos rancheros. By the time Tom managed to drag himself down the hill from his condo, the tables were full, but he nabbed the last spot at the counter. Two mugs of black coffee washed the huevos down in ten minutes flat. He pondered his chronic inability to savor food. *I eat like Stella, the canine shop vac.* As he pictured his chubby corgi girl inhaling kibble, he suddenly realized how he could hide the Monet. *Perfect. Even I won't know where it is.* Tom grinned, doubled the tip for luck, and made tracks to a bench on the Santa Fe Plaza.

As he watched tourists shopping for Indian jewelry on the front portal of the Palace, Tom summoned what courage he could find and dialed Aoife. Her phone went to voice mail. He was fretting whether he was wrong to call her so soon when she called back. "Hey, Tom. Glad you called. I just got out of the shower."

Tom tried not to picture that. "I wasn't sure if I should. But we're both back in New Mexico, and I was wondering whether we could get together and talk things out. You got any time today? I could drive to Albuquerque."

"Today's good, but how about if I wander up there? Since it's a Saturday, I'd like to get out of town. Besides, my students have term papers due Tuesday, and they'd just bug me at home if I stay around here."

"Okay. How about we go up the mountain and take a short hike? If we're lucky, we might find an aspen showing off a bit early."

"You're on. I'll get there about noon. Meet you at the condo?"

"Yeah. I'll pick up some sandwiches or something."

* * *

Tom parked his pickup at the Aspen Vista trailhead, about a mile below the ski area. There wasn't enough fall color to matter, but it was sunny, cool, and Saturday. At least twenty people passed them with bounding dogs, no two alike. The trail was actually a rutted service road, so they were able to stroll side-by-side. An hour and three miles later, neither of them had broached the obvious topic. Aoife spotted a grassy clearing a few yards off the road and stopped. "Time to eat?"

"No, time to talk. Then we can eat." Tom followed her to the clearing, and they sat on dry spots about six feet apart. He wanted to say something appropriate, but the words were hiding out.

"Well, Dad?" Aoife almost choked on the "Dad."

"It'll take some getting used to. Has Grace filled you in on any more of the story?"

Aoife nodded. "She called last night. I was pretty pissed at her. I can see she meant well by not telling me who my dad was, but Jesus, couldn't she have called you herself about the painting? Why send me? And what's with this crap about her not being able to walk? I'm her only child, for God's sake."

"Got no answers for those. Reckon she'll tell you someday, though. You okay?"

"I'll get over it." She smiled for a moment but then scrunched her features into a pensive frown and began to sweep her gaze around Tom's face.

Tom realized she was searching for traces of her own image. He scratched the side of his neck and scanned back. Did she have his cheekbones, or maybe the widely spaced eyes? Tom wasn't good at this sort of thing—he never paid much attention to family resemblances. Still, there must be some. "Find anything?"

"Sure. Didn't you?"

"I dunno. You're a damned pretty woman, but I've never paid much attention to the way I look. I'll take Grace's word for your origin story, but if you've got doubts, we could get a DNA test."

Aoife shook her head and grinned. "No need for that. If Mom filed a paternity suit, the judge would find you guilty in two minutes. Look at those ears!"

"What's wrong with them?"

"A bit large, don't you think? Maybe that's why you got a corgi. I used to keep mine hidden under long hair, but at least they're sturdy enough for hanging major earrings."

Tom never thought his ears were particularly large. He'd check when he got home. "You're welcome, I think." He cleared his throat. "About that night in Boston, after dinner. . . ."

"Nothing happened."

"I mean when we, uh. . . ."

"Kissed is the word you're stumbling for, but nothing happened." Aoife's face turned serious, but she didn't seem upset. "There's no way we're going to forget it, but we didn't do anything wrong, and there just isn't any point in talking about it. Ever. That okay with you?"

"Sure. At least we didn't. . . ."

"Shut up, Dad."

Tom shut up. They wound down the mountain. Aoife climbed into her battered car and blew him a kiss as she disappeared around a curve. Tom headed indoors to begin four weeks of preparation for making a painting vanish.

~ 27 ~

Stella bounded up the stairs of the underground parking garage with gusto but little grace. She was only a foot high, not counting the ears, but she strained at the leash like a hungry husky. Willie opened the glass door for her, and they stepped into an icy blast of late-October wind. High plains weather didn't transition smoothly from one season to the next. The days just oscillated between summer and winter until one day the summer was gone altogether. It was gone now. The trio made their way through the Railyard district, skirting the boutique film theater and crossing the tracks toward the farmers' market building.

Willie tugged at Tom's sleeve and pointed toward the Second Street Brewery. "Couldn't we fortify ourselves with a pint first?"

"Not this time. We're men on a mission, and besides, this is Stella's night."

They moved past the lively brew pub and were jostled by the flow of a crowd converging on the market pavilion. It was a dual-species crowd, dogs and their humans. Many of the dogs were in costume, as were a few of their owners. This was the night of the Barkin' Ball, an annual gala held to support the Santa Fe Animal Shelter.

Tom couldn't stand the idea of buying some ready-made fou-fou outfit for his best girl, so he'd outfitted her as a western sheriff. A woven placemat served as a type of saddle blanket for Stella. She sported a red bandana and a pair of dime-store toy guns in holsters. A shiny star was wired to her harness. The tickets were steep—Tom had shelled out $150 each, and he wouldn't be asking Grace O'Malley to pick up the tab. Fortunately, Stella got in free. She led the brothers inside.

"Well, where is it?" Willie was scanning the walls.

"This way." Tom led his companions through a maze of tables filled with folk art, dog paraphernalia, books, edibles, and dozens of unclassified objects donated to the silent auction. He stopped when they reached a wall of photos, prints, and paintings, also open for bids. In front of them hung a roughly three-by-four-foot Impressionist painting of a pond lush with water lilies-

Willie leaned forward and squinted at a printed note stuck to the wall near Claude Monet's signature. It described the work as a clever forgery, painted on a canvas of the period. "Looks real."

"It was supposed to." Tom had forged a document himself. He'd called in an old favor and obtained a couple of sheets of letterhead stationery from a respected art appraiser in Chicago. The resulting letter declared the painting to be a moderately well-done copy of a Monet thought to have been stolen by Nazis during World War II and never recovered. The minimum bid was $2,000. A brass tag screwed onto the side of the frame declared the artist to be "Unknown."

"Not bad, eh?"

Willie gave a wry smile and slowly shook his head. "Not the right subject for my place. Think anyone will buy it?"

"You bet." Tom steered them to a table of other corgi owners and their dogs. It was piled high with dog cookies, decorations, and donation envelopes. The dinner was enlivened by an obvious canine preference for the carved roast beef over dog biscuits, but there were no casualties. A woman in a "Game of Thrones" outfit, with a cardigan corgi dressed to match, asked Tom for his number. There was a brief pet parade by the dogs and owners who were suitably costumed. Tom sat out the event, but to his surprise Willie grabbed Stella's leash and let her have her moment in the lights.

As the speeches and pep talks were winding down, Tom leaned to his left and whispered in Willie's ear. "Time to go. We need to be out of here before anyone starts talking about who wins what auction."

They slipped away before the festivities wrapped up. En route to the condo, Willie began tugging his right ear. "So let me get this straight, little brother. You figure some rich person is going to buy Mrs. O'Malley's Monet, thinking it's just a copy?"

"Uh-huh. They'll appreciate it for what it is, a fine painting, enjoyable to look at but something of an oddity. Hell, they might even figure it could be one of those forgeries the French made during the war to fool the Nazis. The kind they swapped for Picassos and such to save them from destruction. Wherever it finds a home, the owners will take decent care of it. Probably won't get the place of honor in the living room, but it might grace a study, or maybe a guest bedroom. I don't really care." He glanced at Willie. "The important thing is, we won't know who has it, and we won't ever try to find out. Nobody else will figure out where it went. If enough time passes before the Boston mob boys find out their painting is gone, we'll be in the clear."

"And if enough time doesn't pass?"

"We've still got our guns."

Willie nodded and grinned. "That would be fine by me."

When they reached the condo, Willie hopped out and into his own truck. "See ya, little brother. It's been a hell of a ride." He sped off for his ranch. Tom unloaded Stella and helped her out of her sheriff's outfit. He enjoyed the squeak of the cork as he opened his bottle of Black Bush, but as he was pouring a glass, his phone began singing. It was Kate.

"Toots. How are ya?"

"Lonely. It's Friday night, and I'm by myself. But I've got to be in L.A. by noon Sunday, so I booked a flight west tomorrow morning. I'm overnighting in Albuquerque tomorrow, and I've reserved a nice suite in the Sheraton near the airport. You're invited to share it with me. One night only. I'll text you the details."

"Uh, sure. That seems good."

"You could sound more enthused."

"You just caught me by surprise. Sure. It'll be great."

"Such a silver tongue. I don't suppose you'll give me an update on the Monet?"

"Sorry, but we agreed on five years of silence."

"Once an asshole . . . but never mind. Just show up on time. Meet me at the Sheraton at six-thirty."

Kate hung up.

*   *   *

At five on Saturday afternoon, Kate's phone began to buzz. A visitor was in the lobby. She texted him the room number. Minutes later, there was a light tap on her door. She opened it to a short, wiry man wearing a cheap blue suit. A large, flat cardboard box leaned against his right leg. She flashed him an FBI smile. "Right on time."

The man gave a slight nod to Kate, carried the box into the bedroom of her suite, and eased it down onto the bed. "Special delivery."

Kate handed him a small white envelope. "Here's what we agreed on. You're not expecting a tip, are you?"

"A guy can hope. Besides, you owe me. I had to sit through a goddamned dog banquet last night. It went on for hours. And I'm a hacker, not a social butterfly. Most of those people, the ones not in Rin Tin Tin outfits, were dressed to the nines. In my crummy suit, I stood out like one of the Blues Brothers."

"Ah, poor Jack. No gratuity, though. I'll put in a word for you if your case ever makes it to trial." Kate was pretty sure it wouldn't, but no sense telling him. Jack Jacobsen was a small fish in the hacking world, and his part in a WikiLeaks breach of the FBI firewall was thought to be peripheral. Still, he was good enough to hack Tom's computer. The log of Google searches revealed an unusual focus on something called the Barkin' Ball. Tom had shown interest in the particulars of the silent auction, and it didn't take Kate long to make the connections. A few subtle threats later, Jack agreed to serve as Kate's mouthpiece at the auction, just in case one of the lots was the O'Malley Monet.

"We even, Agent Bacon? For real?"

Kate hesitated a moment, but fair was fair. "Yeah. We're good. Behave yourself."

Jack snorted, but he looked relieved as he slipped out the door.

Kate slit open the tape and removed the water lilies from their box. She admired the beauty of the piece, though she served on the Art Crime Team, she was much more focused on crime than art. Still, this was a major coup. She would live up to her end of the bargain with Tom, at least as long as they remained an item. If that ended, well. . . .

When the painting was secure in its box, Kate slipped it under the bed. She unpacked a black lace nightgown bought just for the evening and held it against the light from the window. She'd never owned anything quite like it, but the young sales girl had eased her through the purchase with a minimum of embarrassment. Maybe it would be better than bare skin, given the glaring scars from her bullet wounds. She stashed the gown in the bathroom and began tidying up the place.

Tom rapped on the door at six-thirty sharp, and Kate counted to ten before she let him in. "Why, Thomas McNaul. What a surprise. Do come in."

Tom handed her a bouquet of Trader Joe's flowers and a bottle of Redbreast single pot that he'd picked up, a rare indulgence for him. "Hey, toots. You look great."

"Why thank you." Kate was in her usual hotel sweatsuit, but she seemed to appreciate Tom's effort. "I think we should postpone the talking for later. What do you say?"

"Fine by me. Like a shot?"

"No, but you have one. Back in a moment." Kate disappeared into the bathroom.

Tom poured himself a double and took off his shoes. In a surprisingly short time, Kate reappeared. He gulped. He'd always considered her kind of sexy, but this was something special, and he was off balance. He set his glass on the dresser as Kate took his hand and led him into the bedroom. Tom wrapped her in his arms. It was the kind of kiss too potent to be remembered. They melted together, and when their lips separated, Kate pulled him down onto the bed.

Tom sensed a distant alarm bell and pulled back a few inches. "I really won't talk about where I hid the painting."

Kate oozed a torrid smile up at him. "Shush, lover. Let's sleep on it."

About the Author

Although **William Frank is a fourth-generation** New Mexican, he spent his childhood at U.S. Naval Air Stations ranging from French Morocco to Guam. He studied aeronautical engineering at MIT and served as a flight test engineer in the Air Force before earning a Ph.D. in Atmospheric Science. He spent thirty years as a professor of meteorology at the University of Virginia and Penn State, studying hurricanes and their somewhat calmer relatives. Along the way, he developed a deep love of storytelling, and in particular, the American detective novel.

He retired from academia a bit early to return to New Mexico and write detective fiction. He lives just north of Santa Fe with his wife, Kathleen Frank, a noted painter of expressionist landscapes, and two corgis.